KAMINISHI

JAN SUZUKAWA

DSP PUBLICATIONS

Published by
DSP PUBLICATIONS

5032 Capital Circle SW, Suite 2, PMB# 279, Tallahassee, FL 32305-7886 USA
http://www.dsppublications.com/

Kaminishi
© 2015 Jan Suzukawa.

Cover Art
© 2011 Anne Cain.
annecain.art@gmail.com
Cover content is for illustrative purposes only and any person depicted on the cover is a model.

ISBN: 978-1-63476-110-9
Digital ISBN: 978-1-63476-111-6
Library of Congress Control Number: 2015904001
Second Edition September 2015
First Edition published by Dreamspinner Press, 2011

Printed in the United States of America
∞
This paper meets the requirements of
ANSI/NISO Z39.48-1992 (Permanence of Paper).

BOOK ONE
LORD OF THE WEST

PART ONE
THE AWAKENING

PROLOGUE

THERE WAS something missing in the eyes. He'd gotten their look essentially right, but the gaze was still lacking some element he couldn't quite put his finger on.

The pencil sketch of the man, inelegantly taped to the wall above his desk, had become his favorite place for his eyes to linger. He didn't suppose a Japanese man in the nineteenth century—even a samurai warlord—would be that tall, but something had made him draw the white silk kimono as though it draped beautifully down long legs. The clean lines of the kimono mimicked the smooth strands of raven hair flowing down below the warlord's shoulders, accentuated by the knotted tail at the top of the head toward the back. The warlord held his curved samurai sword in an odd one-handed grip, horizontally across the front of his body.

The face was classically Japanese, with high cheekbones, dark slanted eyes, and pale porcelain skin like a mask. The man was perhaps thirty years old, and the look in his eyes was that of a born leader.

Michael rubbed his eyes tiredly, turning back to his textbook on the late-Edo period in Japan and trying to find where he'd stopped reading. Finals began in three days, and in the midst of studying, filing the necessary forms to graduate, and everything else, he'd been having unexplained dizzy spells; one moment he'd be fine, and the next he'd be leaning against the nearest wall or solid piece of furniture. After a few moments of closed eyes and deep breathing, it would go away.

Stress-induced vertigo, Ellen would say. *Get out and ride a bike; go for a walk in Tilden Park. Stop living in your head.* She was a civil engineering major and a black belt in karate, equally qualified to build a bridge or kick your head in. He wasn't sure if he had eventually bored her into stopping the sexual part of their relationship or what else exactly had gone wrong. Ellen was less emotional than he was and had never told him. The name "Nakamura" was still under "Holden" on his mailbox downstairs, and she still had the key to the apartment. *Let's just be friends for a while and see what happens*, she'd said on her way out the door.

He stared up at the sketch again. For an Asian studies major, he supposed it wasn't actually odd to dream about a samurai warlord, although he would've felt more comfortable if he'd dreamed about geishas instead.

Michael blinked. Where had *that* thought come from?

He needed a break.

He went to the bathroom and bent over the sink to wash his face. He grabbed the hand towel, dried himself off, and looked in the mirror.

His eyes were bloodshot, and his face overall was looking a bit haggard. Finals would be over soon, and he could sleep then.

Until then, however, his schedule sucked.

Michael closed his eyes, then opened them once more to really look at himself.

His light brown hair had gotten shaggy; he needed a haircut. His blue eyes and even features stared back at him from the mirror. Ellen hadn't been the first girl who'd told him he was attractive, but he still couldn't see it himself. The looks he got from girls, the hints they dropped around him, and the invitations to social functions and hiking clubs and other coed group activities had always left him cold.

It wasn't that he disliked the young women who invited him to these things with their eyes hopefully gazing up at him. He just didn't feel any real pull toward any of them.

That he wasn't sure what he was going to do next in his life added to his sense of being unsettled. His circumstances allowed him to do whatever he wanted without thinking about money. Ironically that left him more indecisive than ever.

He could take a year off, travel to Japan and around Asia, then maybe apply to grad school. His grades were good enough to get into the better universities. Maybe he'd try the East Coast schools. He'd always lived in California. Perhaps a change of scenery would help....

He returned to his bedroom and to his desk, resolving to get down to his studies again.

Suddenly the dizziness was back. He was glad he was sitting down. Closing his eyes, he rubbed his temples briefly and then lowered his head to the book, resting his forehead on the open pages.

Just a few moments... and it should pass....

THE FIRST thing he noticed was the smell of wet earth.

He could feel that he was lying on his back, which didn't make any sense, because he'd been sitting at his desk. Even stranger, his clothes felt damp.

Michael turned onto his side and cautiously opened his eyes. *What the...?*

He was in a field of tall grass, lying in a patch of mud. It was broad daylight. The soft sound of gently moving water pooling around rocks and trickling downstream reached his ears.

The bright sun hurt his eyes, so he shut them, thinking, *She was right. Now I'm seeing and hearing things.*

But how is it that I'm feeling *things?*

He opened his eyes again and half raised himself to look around. Slowly he got to his feet.

He was standing in the middle of a valley bounded by mountains on three sides. The stream he heard was to his right, which he somehow knew was east, although he couldn't say how. To the west he saw something he'd only read about: water-drenched fields of rice… with people wearing conical straw hats… like out of a… a….

This can't be real.

One of the peasants turned in his direction, and Michael hurriedly crouched down in the tall grass. The mud squelched unpleasantly beneath him. His pants and shirt were sticking to him.

A small copse of trees stood upstream in the distance. He moved cautiously through the grass until he could hide under the tree closest to the stream, and pulled off his shirt.

This is just a very real-seeming dream. It was nighttime, I was studying, I fell asleep at my desk, and my imagination has taken me to historical Japan. Very funny—hysterical, really. How did this mud get into my pants?

He took off his shoes and socks, pants, and finally his briefs, then tested the stream with his hand. The water was cold, but not agonizingly so. He threw water over his arms, shoulders, and neck.

Shouldn't cold water wake a person up?

He rinsed the rest of his body, the water bracing him. Finally he dashed water on his face, thinking, *This should do it. Wake up, already!*

A little prickly feeling on the back of his neck made him turn around.

He'd seen illustrations of samurai, photographs even. Once Commodore Perry had arrived to open Japan in 1853, all manner of Western goods and technology had flooded into the previously closed society, including daguerreotype cameras. But seeing pictures of samurai and seeing a group of them standing ten feet away from you were two different things.

They were dressed in kataginu, the sleeveless open-sided vests, and hakama, the divided skirt-like pants worn by late-Edo-period samurai. They were of different heights, none as tall as Michael, though what they lacked in height they more than made up for in sheer ferocity of appearance. Their hair was long and tied in a variety of topknots, and they carried the traditional two swords, one long and one short. He stared at them. They stared back at him. "Gaijin," one said in amazement.

Michael opened his mouth to say something. "Shit," he finally managed.

The samurai leader—a fiery small man—glared at him. "Toraero!" he barked to the others. In a heartbeat they were on Michael, and threw a large blanket over his head and body. "Shiro e tsurete ike!"

Okay. Now it's for real.

MICHAEL COULDN'T see or hear under the blanket. He sensed he was being walked down a street and there were people and buildings on either side of him. If he had heard the leader right and he was being taken to a castle, then this was the main street of the castle town. He tried to envision the scene outside his blanketed world: farmers, merchants, traders, ox carts, foodstuffs and goods for sale. And all of them staring at the naked man under the blanket being hustled along by the daimyō's men.

He nearly stumbled as he was moved along, occasionally pushed from behind.

The noises from the street faded. Michael heard a door open as they entered a more enclosed space.

The blanket was whipped off, and Michael saw they were in a dank corridor. He guessed this was the lowest level of the castle.

Finally they entered a room. Two samurai got his arms behind him, and he was held fast.

The leader slowly walked up to him. The men behind Michael gripped him tighter.

The man was about three inches shorter than Michael, making him perhaps five feet seven, and he had most of his long black hair coiled into a seamless topknot. He had a bushy mustache, and his small beady eyes fixed on Michael with personal malevolence, as though Michael had stolen something precious from him.

The leader unsheathed his sword, drawing it out slowly, giving Michael time to watch and think about it as the silver blade glinted in the sunlight slanting in from the small high window.

He placed the tip of the blade beneath Michael's chin. Michael stood completely still. "Doko kara kita?"

Where do you come from? Michael thought quickly. Should I answer him in Japanese or in English? Would he understand where California is? Should I say nothing at all? He stared at the man, his thoughts a jumble with no clear answer.

Taking Michael's silence as a challenge, the man slapped him across the face. "Gaijin," he spat. He nodded at the other samurai, and Michael was pushed to the floor. Terror overtook him. He struggled as first his wrists and then his ankles were bound.

"Tōru," someone called.

Michael saw the leader—Tōru—turn and go to the doorway and speak to someone just outside in the hall as hands kept Michael down.

He tried to look, but his face was held fast against the floor. Panting, he tried not to panic as he heard footsteps approach.

Abruptly he was pulled up to his knees. He lifted his head, but a hand shoved it down, forcing his chin to his chest and leaving him staring at the floor. He heard the other samurai leave the room.

A lone set of soft footfalls approached, almost silently. Michael's knees ached on the wooden floor, and he felt cold for the first time, kneeling naked with his ankles and wrists bound. The one saving grace was that his wrists were bound in front of his body, allowing him to cover his privates with his hands.

He kept his eyes downcast as the man came closer. The feeling of complete unreality was back, like in the muddy field.

The man stopped a few feet in front of him. Silence filled the room as the man regarded Michael.

Finally the man said, "Kao o agero," and Michael looked up.

It was the samurai warlord he had drawn in his sketch—the one from his dream.

CHAPTER ONE

HE LOOKED very tall—given that Michael was kneeling at his feet—and he wore a light-colored raw silk kosode, a loose-flowing garment banded with an obi-style tie at the waist. The hair was as Michael had drawn it, the long black strands gracefully splaying about the warlord's shoulders and down his back, with a loosely coiled topknot from which a few tendrils had escaped. The face was even more striking than he had captured. The eyes in particular were beautiful, with an inquisitive, lively spark in their black depths, and he had flawless skin on a narrowly drawn face. He was an exceptionally handsome man, beautiful even.

The warlord stared hard at Michael, almost as if recognizing him as someone he knew or had known. He seemed startled for a moment and turned away. The sight of his profile made Michael forget to breathe: the upswept hair and regal profile made him look every bit the nobleman of ancient times.

He was the most perfect man Michael had ever seen.

He looked to be around thirty years of age, as in Michael's dream. Michael realized he was staring and quickly looked down again. He watched the warlord's feet—wearing tabi, those odd toed socks favored by the Japanese—pace back and forth in front of him.

"Namae wa nan da? Doko kara kita?"

Michael took a deep breath. "Holden Michael desu. Watashi wa Amerika kara kimashita."

The man stopped in his tracks and stared at him. "What did you say?" he asked in Japanese.

Michael repeated his name and where he was from.

"How is it that you speak Japanese?" The warlord stared at him as though he were from outer space.

"I-I study it." He wetted his lips nervously.

The warlord stared at him for a long moment. "You are my prisoner now," he said calmly. "I do not know who sent you, but you will never see them again."

"I'm here on my own. I'm not a spy, and I wasn't sent by anybody. My lord," Michael added, hoping to appease him. He swallowed.

The warlord walked to where Michael's muddied clothes lay on the floor and leaned down to pick them up. Michael's eyes traced the long line of the warlord's back as he bent over, the straight black hair spilling over his shoulder.

Frowning, the warlord straightened up and examined Michael's blue button-down shirt and jeans. Then he took the wallet from the jeans and opened it.

Michael watched as the warlord stared at his driver's license, thumb caressing the plastic curiously, and then his student ID card. The warlord's face was a study as he took out the paper money, fingering the twenty-dollar and one-dollar bills with a bemused expression.

The warlord set the items down and came over to Michael. "Who are you?" he asked. "I don't understand any of this."

His simple, honest statement made Michael feel an odd kinship with him. "My lord, I don't understand either. I... woke up and found myself here...."

All speech left him as the warlord stopped in front of him, staring down at him with an unreadable expression. It was a moment suspended in time, the warlord standing above and Michael kneeling below, gazing up at this man who held him in his complete power. His mouth went dry.

Michael blinked, and his eyes met the warlord's, confused. The two men stared at each other for a moment. Then the warlord's eyes unexpectedly softened. Abruptly he turned and walked out of the room. Michael felt himself breathe again.

He heard a quiet conversation, too low to pick out words, in the hallway outside the room. Then Tōru reappeared, strode over to

Michael, and crouched down beside him to efficiently remove his bonds. "You will remain in this room at all times," the warlord's second said. "You will not leave this room unaccompanied. You will do as you are commanded, and instantly. A woman will see to your needs."

He left the room then, and Michael sat on the floor, rubbing his wrists. Presently a young woman entered, carrying clothing and other items. In the Japanese traditional manner, she opened the sliding door while seated on the hallway floor, then set the items inside the room. She then moved into the room on her knees and shut the door. Michael remembered he was naked and drew his legs toward his body, but the woman kept her eyes averted, as if used to carefully not seeing what she wasn't supposed to see.

She placed a folded yukata near him for him to wear, and bowed her head in his general direction before exiting the room in the same manner as she had entered it before.

MISAKO SET about preparing miso soup, but in her mind she kept seeing a young man looking scared and alone, seated on a tatami mat and trying to hide himself from her. A gaijin, with light brown hair spilling over his face and big blue eyes. She had gotten a fleeting impression of broad shoulders on an otherwise slender frame, and long coltish legs. She wondered if all gaijin were this attractive; certainly this one didn't fit the description of the "foreign devils" they were all warned about.

A handsome young male, even a gaijin, might deflect some of Lord Shinjirō's attentions away from her for a time. Misako permitted herself a small smile as she chopped green onions. *But in the end, you'll still be here*, she thought, and her smile faded.

AN EVENING meal of some kind of fish, rice with nori seaweed, and miso soup was brought to Michael, along with a futon and blankets. The young woman moved in and out of the room silently with the items, and Michael tried not to stare at her. She even removed the pot that had been left for his toilet, then returned with it cleaned and functional again, with a small damp towel hanging from its rim. He felt his face grow warm, but the woman did not look in his direction.

SOMEHOW HE slept through the night and did not dream.

In the morning he lay on the thin futon, staring up at the ceiling. If this had been a dream....

If this had been a dream, he would've woken up in his own bed or at his desk in his Northside Berkeley apartment with books scattered about his head.

If this had been a dream, he wouldn't be feeling the rough, cottony texture of the futon beneath his naked skin or the soft morning sunlight on his neck, streaming in from the high small window in the cell.

Somehow, he was really here in samurai-era Japan, the apparent prisoner of a warlord he'd seen in a dream and then drawn a sketch of. Michael closed his eyes and pulled the blanket over his hips. His thoughts went around and around, but nothing made sense.

A sixth sense alerted him to a presence in the doorway. The door had been opened silently, and Tōru stood staring at him. "Prepare yourself to meet with Shinjirō-sama." Then he was gone.

Shinjirō. At least now he had a name....

THE WARLORD was seated on the floor, wearing the same light-colored kosode as the day before, and did not look up as Michael was led in.

A hand on his shoulder pushed him down to the floor. The warlord was sitting cross-legged. Michael arranged himself in the traditional seiza position: knees together and resting his behind on his heels. It was uncomfortable almost immediately, but this was the position that showed respect; he hoped the warlord would recognize that the gaijin was aware of this and had chosen it deliberately. He smoothed the ends of his yukata over his knees, folded his hands and laid them in his lap, lowered his eyes, and waited.

He felt Tōru leave the room behind him, probably in response to a nod from the warlord. He kept his gaze downward until the warlord said, "You may look at me."

Michael raised his eyes.

"I see that you are still here."

Michael blinked, and the corners of the warlord's mouth quirked. "I had thought that perhaps you were an apparition, that you would disappear sometime during the night."

Michael opened his mouth but found he had nothing to say.

"You are like a bird dropped in from the sky. Our borders are watched. No one saw you cross them." His face showed genuine curiosity. "Tell me who you are."

The warlord's sense of presence was overwhelming; he radiated authority and charisma, though the latter was controlled, like a banked fire.

Michael took a deep breath. "My lord," he began. "I am a student of Asian studies at a university in America. I live in a place called Berkeley, near San Francisco, California."

"California…. Is that where people found the gold?"

The warlord's look of mild interest distracted Michael. "What…? Oh." *Sutter's Mill—the great Gold Rush of 1848. So this must be sometime after that year.* "Yes. Yes, my lord. But that was a long time ago." He stopped suddenly. *That was a slip.* Seeing the curious look in the warlord's eye, he hurriedly continued. "I was studying at my desk late one night and fell asleep. When I woke up, I was here." He hesitated. "There's something else, my lord. I had a dream in which… I saw you."

The warlord stared at him.

Michael rushed on. "You were standing, holding your long sword across your body, looking at me. I couldn't forget your image—I even drew a sketch of you."

"So I appeared to you in a dream," Lord Shinjirō said. "Interesting. Perhaps we were destined to meet." His eyes flicked to Michael's primly set-together knees, as if noticing his seiza position for the first time. "Please make yourself comfortable." He patted his own knees, referring to his cross-legged position, and Michael understood.

He moved to sit cross-legged, flipping the ends of his yukata to cover his privates. The warlord coughed and put a hand over his mouth. Michael looked at him curiously before remembering himself and dropping his eyes.

"My name is Shinjirō Kaminishi. I am the daimyō of this han, which has been my family's responsibility to lead for almost two hundred years."

"Han" meant domain or region, Michael remembered. Lord Shinjirō's limpid gaze captivated him.

"We are an old and traditional han, not particularly influential these days, as most commerce now takes place in Edo." A small wry smile graced the daimyō's beautiful features. "We are west of Kyoto. The people who live here are farmers and the merchants who support them. We are at peace with our neighbors—well, all but one." He said the last with a slight grimace.

"Shinjirō-sama—if I may inquire—what year is it?"

The daimyō blinked. "It is Kaei 4."

Michael quickly calculated in his mind. *1851. Two years before Perry and the black ships.*

"I believe in your part of the world the year is known as 1851, yes?"

"Yes, my lord."

"There are so many things I would like to know about your country," the daimyō said. "We are fortunate in some ways here in Japan to be on our own as a people and as a nation. But I cannot help but wonder if we are missing valuable experiences by looking solely to ourselves."

His expression was wistful, and Michael heard himself say, "It will not always be so, my lord." Japan would be opened to the world within years; the daimyō would be a middle-aged man when that happened and would live to see it.

Michael glanced up to find the daimyō staring at him. *Uh-oh. Probably shouldn't have said that....*

"Do you know this for a fact, gaijin?" Lord Shinjirō said. Fortunately he looked more amused than serious.

"No, my lord. It's just something that I believe."

The daimyō's face was expressionless for a moment; then he permitted himself a small smile. "So. You dreamt about me... you came from America but don't know how you got here... and you appear to be from a future era."

"My lord?"

Lord Shinjirō's countenance grew stern. "I can read Western numerals, gaijin." He held up the wrinkled currency from Michael's wallet. "These notes are dated 2009."

Michael stared at the bills, then swallowed nervously. "Yes. You are correct, my lord. The last thing I remember was that it was June of the year 2010 by the Western calendar." The daimyō's face remained impassive, and Michael hurriedly added, "I was... reluctant to tell you that I was from the future. It is already difficult to accept that I would be here from the America of this time period. To say that I was from the year 2010 as well... well, I was afraid you might think I was completely insane."

The daimyō blinked. Michael slowly felt himself breathe again. "This is... highly unusual," Lord Shinjirō finally said. He turned his face away for a moment, and Michael waited, gazing at the fine profile in repose.

A look of realization came to the daimyō's eyes. "So, you are from the future. This is interesting."

Michael didn't think he'd like what was coming next.

"Perhaps you can tell me what will become of my country, then."

"I'm sorry, my lord. I don't know what you—"

"I think you understand me, gaijin. Tell me the future of Japan." The daimyō's tone brooked no argument.

Michael took a deep breath. "No."

The daimyō blinked. "Nanda to?"

"No one should know what will happen in the future. It's… not right." Michael closed his eyes.

I am so dead.

Lord Shinjirō stared for a moment, and then unexpectedly he laughed. He sounded much younger when he laughed.

"Very well, gaijin," the daimyō said politely. "There will be time enough for that. We will talk again."

CHAPTER TWO

OVER THE next few days, the mystery that was Lord Shinjirō Kaminishi began to be revealed little by little, and Michael found himself more deeply intrigued. In some ways the daimyō fit the stereotype of what one expected from a samurai leader: he was austere, sometimes stern and forbidding, and always the epitome of calm. But he also showed moments of humor and unexpected kindness. Michael was reminded that yasashisa, or gentleness, was a trait valued in both sexes by the Japanese, and that even a samurai warlord could be kind without being seen as weak.

Lord Shinjirō was born in 1819 and was thus thirty-two years old. As the only son of the daimyō of the Kaminishi Han, Shinjirō had been raised by several female caregivers and a male tutor with a combination of strictness and indulgence. Michael noted that he never mentioned his mother. The young future daimyō had received instruction not only in sword skills, martial arts, and weaponry but also in calligraphy and ikebana, the Buddhist-inspired art of flower arranging.

As a child he had felt his father's love, but distantly, like music being played at the other end of the castle late at night. His childhood had been cut short by his father's death, with the burden of ruling the han passing to his shoulders at age sixteen.

Though his father had prepared him well, the challenges in the first few years were many. The greatest involved his first advisor, a longtime aide to his father whom Lord Shinjirō had trusted. That trust turned out to be misplaced, as the advisor was discovered to be coercing tributes from the town's farmers and merchants under the guise of taxes to the daimyō and keeping the money himself. Lord Shinjirō had cut off the advisor's head with his own sword.

There were bad crop years, increasing tributes demanded by the Shogun in Edo, and occasional unrest in the castle town. A continuing border dispute with the neighboring han to the east ruled by the Shirakawa clan was a particular irritation, as the Shirakawas believed that the Kaminishi Han had become vulnerable upon the death of Lord Shinjirō's father and that control of it could be seized. A young Shinjirō had led his men into battle to prove them wrong, and now, though the Shirakawa clan continued to dispute the borderline, there had been no major violence on the border for many years.

Michael thought the daimyō was merely being polite as he asked Michael many questions about his early life. He didn't see anything about himself that would be of interest to a man like Lord Shinjirō, but the interest did seem to be genuine.

"So your parents no longer live with one another?"

"Yes, my lord. They are divorced."

"And you are the only child?"

"Yes."

The daimyō contemplated this for a moment. "And you say you are still in school?" *At your age?* Michael sensed the rest of the daimyō's thought without it being said.

Lord Shinjirō had been ruling his family's territory for sixteen years, responsible for the lives and well-being of thousands of people at the age where Michael found himself still living a student's life: studying, writing papers, wandering down to his favorite Northside café for a latte every morning.... He lowered his eyes, embarrassed, but the daimyō only laughed. "Yes, America must be an interesting place indeed," he said, "to study at leisure for so many years. Or is it that you are a scholar by profession?"

"I... I don't know yet, my lord."

"And the time to consider it as well. Interesting," Lord Shinjirō mused.

A gentle breeze wafted in. The daimyō's receiving room opened onto an inner courtyard within the castle, and the shōji door had been opened all the way to allow the most air and sunlight inside. Michael was unable to resist looking out at the courtyard, only a portion of which he could see: a neatly trimmed garden with grass and rocks. A sound like a stream of running water reached his ear, but it sounded too close to be real. It almost seemed to be inside the castle walls, which didn't make sense.

He came to himself with a start; the daimyō was staring at him. "Mōshiwake gozaimasen, Shinjirō-sama," he apologized quickly, bowing his head. His inattention was at the very least a sign of disrespect. *This man has the power of life and death over you. Try not to forget that again.*

When he dared to lift his head, he found Lord Shinjirō gazing at him with a quiet, neutral expression. "We shall speak again," he said, the standard words indicating their conversation was over for the day.

"Thank you, Shinjirō-sama."

The daimyō called for a retainer to escort Michael back to his locked cell. Michael bowed more deeply than ever before, then left the room, the retainer following behind him.

You are officially an idiot. How could you lose focus like that? God. He mentally berated himself all the way back to his cell.

FOR SEVERAL long minutes, the daimyō remained still on his cushion on the floor, staring at nothing.

Then he stood up slowly and looked out toward the open space of the courtyard.

DINNER HAD come, Michael had eaten it, and the tray with its bowl and cup had been taken away.

He sat with his knees pulled into his chest, arms folded over them, with his chin resting on his arms, as if trying to take up as little space as possible. A small shaft of moonlight angled down from the little, high window.

It had been six days since his... arrival in Japan, in this time period. There was nothing to write with—or on—in his cell, so he kept track in his mind of the passage of time.

Keeping track of his thought processes and changing moods was another thing. The unreality of the situation predominated at first, but as the days passed—slowly—something inside of him came to accept this new life, this interlude—whatever it was—as a kind of lucid dream that he stopped questioning. His body felt real when he touched it; its functions were real, the food was real, everything from the shaft of sunlight coming in through the high window every morning to the daimyō's beautifully modulated voice every afternoon was as real as anything Michael had ever experienced.

He wondered if time was passing at the same rate back home. Had he missed finals? Was Ellen wondering where he was?

He touched the back of his hand. He had done this numerous times in the first few days, trying to see if this place were real and if his hand felt the same "here" as it did at home.

If this lucid dream never ended, this place would *be* home, forever. Could he live with that?

He didn't particularly believe in the paranormal, although at this point he might have been crazy *not* to. Somehow he had ended up here and now, in this time.

He had no illusions about his position. He was a gaijin, a white foreigner, here in Japan fully two years before the country would be opened to the West. Save for a small number of Dutch traders in Nagasaki to the south, there would be no other people who looked like him anywhere he went. If he were ever allowed to leave, that is. The daimyō might decide to keep him in this cell forever.

That was why.... Michael grimaced as he thought again about his lapse in the receiving room. The garden had beckoned to him, and he had momentarily been lost in its beauty, staring out at the courtyard, at the vista of fresh air and sunshine that was denied him for twenty-three hours a day in his cell. He had forgotten that he was the daimyō's prisoner and he had no rights.

Michael lowered his head and closed his eyes.

LATER THAT night the door opened unexpectedly, and Michael came to with a start.

It wasn't Tōru this time but another retainer, a slightly taller and somewhat younger man. His face carried a mild expression, and he blinked and stood still for a moment, looking at Michael with simple, unabashed curiosity. "Please prepare yourself to see the daimyō," he finally said.

Michael's mind was a jumble as he walked down the hallway, the polite retainer following behind at a short distance.

The daimyō had never before requested his presence in the evening hours. The only thing Michael could imagine was that his offense of that afternoon had been so egregious that some kind of punishment awaited him. He waited numbly as the retainer entered the room and announced his arrival.

Lord Shinjirō was standing in the middle of the room as Michael was escorted in. Before, he had always been seated during their sessions.

The daimyō dismissed the retainer, then turned his full attention to Michael.

Michael started to kneel. "You may remain standing," Lord Shinjirō said. They stood apart at a distance of around ten feet. Michael realized he had never stood eye-to-eye with the daimyō before; they had either both been seated or Michael had been kneeling before him. Lord Shinjirō was truly tall for a Japanese man, particularly for the nineteenth century; he was at least Michael's height and probably an inch or two taller. Even in an informal yukata, his regal bearing was imposing.

The daimyō turned and walked to the sliding door that opened onto the courtyard. He slid the door to the side, giving Michael a tantalizing glimpse of the moonlit garden outside.

"Come," Lord Shinjirō said.

THE SOUND of gently moving water greeted Michael's ears as they walked outside. His feet met perfectly fitted wooden slats that formed a walkway that bounded the three sides of the garden that Michael could see, as the courtyard and garden wound around a corner to an area that was out of sight.

In the middle of the courtyard, a sculptured garden of short soft grass with patches of sand here and there wove around a small trickling stream. Native plants and flowers surrounded the stream, which flowed through some rushes and disappeared under the slats at the near end of the courtyard.

"It's an underground stream," Lord Shinjirō remarked. "My father discovered it and was able to direct part of its flow through this garden area. This means we have our own water supply in the castle." He stepped onto the short grass and approached the stream, turning his head to glance at Michael. "Please."

At his gesture of invitation, Michael stepped forward, following the daimyō, noting the soft drape of the informal yukata down his back. The grass was like velvet under his bare feet; the daimyō was also barefoot.

Lord Shinjirō crouched down and played his hand gently through the moving water. Hesitantly Michael bent his knees and lowered himself to the water's edge about two feet from the daimyō. He peered into the shallow stream. The water glittered in the moonlight, and the sound of it moving over the rocks was intoxicating.

"I sensed this afternoon that you desired to see this stream," Lord Shinjirō said, still looking down at the moving water. His tone was unchanged as he continued, "If you wish to kill me, now is the time. I have sent all my retainers to bed. The only guards on duty are outside the castle."

"I have no wish to harm you," Michael replied. His own calmness surprised him. "It is as I have said. I am a student, not an assassin. I have never been trained in martial arts or in the use of weapons of any kind. I don't believe in violence."

The daimyō laughed, a small surprised huff. "You do not believe in violence," he repeated, as if the sentence needed to be said again to be comprehended. "If you do not believe in violence, does that mean violence cannot touch you as a matter of course? What world do you inhabit, gaijin, where your magical belief keeps what you prefer to avoid away?"

He's calling me "gaijin" again. Uh-oh. "Forgive me, my lord," Michael said, bowing his head in the daimyō's direction. "I meant no disrespect. The world I come from is indeed… different from this one. There are many positive aspects there, as there are here in this time and place. Where I come from, if you respect the law and your fellow citizens, you are usually safe from violence."

"There is order in the streets, then."

"Yes."

The daimyō paused, thinking it over. "That is good," he finally said.

Michael's breathing eased infinitesimally.

"We are supposed to be in a time of peace ourselves. However, between our land and the Shirakawa land, there is never a completely quiet time. We have long suspected our neighbor to the east of instigating various incidents on the border, but without direct proof…." The daimyō trailed off, then gave a soft sigh. "The world is based on power—how much power one has, how much your enemy believes you have. There never was a time when that was not so." He rose to his feet, and Michael followed suit.

"We all have our roles to play in this world. What is yours, Maikoru?"

Michael stared. It was the first time Lord Shinjirō had used his name, and his Japanese pronunciation of it took a moment to sink in. "I don't think I have any," he found himself saying.

Lord Shinjirō stared at him.

"I'm nobody, really. Just another person living on this earth. What can I say? I'm an American college student. My mother is very wealthy; I went to the best schools. She's absorbed in her society activities, her charities. I was an afterthought to her. She divorced my father when I was very young and paid him off— paid him to leave us, really. I've barely seen him since. I have a great interest in East Asia, especially Japan, so I've been studying the subject. My family set me up with a trust fund, so I don't need to work. I'm basically useless in this world." He looked down at the stream.

Michael turned to find the daimyō standing very close. They regarded each other silently.

An odd sensation lit in his stomach, like butterflies. The daimyō was so near that Michael could almost feel the warmth emanating from his body. The features of his face, the beautiful eyes, bone structure, and flawless skin framed by the soft upsweep and then the long fall of hair past his shoulders.... Michael realized he was staring and would've been embarrassed save for the fact that the daimyō was also staring at him. *Not the fairest of bargains. I've got nothing special.* He shook himself mentally. *You know, he's a guy. A samurai warlord, yes, but still a guy. You're staring at him like....*

"Are you typical of the men of your country, Maikoru?" The daimyō's voice was soft.

"I.... Yes, I suppose I.... What do you mean?"

The sound of the water faded. All he saw were the luminous dark eyes, which regarded him with utter seriousness. Then a gentle glint of humor softened the look.

"It is late," Lord Shinjirō said. He looked away a moment, then turned back to Michael. "I don't believe that you are 'useless' in this world, Maikoru. Something tells me that you will play an important role in my life and those of many other people." He gazed at Michael with kindness in his eyes.

"What if the things I do hurt others?"

The daimyō stared for a startled moment. Then he laughed. "Do you not understand? That is unavoidable in this world. You will do both good and harm while you are alive. There is no one who is above that conundrum."

He gazed intently at Michael. "To live fully, you must enter into the river of life with the rest of us. No one can say what the result will be. But you cannot be afraid to be a part of life."

Michael stared at Lord Shinjirō as the daimyō's hand slowly reached to his face. A single finger trailed down his cheek as the daimyō's eyes held his own in a locked gaze.

"Being afraid to live is the only sin."

SHE UNLOCKED the door and cautiously peered into the room.

The room was almost dark. A thin fall of early morning light slanted down from the high window, softly illuminating the long formless mass lying under the blanket in the corner of the room.

She set the tray down and checked the bucket—nothing solid yet. The room was as bare as always. The man on the futon moved restlessly, turning his body to face her, his eyes still closed.

The light brown hair fell softly across his face. Misako stared, free from inhibition, as he was still sleeping. She crept closer.

He was even younger-looking up close. Having never seen a gaikokujin before, she had nothing to compare him to, but she guessed he was in his late teens or perhaps early twenties. Unlike Japanese men, he had a firm jaw and a more defined nose. The light color of his hair fascinated her; she longed to touch it.

No. She sat back, pulling herself together. She had no idea what Shinjirō-sama planned to do with this gaijin. Best not to get involved.

But she was unable to move away when the eyes opened.

Blue eyes gazed at her steadily, and when she tried to turn away, he lightly grasped her wrist. She stared, frozen in place, at the young man's hand on hers.

"I won't hurt you."

His voice was soft and kind.

"What is your name?"

Her lips parted, but no sound came out.

"Maikoru desu." He let go of her then, and she withdrew her hand.

He blinked, sleepily. She let out the breath she'd been holding. He looked so innocent lying there.

"My name is Misako," she said.

MICHAEL WATCHED as she moved the tray to its usual place before lifting the bowl of rice and other items and arranging them. He lay quietly under the blanket, not wanting to do anything that might threaten or intimidate her.

"Thank you, Misako-san," he said.

She smiled slightly but didn't meet his eyes. Her hair was swept up and back, but a stray lock fell across her cheek.

Michael blinked. He turned his head to look at her more directly, and a few strands of his own hair fell down the side of his face.

It seemed like one moment she was a few feet away, and then she was close. Michael felt rather than saw her hand moving to sweep the hair from his cheek and move it behind his ear. The movement caused a little tickly feeling, and he drew in his breath sharply, almost a gasp. She blinked, startled, and then her hand flew to her mouth.

"It's okay," he reassured her.

Her face colored, and her eyes were wide. "Sumimasen," she said, eyes lowered.

"No harm done," Michael said.

"I'm not allowed to touch any man except...."

He stared, comprehension dawning slowly. "Oh."

Her body posture was rigid, and she still wouldn't meet his eyes.

"I won't tell," Michael said gently. "You have my word."

"Thank you," she choked, then fled from the room.

He sat up slowly. An unsettled feeling came over him. His physical space hadn't been violated in his first few days here, with the exception of the day he'd been brought to the castle. Now he had been touched by Lord Shinjirō and by Misako-san. He knew he was naïve in some ways, but he wasn't *that* naïve. Fortunately the daimyō had stopped with that single-fingered caress on his face, leaving Michael to be escorted back to his cell immediately thereafter.

And now this morning with Misako. From what she'd said, she must be Lord Shinjirō's....

The door opened suddenly. Michael turned to see Tōru smirking at him, with another samurai behind him. "Prepare yourself to see the daimyō."

LORD SHINJIRŌ was leaving for Kyoto that day.

He was to return in two days, after concluding his business with the Imperial Court. They were meeting earlier in the day than usual due to Lord Shinjirō's trip. Seated now in the daimyō's receiving room, Lord Shinjirō's demeanor was as calm and settled as always. Michael looked for signs of the daimyō's sexual interest in him but found nothing; the daimyō's face was at its most impassive.

"Misako will see to your basic needs while I am away."

"Thank you, Shinjirō-sama."

A pause. "I trust that her services will be sufficient," the daimyō continued.

Michael hesitated, then nodded. There was a silence, which he felt he should fill somehow, but his position dictated that he remain silent until the daimyō spoke first.

"I sense there is something you would like to say to me," Lord Shinjirō said. His voice was deceptively soft.

Michael lowered his eyes. Lord Shinjirō's action the night before and Misako's this morning, and Misako's indirect admission of what she was to the daimyō, all warred with each other in his thoughts.

He knew he shouldn't say anything, but he sensed that Lord Shinjirō probably wouldn't let him remain silent. *I'm screwed either way. May as well say it.*

"Misako is my concubine," Lord Shinjirō said.

Michael looked up at the daimyō, startled.

"My wife and daughters are in Edo. I will be with them again next year," Lord Shinjirō continued. "My wife has been unable to produce a son. As I am the last male in my line, I am hoping that Misako will be able to give me the son that I need." His gaze was placid, but there was something stirring beneath its surface, some indefinable thing that made Michael's pulse quicken as if in the presence of danger.

"I see," Michael said neutrally.

The daimyō's eyes narrowed. "It is extremely important that I have a son," he said. "It is a matter that I cannot ignore or leave to fate."

Michael didn't miss the edge in the daimyō's tone. "Forgive me, my lord," he responded. "I meant no disrespect. Again, it is a matter of my coming from a place—and time—where this is not the norm."

"You are disturbed by this, however. I am curious as to why."

Michael hesitated, then plunged in. "In my time, women make their own decisions about how they want to live, including whether to live with men or to live alone and whether to have children or not have children at all."

Lord Shinjirō stared. "I don't understand. What about their duties as women?"

Michael opened his mouth, then closed it. *How to explain this?* "There are still many women, the majority in fact, who choose to be married and bear children. That hasn't changed, either in my country or in yours, my lord."

"You speak of choice. What about duty? I am the ruler of this han, and yet I have duties that I must carry out, responsibilities that were destined to be mine from birth. You speak of 'choices' that the people in your time have, but life is not about such selfish acts."

The daimyō seemed merely piqued now instead of dangerously angry.

Michael breathed a little easier. "I think that if you could observe the society I come from, my lord, you would call both the women and the men selfish. We live very differently from this society. Individual freedom is considered important."

"Freedom from what? There are always those who abandon their responsibilities and their own blood kin. They are lower than dogs. An individual's wishes can never be more important than the group he supports. A man is nothing if he has no one other than himself to protect." Lord Shinjirō collected himself, then continued. "Misako is under my protection, as is everyone in my home, in this town, and in this han. This is a duty that I would defend at the cost of my own life, without a moment's hesitation. You would do well to remember this as you consider Misako and her position in this household."

"Hai, my lord." Michael bowed his head.

"I will return in two days. Tōru, please see our guest back to his room."

THE AIR was hot and muggy, unrelieved by the shade of the tall green bamboo trees in the small grove. Tōru stood still in the densest part of the grove, listening for approaching footfalls on the soft dirt path.

At the sound of movement, he glanced over and saw the man moving cautiously along the path.

He was in his midthirties—older than Tōru, who was twenty-eight—and the man's face held a worn and tired expression.

So Lord Ryū is still quite the taskmaster.

Tōru stepped out onto the path, noting Kenji's startled expression. *What an incompetent.* "Kenji-san," he said.

The man had nervousness written all over his features. "Tōru-dono," he replied. He released his grip on his sword handle. "Ryū-sama sends his regards."

"Thank you. I trust he is well."

"Yes."

Tōru exhaled, a bit impatiently, and the other man jumped a little. "Oh. Yes." He dug into the small bag attached to the tie-string that held up his hakama trousers.

After extracting a yet smaller bag, Kenji held it out to Tōru, who could barely restrain himself from snatching it out of his hand.

As he counted the iron mon coins, Tōru considered insisting on gold or at least silver for the next payment. Mon were the coin of the realm, but precious metals were better still.

"Shinjirō has left for Kyoto."

"How long will he be gone?"

"He is returning two days from now."

Kenji blinked.

He looks like a tortoise in the sun, Tōru thought contemptuously. *Slow and stupid, a creature made to die.* "I believe it is his usual business with the Emperor, a report on the domain and what it has produced so far this year. Nothing out of the ordinary. However...."

"Yes?"

"There is something that Shirakawa Ryū-sama may find of interest. A guest whom Shinjirō is keeping in the prisoner's cell."

"And what of this prisoner?"

Tōru smiled.

FOOTSTEPS APPROACHED the door.

Here it comes.

He'd been expecting this. He'd seen the look in Tōru's eyes earlier that morning.

The door opened, and Tōru entered, accompanied by two other samurai. Michael looked up, meeting Tōru's eyes without flinching.

"Yō, gaijin." Tōru smirked.

In a flash they had him on the cold floor on all fours. Someone lifted the hem of his light yukata and threw it back over his hips, exposing his bare buttocks, his sex organs covered only by the sling-like fundoshi undergarment.

Tōru walked around in front so Michael could see him. "You see, gaijin," he said conversationally, "you think you are safe, that you have Shinjirō-sama's favor." He crouched down. One of the samurai grabbed Michael's hair and yanked his head back.

Michael winced, and Tōru smiled. "But you are wrong about so many things, gaijin," he said.

The samurai who held Michael around the waist tightened his grip as Tōru brought his face close to Michael's. "Shinjirō-sama is playing with you," he breathed. "Like a cat plays with a mouse. There's only one thing he wants you for."

Tōru grabbed Michael's jaw and forced his mouth open, then slowly placed two fingers inside. He moved the fingers in and out rhythmically as Michael choked and fought to breathe.

He opened his eyes and glared at Tōru, who snickered. "Poor little gaijin," he crooned.

Michael narrowed his eyes—and then bit down.

There was a moment of silence; then Tōru roared something unintelligible before backhanding Michael across the face. "Hold him," he snarled to the other men. He grabbed Michael's jaw to glare into his face one last time. "Time to make you my woman."

Someone pushed Michael's face to the floor, and he turned his head to the side, trying to stop his skin from getting scraped. He was being held down. He couldn't see where Tōru had gone, but he could guess.

He felt his fundoshi being ripped off and tried to struggle, but his position made it impossible. *He's not serious. If I get ripped up back there, it'll leave abrasions, bleeding, evidence. He can't mean to do this.*

Shinjirō wouldn't allow this. He had to believe that.

"Let's see how tight you are," Tōru said.

He thrust a finger up Michael's anus, brutally and without warning.

God. He cried out and heard the samurai laugh. The jabbed intrusion hurt, but it was the sense of invasion that wrung the sound out of him. He hadn't thought Tōru would actually do anything, just taunt and push him around a bit. He didn't think anything would really happen to him.

Maybe it was true. Maybe Shinjirō told him to do this….

No. He refused to believe it. Shinjirō wouldn't do that.

Any further thought was pushed out of his mind by the addition of a second finger, and he bit his lip to keep silent as he felt the tight space split open too wide. Pain shot through his anus as the dry fingers jabbed roughly in and out.

Michael tried to breathe through the pain. Tried not to give Tōru any satisfaction.

"What do you think, gaijin? You like this?"

"Kutabare," Michael ground out.

He hoped he'd remembered "fuck you" correctly in Japanese.

The other samurai gasped in shock. Probably the rumor had gone around the castle about the gaijin speaking nihongo, but he supposed knowing this and actually hearing him speak Japanese was another thing altogether.

Rough fingers grabbed his balls and squeezed, and he couldn't have stopped the hoarse yell that tore from his throat if his life depended on it. The pain was so intense he couldn't breathe.

A dry cough in the doorway.

"What is it, Norio?" Tōru asked, sounding annoyed.

Through a haze of pain, Michael looked up and saw the mild-mannered retainer, the one who'd come to escort him the night Shinjirō had taken him to the garden. Norio met his eyes for a moment; then he looked again at Tōru.

The torturing hands were withdrawn from his anus and from his balls, allowing Michael to draw a ragged breath, lowering his head.

"Some of the farmers from the borderland wish to speak with you."

Norio's tone was even and mild.

Tōru made an impatient sound. Then, as swiftly as they'd entered the room, he and the other samurai left along with Norio.

The door was shut and locked again.

Alone, Michael collapsed on the floor. He lay there for a minute or two, recovering. Then he sat up. *I should check for blood.*

He reached around and touched his anus gingerly. It was sore, but he felt no wetness.

He dragged himself over to the futon and lay down, closing his eyes.

MISAKO ENTERED the room with trepidation.

The young gaijin lay on the futon, sound asleep.

She set the wash bucket and towels down and kneeled by the young man's side. He was breathing lightly and evenly. The yukata had fallen open, and Misako stared, fascinated by the light downy hair on his chest.

Norio told her there'd been... an incident involving Tōru and his men but that it hadn't gotten out of hand. He'd instructed her to bring the wash bucket and towels and simply leave them for the prisoner.

The gaijin looked so peaceful in his sleep. It was late afternoon, and waning sunlight slanted in through the small high window. Misako settled back on her heels in seiza position and contemplated the young man.

There was no way that a Westerner could be in Japan legitimately, save for the few Dutch traders that disembarked for trading activities down in Nagasaki. But Nagasaki was far, far to the south, and the Kaminishi Han was barely a half-day's journey from Kyoto, the capital of the country and seat of the Emperor himself. The centuries-old edict against foreigners being in Japan was still the unquestioned law of the land.

How did this man come to be here? Why is he here?

The young man started in his sleep, gasping, and Misako reared back, her hand knocking against the bucket.

The sound woke him. He opened his eyes, blinking.

His eyes lit on Misako, and she saw him relax. *You thought it was Tōru again.* "Sumimasen," she said. "I didn't mean to disturb you."

"Iie. You didn't disturb me," he replied.

It was still strange to hear Japanese being spoken from that very different-looking face; her expression must have shown her bemusement, because the young man smiled suddenly. He had beautiful white teeth, like a child's.

"I brought you a wash bucket and fresh towels," Misako said.

"Thank you."

He regarded her with a serious look and then another gentle smile that made her heart pound a little. He was looking at her as if he actually saw her, saw her as a person apart from her role as provider of meals and wash items. The only other man who had ever looked at her that way was—

Her hand flew to her mouth.

"What's wrong? Are you all right?"

"Yes. I-I'm fine. Shitsurei-s-shimasu," Misako stammered. She gathered the folds of her kimono, preparing to rise, but his voice stopped her.

"Please stay."

He spoke to her as if she were his equal. That, coupled with his startlingly different gaijin face, made Misako feel as if she had entered an odd dream of some kind.

"Where are you from?"

"I am from the Shirakawa Han, to the east of here."

"That would be on the way to Kyoto, yes?"

"Hai." She lowered her eyes. The gaijin had a way of staring at her, instead of the way a nihonjin would gently nod throughout a conversation or look down or away. Seeing his blue eyes gazing at her so frankly made her think about things she shouldn't be thinking about, not about a man other than Shinjirō-sama.

"Are you happy... here?" he was asking, and Misako, surprised, looked directly at him. "I'm sorry, I probably shouldn't ask, but—"

"Iie.... It's all right. Shinjirō-sama is a very kind man. My family receives compensation and other benefits from my... being here. I am content with that."

"Do you miss them?"

She paused. "Yes, sometimes. Actually, it's not them, but...." Misako stopped, realizing belatedly that she was entering dangerous waters. "Sumimasen. I should go."

But she couldn't seem to leave.

"There is someone back in my village," she continued finally in a soft voice. "I was the receiver of his affections, and I thought that perhaps...." She glanced up at the small high window. "But I have been here for many months. It is likely that he has forgotten me by now."

She turned her attention back to the young man, who was staring at her intently. His blue eyes regarded her with sympathy and interest. "It must be difficult for you."

"Iie.... I... I must go now."

She left the room, feeling the gaijin's eyes on her back.

SHE GOT as far as the hallway leading to the stairs that went up to the main floor of the castle before a hand suddenly covered her mouth.

In shock she felt herself being dragged backward and into the storeroom. Rough, masculine hands turned her and pushed her against the wall between a bag of onions and a barrel of wild mountain yams.

She shut her eyes, terrified and not knowing what to expect. Slowly she gathered her courage and opened her eyes.

"You stupid female," Tōru said.

CHAPTER THREE

THE DAY after his conversation with Misako, his morning and midday meals were brought in by an elderly woman. Although there had been a few occasions before when this had been the case, it was usually Misako who brought his meals and saw to his wash supplies.

Michael felt a slight uneasiness, though he couldn't say why. There wasn't anything that unusual about Misako's absence, so by midafternoon he concluded that there was nothing to it.

Tōru and his minions hadn't returned either. Michael had been bracing himself for another unwanted visit, but there had been nothing forthcoming from that quarter. Either Tōru had had enough fun the day before or other matters required his attention.

So it was somewhat unexpected when the door opened and Misako silently entered the room, head bowed, with the fish and rice that served as his supper. It was late afternoon but earlier than usual, and Michael stared at the young woman as she set the tray down carefully.

She didn't look at him.

He continued to watch as she straightened the futon—he was sitting against the wall across the room—and smoothed the cloth out, a purposeless task. He was a prisoner; it wasn't likely that a neat futon for him was among the priorities of her job.

The silence grew until Michael couldn't take it anymore and broke it. "Are you all right, Misako-san?"

Her hands on the futon stopped; then she folded them on her lap and spoke calmly. "I am fine. I do wish... to speak with you, Maikoru-san, if I could."

"Of course."

She bowed her head. "This morning, I spoke with an old friend near the border. This friend has kindly arranged for me to return home."

"What?" Michael stared.

Misako cleared her throat. "I can go home... tonight. My family will be waiting for me at the border. It's been arranged."

"I don't understand."

She still didn't look at him. "I... I am afraid to go alone, Maikoru-san. Will you come with me?"

ODDLY IT had never occurred to Michael to try to escape.

He was a prisoner trapped not only physically in a cell but by time itself. Finding himself in another era as well as in a foreign country, as the days passed he had felt strangely as though he were in the right place, as if he were supposed to be here.

But if he never left here... he might be a prisoner forever.

In the end, it wasn't about escaping or his freedom or even why he was here, having this apparently real experience of being in Japan in 1851.

It was that man. Lord Shinjirō. Michael didn't want to leave him.

"I'll see you to the border," Michael had told Misako, "and then I'll return to the castle."

"No! If you do—"

"Don't worry about me. I'll be fine."

Finally with tears in her eyes, she had nodded and bowed her thanks repeatedly, while Michael smiled, trying to act reassuring.

He wasn't quite as sanguine as he made himself out to be. He knew that daimyō in this time period had life-or-death power over their subjects, answering only to the Emperor and the Shogun. A samurai like Tōru, for example, could kill an ordinary citizen in the town for giving a disrespectful look—or one Tōru considered disrespectful. That was an ordinary citizen; Michael was a prisoner. He had even fewer rights. Actually he had no rights at all.

So Lord Shinjirō, as daimyō and lord over this entire region, was empowered to do anything to him should his aiding of Misako's escape be discovered. It was only Michael's belief in Lord Shinjirō's essential fairness that enabled him to decide to help her.

That, and the belief that Misako deserved her chance at love as much as anyone.

He wasn't sure if he believed in love for himself, or that he even knew what love was. A barely there mother and long-absent father had taught him that if there were such a thing as love, he would have to find it later and elsewhere.

A stray memory came to him: Maria. That was her name. A Filipino nanny his mother had hired when he was very little. She used to push his hair back behind his ear with her finger, giving him a little tickly feeling… just as Misako had done the morning before Lord Shinjirō had left, when she'd brought in his breakfast early. That was it; she had reminded him of Maria.

He had loved Maria. She smiled at him with her warm brown eyes and played with him whenever he wanted. He could tell that she really enjoyed him; while his mother forced a smile when others were present to see, Maria laughed openly with him. Even at three years old, he could tell the difference.

One day, a day like any other day, Maria was playing with him and they were laughing together when he felt a shadow fall across the room. He looked up and saw his mother staring at them from the doorway.

The next day Maria disappeared and never returned.

He wandered all over the huge house looking for her. He cried himself to sleep every night for a week. It wasn't until years later that he understood the look on his mother's face. Jealousy.

He had run to Maria's arms more often than to his mother's arms. His mother couldn't accept that the *paid help* was his focus of devotion. So she sent Maria away.

Misako's caring for his needs, her vulnerable position in the household, her status as a concubine, all had affected Michael, who was already a believer in feminist rights (he had to be—he'd had

Ellen as a girlfriend, after all), and thus his decision had been made. No matter what happened to him afterward, he would help Misako.

Michael strained to see in the dark grove, the moon being a sliver in the black night.

Behind him, Misako clung to his shirt, head lowered.

The two made their way eastward through the darkness, one with a quiet but firm resolve, and the other with a conflicted and heavy heart.

They reached a small clearing in the bamboo grove and silently waited in the bushes.

The clearing was lit by moonlight, and the night air was cool and pleasant to breathe. In spite of the reason for the long walk and the tense situation, Michael found it invigorating to finally use his limbs and walk freely in the outdoors again.

He glanced at Misako, who sat quietly in seiza position in the dirt, her head inclined downward. He couldn't see her expression.

"Misako-san, I have appreciated knowing you. I wish we could have spent more time together." He kept his voice very low.

She didn't look up.

"You are a good person, and I wish you every happiness."

One of her hands that rested on her thighs clenched.

A single tear fell.

She raised her head and looked directly at him.

"I am nothing."

As Michael stared at her, a rustling noise sounded from across the clearing.

STAYING IN the shadows, his face obscured by the rough shawl Misako had given him when they left the castle, Michael watched as Misako embraced her father and mother.

He smiled at her and waved his hand as she looked in his direction.

She nodded briefly, and then her face crumpled as she turned to leave with her family.

Michael waited for a few minutes, then stood up and started back in the direction of Kaminishi Castle.

Misako had let him out of his cell, then taken him down a secret passageway that led outside the castle to the forest and dense underbrush. A path choked with overgrowth led away from there into the woods. It was a common feature of castles and other important buildings in Tokugawa-era Japan: the castle occupants needed a safe and hidden means of ingress and egress in case of attack or siege.

He could, therefore, if luck were with him, reenter the castle and return to his cell before anyone noticed he'd been gone. The cell door being left unlocked would be attributed to Misako, who was now safely with her loved ones. The samurai would think that Michael had been too frightened or stupid to try to escape.

A cloud passed over the moon, and Michael shivered.

A noise sounded behind him. He froze.

THE DAIMYŌ returned at midday, having left Kyoto before dawn.

It had been an arduous return journey through the mountain passes, and Shinjirō was in no mood to deal with any additional headaches.

So it was with a sense of displeasure that Shinjirō noted Tōru lingering nearby as he opened the receiving room's sliding door to the courtyard outside. "Was there something else?" he asked curtly.

His second in command bowed his head. "My apologies, my lord. There is a situation that I must inform you of."

THE GAIJIN lay naked on the futon, his wrists bound behind his back, with his ankles similarly tied.

He was facing away from the door but turned his head to look as Shinjirō entered the cell.

Shinjirō stared at him without expression.

He was dirty, his face covered in a light sheen of sweat, but he met Shinjirō's gaze without flinching.

Shinjirō narrowed his eyes, then turned and left the cell without a word.

"See to his basic needs," he said to the elderly woman who stood outside the door.

MICHAEL WAS released from his bonds and allowed to eat and drink and wash himself.

After he was seized, Tōru and his men had taken him back to the castle, forced him into his cell, and bound him. Though he had braced himself for more, Tōru inflicted no further abuse on him.

He guessed that his summary execution would probably be sufficient to satisfy even Tōru's bloodlust.

Using the hem of his yukata to finish drying himself off, Michael felt oddly at peace. *The worst that can happen is that I die.* He didn't know why he had been sent to 1851 Japan. What if helping Misako had been the reason?

It would make as much sense as anything else about this whole experience.

He heard footsteps coming downstairs. He straightened his back and stood facing the door calmly.

The door opened and the daimyō entered, his face unreadable. He nodded to Norio behind him, and Norio exited and shut the door, leaving the two men alone in the cell.

"Remove your clothing," Lord Shinjirō said.

Michael stared at him, then untied the yukata and dropped it to the floor. Realizing it would be a good idea if he were to follow suit, he then sank to kneel on the floor with his head lowered and his arms at his sides.

He kept his gaze to the floor as the daimyō paced back and forth.

"Tell me what happened," Lord Shinjirō finally ground out tersely.

He came to a halt in front of Michael, who still had his eyes lowered.

"Hai, Shinjirō-sama," Michael replied. "Misako-san told me that there was a man in her village—"

"—whom she loved. Yes, I am aware of that fact."

Michael looked up at the daimyō's face. It was a mask, and Michael blinked. "You knew that she left someone behind to come here and be your—"

"The bearer of my child, yes. Did you willingly help her to escape?"

"Yes."

Something was in Lord Shinjirō's hand. A bamboo rod.

Michael shut his eyes. "I wanted to help—"

"Do not speak, unless you are asked a question."

"Sumimasen." He shut his mouth and waited, opening his eyes but lowering them again.

The daimyō seemed a little calmer now, but Michael wasn't sure that was a good thing. "Do you recall that I told you that Misako was under my protection?"

Michael glanced up at Lord Shinjirō, startled.

"Yes, my lord."

"Did you consider that returning her to the Shirakawa Han might be dangerous for her?"

Michael stared at him dumbly.

"The man she wanted to be with no longer returns her affections. Her family is under no obligation to take her back."

"Where is she now? Is she all right?"

A sudden fire streaked across his left arm, so agonizing that he couldn't even draw breath. The rod was already back at Lord Shinjirō's side, hanging down from his grasp. "I said do not speak unless I ask you a question." Michael managed a tight nod, keeping his face lowered, fighting the urge to hold his arm.

"Misako has been taken in by a family friend. But she will not be able to stay with them for long. Her presence in the village shames her family, so she will have to leave soon."

Where will she go? Michael wondered. But he was forbidden from saying it.

"It may be a matter of no consequence to you, but your actions have shamed not only myself, my family, this castle, and this town but the entire han that has been my family's responsibility for generations. What do you have to say to that?"

"I'm sorry."

"You are expressing regret for what, exactly?"

Michael stared at the floor. "I regret that Misako's choice did not lead to the happiness that she sought," he said softly.

There was absolute silence above him; then he felt the daimyō moving toward him. Suddenly he was beside Michael, and Michael's face was pushed to the floor.

A hand held the back of his neck. "Do not move," he heard, and then the first blow struck his back.

The searing pain again, this time using more of the rod, leaving a long line of agony across his flesh. He stifled a gasp. Another stroke.

Don't cry out. Michael tried to focus on keeping silent, for lack of being able to do anything else to help himself. *Four... five....* It felt like his back was being flayed open with every stroke. He crossed his hands together on the floor and laid his forehead on them, trying to keep breathing in and out.

Six... seven... eight....

Above him, Lord Shinjirō said nothing as the rod swished through the air again, then once more, then stopped.

Sweat broke out on his face, and he panted heavily through his mouth as the daimyō stood up and walked away. He raised his head from the floor, holding himself up with his hands. He didn't dare look at Lord Shinjirō.

When he finally gathered the courage to look, he saw the daimyō standing at the far end of the cell, his back to Michael. Unbidden, Lord Shinjirō's words came back to him: *"It is extremely important that I have a son. It is a matter that I cannot ignore or leave to fate.*

"You speak of choice. What about duty? I am the ruler of this han, and yet I have duties that I must carry out, responsibilities that were destined to be mine from birth. You speak of 'choices' that the people in your time have, but life is not about such selfish acts.

"An individual's wishes can never be more important than the group he supports. A man is nothing if he has no one other than himself to protect. Misako is under my protection, as is everyone in my home, in this town, and in this han. This is a duty that I would defend at the cost of my own life, without a moment's hesitation. You would do well to remember this as you consider Misako and her position in this household."

Michael stared at Lord Shinjirō's back.

It was true. What he had done was both selfless and selfish—selfless in that he had helped Misako, and selfish because he had considered only his own beliefs to the exclusion of the daimyō's needs and responsibilities.

He would do it again. But not without recognizing the cost to Lord Shinjirō.

At that moment, Lord Shinjirō turned around and looked at Michael. Michael immediately bowed his face to the floor, his hands on the floor with elbows out in the most submissive position possible.

"My lord, may I speak?"

"Yes."

"I am deeply sorry for offending you with my actions. I was thinking only of what I believed in without taking into account your position, the respect that is due to yourself and to this society, and your wishes. I humbly ask your forgiveness and accept whatever punishment you see fit to give me."

He remained in that position, head and body bowed to the floor, for what felt like an eternity before he heard Lord Shinjirō walk past him and out of the cell.

The next thing he knew the elderly female servant was entering with a bucket, washcloth, and jars of ointment for his wounds.

His punishment was over.

CHAPTER FOUR

IT WAS a week before he saw Lord Shinjirō again.

The wounds on his back had healed sufficiently that he could wear the yukata again. At least several of the strokes had drawn blood and scabbed over. If the stroke on his arm was anything to go by, the ones on his back might leave scars.

One day he was taken from his cell by Norio and, to his surprise, brought upstairs to a room on the main floor.

"This will be your room from now on," Norio said, then took his leave.

The room was about the same size as his cell but had a shōji door that opened onto a side area of the courtyard. This small area was private, being in a corner where two of the castle's high walls bounded it, and Michael saw a vegetable garden planted there. He could hear the trickling sound of the stream coming from around the corner in the main part of the courtyard.

There was a futon, and the bucket with its wet cloth, and some new clothing neatly folded on the futon. Other than those items, the room was empty. Altogether it was similar to the cell, with the exception of having access to the outdoors and having a sliding door that did not lock on the outside.

It appeared that he was no longer a prisoner; or rather, he was still a prisoner but one who was trusted now not to run away. He wondered at that, having betrayed the daimyō only a week before. What had changed? Lord Shinjirō was within his rights to execute him for what he'd done. Yet now Michael had been moved to a room closer to the daimyō's own, and with an unlocked door to boot.

It was odd.

Lord Shinjirō also resumed their conversations in the receiving room.

What Michael had done, and the topic of Misako, was never raised again.

The daimyō asked him about the twenty-first century, about America and the Western nations. Michael responded as informatively as he could. It was difficult, and he found himself making instant decisions on how much to tell and how to phrase what he said so a mid-nineteenth-century Japanese daimyō wouldn't be corrupted by what he heard.

And all the while he waited for the other shoe to drop, for Lord Shinjirō to start asking about Japan again.

LATE ONE night, Michael felt another's presence in the room.

He kept his eyes closed.

The person approached his futon quietly, coming to kneel beside where he lay. For a while nothing happened. Then a hand reached out and touched the side of his face.

Michael felt oddly calm, because he knew who it was.

He opened his eyes. The room was dark, but moonlight lit the paper door that led to the garden, and he could easily make out Lord Shinjirō's features hovering over him.

For a moment the two of them looked at each other; then the daimyō moved his hand to pass over Michael's eyes, gently bidding him to close them again in an unspoken fashion.

He did so.

Lord Shinjirō stroked Michael's hair and then brought his face down so his lips ghosted around Michael's ear and neck. Michael lay there, letting himself enjoy the sensations, breathing in the scent of the man's skin and hair, so close to him now.

For a moment Michael wondered if it was a dream. But it felt too real. He didn't know why he wasn't objecting. It just felt natural, so he let it continue.

Since the daimyō bid him close his eyes, Michael assumed he wasn't allowed to move either. So he let him do all the touching.

The blanket covering him was laid aside, and Michael felt the daimyō go still.

Oh. Michael supposed a circumcised penis must look mutilated or damaged in some way to Shinjirō.

Abruptly Lord Shinjirō disappeared from the room as quietly as he had appeared, and Michael opened his eyes.

Was it a dream?

HE OPENED the door to the garden the next morning. The summer air was sweet to breathe in.

The garden was developing nicely. Michael had worked at a community garden in Santa Barbara growing up, and he recognized the various plants and their bounty: cabbages, green onions, turnips, and cucumbers. He also noticed the local Kyoto varieties of sansai or kyō yasai vegetables like mizuna, Kamo eggplant, and Shishigatani kabocha pumpkin. Despite the great variety of plants, the garden had an orderly look to it. The plants were set and staked in neat rows with raised lines of dirt separating them.

A small rounded back appeared at the far end of the garden, barely visible above the stems and leaves.

Michael watched for a moment, but the person did not turn around or look up.

The dream—or whatever it was—from the night before came back to him. Despite the fact that he had initially been asleep when Lord Shinjirō entered the room, he was certain it had actually occurred.

The daimyō was sexually attracted to him.

And Michael wasn't sure how he felt about it.

He'd never had a relationship with a man, but oddly the idea didn't offend him. He had never considered himself anything other than heterosexual, but there'd been times when he'd felt a stirring in his groin when noticing another man. It was a certain aesthetic that did it to him, a kind of austere strength and intensity. It wasn't something that most men had or projected, so he hadn't been faced with it too much. But Lord Shinjirō was another matter.

The daimyō presented Michael with the ultimate image of these things.

Michael considered himself to be an analytical type of person. But analyzing himself had never been easy. With his father having left the family at an early age—and a mother who was, to say the least, difficult—he could guess that maybe he had a father complex, or a missing authority figure complex, perhaps. But did that translate to one's sexuality?

He closed his eyes, letting the morning air waft over him, breathing it in deeply. Was he attracted to the daimyō?

"TELL ME about Japan," Lord Shinjirō said.

Michael started. He had just settled onto the tatami mat for one of their conversations. "My lord—"

"It is important to me that I know."

"I apologize, my lord. It is difficult for me to—"

"I understand you are apprehensive that some harm will be done by our discussing this. But I need to know."

"Shinjirō-sama, my concern is for your safety. If you discover things about the future it may bring you to harm."

The daimyō blinked. "So you are being protective of me, Maikoru." An ironic smile came to his face, then disappeared as soon as it had arrived. "Be assured, I am more than capable of handling whatever results from what you have to tell me."

Michael looked down. He didn't know where to start, or if he should start, though it seemed he had little choice.

"In two years, an American naval commander named Commodore Perry will arrive in Edo Bay with large black ships with huge guns. This visit will begin the process that will lead to Japan opening its doors to trade and commerce with the outside world again...."

He told Lord Shinjirō of the fall of the Shogunate and reestablishment of the Emperor's rule, and of the rise of Japanese militarism: the first Sino-Japanese War, the Russo-Japanese War over control of Manchuria and Korea, the turn to fascism and the start of World War II.

Michael spoke with a lowered head, not daring to look at the daimyō as he recounted the facts of history. But the most difficult part was still to come.

"In 1941, Japan commits a surprise attack against America in the Hawaiian Islands, at Pearl Harbor. The world continues to be at war for another four years... until...." He stopped, unable to go on.

Michael looked at Lord Shinjirō. Lord Shinjirō was staring at him with an unreadable expression, almost as if he were in shock. "Go on," Lord Shinjirō said. Even his tone was unreadable.

"The war finally ends in the European theater in late spring of 1945. Major cities in Japan are bombed by airplanes. Kyoto, Nara, and Kamakura are spared because of their historical significance."

He straightened his shoulders and looked the daimyō directly in the eye. "Many cities are firebombed, killing countless thousands of people. But the most powerful bombs are dropped on Hiroshima and Nagasaki, killing many, many thousands. It is a new kind of weapon—a kind of superbomb. And Japan surrenders. That finally ends the war."

The daimyō stared at him. "Sonna," he intoned.

Michael nodded. "I know that it sounds unbelievable," he said. "I'm sorry. But the story isn't over, not by a long shot. Japan is occupied by American forces for a number of years, but regains its autonomy in the 1950s. After that, Japan brings itself up in the world, recovering from its war losses to become an economic powerhouse. It turns completely modern while still retaining many of its historical landmarks and traditions. Tokyo—what you know now as Edo—becomes an international city, and the largest city in the world. It's a beautiful place, Shinjirō-sama." He stopped as he saw that the daimyō was still simply staring at him.

"Please believe me. The rehabilitation of Japan after this last world war is complete. Japan is now respected among nations, standing shoulder to shoulder with everyone else in the world." Michael heard the pleading tone in his voice and shut his mouth.

Lord Shinjirō's gaze finally broke. He stood up and walked to the open doorway leading to the garden.

Michael watched the daimyō, concerned. "My lord—"

"Please, do not speak."

The daimyō turned his face toward the garden.

Michael lowered his head. *I knew this would happen.*

The whole crazy deal with him being here at all…. Was this really a lucid dream he was stuck in? Could he actually be here in Japan, in 1851, the prisoner of a samurai warlord some miles west of Kyoto? And what was the purpose this conversation? Was this the reason he had traveled through time?

Lord Shinjirō's back was still to him, but Michael saw his shoulders shaking.

I am sorry to have told you this.

"Can nothing stop this?"

"My lord?"

"This terrible thing. If what you say is true, then the country I love will be lost."

Michael swallowed. "Not lost, my lord. Changed, yes, but not lost. And in the eyes of the world, a better place."

Lord Shinjirō turned around then, and Michael saw tears in his eyes. "No. What you have described is a tragedy. I see nothing but suffering for my people in the future you have told me—wars, civilians killed, the defeat of our people. The terrible bombs dropping out of the sky. There will be no future for Japan if these things come to pass."

"My lord—with all due respect—I did say that this nation will rise again economically, though not militarily, and will stand at the top among nations in a way undreamed of even by the Shogun or the Emperor in any era. Yes, Japan will see great changes, some of them caused by tragic events. But those events will turn out to be the catalysts for change that were necessary for Japan to join the nations of the earth. You can't let your feelings—"

"The Shogun whom I serve will be no more, seventeen years from today. And one hundred years from now, the Emperor will be a mere figurehead of this land. This nation will be occupied for years by a foreign power. And then, you say, our cities will rise again. But what will we have become by then? How can we still be who we are after such deadly changes?" The daimyō paced back and forth. "I see nothing but suffering in my nation's future, and it is all due to this 'opening to the West' that you speak of, which will take place two years from now."

Michael remained silent.

"I am filled with dread over this future. This must be stopped. I must warn the Shogun of this tragedy to come, so he can gather all the daimyō together. We must join together to prevent this from happening."

"Shinjirō-sama, please reconsider. I don't believe that any action you could take would change the outcome."

"There is no way I can sit still and do nothing, given what I know now."

"My lord, is it likely that anyone who hears your words would believe you? Please—"

The daimyō glared at him. "If the outcome is likely to be unsuccessful, is that an honorable reason not to try at all? This cannot be what you are saying."

Michael sighed. Wasn't this exactly the result he'd been trying to avoid? He gave it one last try, choosing his words carefully.

"I've said this before. I don't know how or why I am here in the past, in your country. I think sometimes that this is just a dream I'm having and that I'm not really here. I don't know. But I can't believe that I would be here because you are supposed to change history. My lord, I am simply asking you to think again before you take action. Please."

He stopped his words and looked at Lord Shinjirō, mutely pleading with his eyes.

The daimyō returned his gaze evenly.

"I thank you for sharing this with me." He raised his voice. "Norio, please see our guest back to his room."

THE BAMBOO grove was still. Small streaks of sunlight streamed down between the tall, reedy trees.

Tōru stood impatiently in the shade of the tallest tree. *Late again.* How much of his life would he waste waiting for idiots like Kenji? He had been waiting for over an hour. If Kenji didn't come soon—

A rustle of leaves, and then Kenji appeared at the edge of the grove. "Toru-dono, my apologies. I was delayed by Ryū-sama's change in plans." The man was more tired-looking than usual. At Tōru's pointed look, Kenji started. "Ah, forgive me."

He extracted a small packet from his waist bag and handed it to Tōru. Tōru opened it and emptied the silver coins into his palm to count them.

A slight wind rippled through the grove. "Good," Tōru said. "Now. I think it's time we had another disruption on the borderlands."

"Yes," Kenji said. "Oh. About the gaijin—"

"What about him?"

"Ah. He is…. Is he…?"

Tōru exhaled impatiently. "He's still alive. My lord has shown exemplary leniency in this situation, unfortunately."

"I see." The older man seemed surprised.

Tōru snorted. "Shinjirō's judgment has been affected by this gaijin. It is extremely regrettable." He narrowed his eyes. "But this may be something we can use to our advantage."

THE GARDENER was working in the garden when Michael was returned to his room.

Cicadas chirped noisily, and the sun was beating down on the patch of ground that was his only window on the outside world.

He walked to the open doorway, then hesitated. He hadn't specifically been told to stay in his room, but he knew he was still a prisoner. A bit nervously, he stepped outside.

Michael walked to the edge of the garden and crouched down to look at the growing plants.

Fifteen feet away, the gardener remained hunched over, hands working in the dirt. Michael could see the small rounded back, mostly obscured by plants.

He hesitated, then stood up and slowly walked around the garden to where the figure crouched in the dirt.

He was a small man who wore a gray-striped peasant kimono over rough trousers and was pulling weeds, working a small metal digging tool around the base of each weed to get it out.

His back was still to Michael, and Michael, not wanting to startle him, cleared his throat politely.

The man turned and glanced up at him. His eyes widened. He was in his forties, Michael guessed, though his features were still boyish.

"Sumimasen," Michael said.

The man's mouth fell open, and he sat down abruptly in the dirt.

"I'm sorry to disturb you," Michael continued in Japanese. "Your garden is beautiful." He crouched down, a few feet away so as not to startle the gardener any further. "I've been admiring it. How long have you been growing these plants?"

The man had closed his mouth, but he still stared at Michael as though he were from outer space. Then, as if not knowing what else to do, he turned back to his plants and resumed weeding again.

Michael blinked. He supposed having a gaijin turn up out of nowhere and then actually speak Japanese must be a shock to anyone in 1851 Japan. He decided not to take it personally and settled in to pulling weeds himself.

The two men weeded the garden comfortably, in silence, for the next hour or so.

ONE NIGHT, there was an unexpected invitation for him.

Michael was called to the daimyō's receiving room. It was unusual, though not unheard of, to be called to converse with Lord Shinjirō in the evening. They had not spoken about Japan's future again after the one time, and Michael couldn't help but wonder for a moment if this evening he was to be grilled on the subject again.

What was really unusual was that Norio had brought him more substantial clothing to wear than the usual yukata—a dark blue kimono, with a deep royal blue kamishimo to wear over it, both made of the finest silk. The kamishimo was a two-part garment consisting of an open vest with wide shoulders and hakama pants.

Michael put them on, and they fit well. They must have been Lord Shinjirō's, since no one else in the castle was as tall as he. He estimated he was about two inches shorter than the daimyō, so the fit was near perfect.

He walked with Norio down the hall to the receiving room, feeling different because of his dress. It was odd, but he felt as though he were about to take part in a ceremonial meeting or event.

When Norio slid open the door to the room, Michael had to suppress a gasp.

The daimyō was wearing a deep blue outfit, similar to Michael's but with the addition of a blue and white brocaded kamishimo with an elaborate design of cranes embroidered in silver thread. It was a beautiful piece of clothing, and the daimyō was utterly, breathtakingly beautiful in it.

Michael was distantly aware of Norio stepping discreetly back into the hallway behind him as Lord Shinjirō walked forward to greet him. "I wanted to see you wearing this," he said, using formal Japanese and gesturing gracefully toward Michael's kamishimo.

"My lord," Michael said. He was incapable of saying anything further.

This is a beautiful, beautiful man.

THE NIGHT air was still, and crickets chirped their gentle song.

Norio had led the way out of the castle through the underground passage, carrying a lantern. Guards bowed their heads as they passed, and Michael was glad for the scarf that covered his light brown hair and hung over the top portion of his face.

They walked through the forested area, emerging onto a mild, rocky upslope that became a gradually steeper ascent to the mountains.

Eventually they came upon a grouping of boulders, and the soft sounds of bubbling water reached Michael's ears. Lord Shinjirō nodded to Norio, who bowed and departed, leaving the lantern behind on a rock.

It was an onsen, or natural hot springs. Steam rose up from the slightly milky-looking water. The area was surrounded by trees, giving them privacy—or at least the illusion of privacy, as Michael was sure that many guards were keeping watch all around them somewhere in the distance.

It was enchanting.

He turned to find the daimyō watching him, a small quirk of a smile on his face. "It's beautiful, Shinjirō-sama," he said simply.

The daimyō smiled, then began removing his clothes. "Then let us enjoy it."

THE NIGHT sky overhead was full of stars, and Michael leaned his head back against solid rock, enjoying the view.

Next to him, the daimyō was more relaxed than Michael had ever seen him, the responsibilities of leadership off his shoulders for a few precious moments.

The water was heavenly—hot and just the right temperature. Michael felt his muscles let go and become heavy and soft in the water. He closed his eyes.

He felt a featherlight touch on his temple; then a hand began stroking his face. He was still for a moment; then he turned toward the caressing hand and opened his eyes.

Lord Shinjirō was gazing at him, his body next to Michael's. It was the closest he'd ever been to the daimyō, with the exception of the time he had been whipped.

Punishment didn't seem to be what was on the daimyō's mind at the moment.

Michael held his breath.

A warm hand reached behind his head and gently pulled him forward. Then the daimyō's lips were on his. Michael closed his eyes again.

He was surprised at the sensation of kissing someone who was bigger than him, someone big and strong and very male. He opened his mouth without resistance, and then the daimyō's arms were around him. Michael reached his hands under the water for Shinjirō's body. He grabbed hold and hung on, his mouth captured by the daimyō's mouth.

Shinjirō's hands were moving on his back. Michael pulled Shinjirō closer against him, feeling the man's hardness pushing into his pelvis. His own cock was getting there, and the pressure of being up against Shinjirō's hard body only aided in this.

He threw his head back, breaking the kiss, and Shinjirō responded by mouthing his exposed neck. His hands moved down to Michael's ass, grabbing for a handhold in the water. He brought their hips together, holding them fast against each other. Michael gasped at the delicious sensations.

Shinjirō's eyes held Michael in an almost hypnotic gaze. He began moving against Michael, grinding their groins together rhythmically. Michael couldn't look away.

He was beyond hard now, both of them were. Shinjirō rocked their hips together faster and faster until they came, Michael first and then the daimyō, who gasped his release.

When Michael could think again enough to open his eyes, he found he was still in Shinjirō's embrace. He laid his face on the daimyō's shoulder, not having any words for what had just occurred.

He'd just had sex with a man.

His heartbeat slowed gradually, and lassitude came over his muscles. It was difficult to keep above water, his leaning on Shinjirō the only thing holding him up.

"Was that your first time?" the deep voice said next to his ear.

"With a man... yes."

"Ah," Shinjirō murmured. Then he chuckled.

"What?"

"I sensed that you were not experienced with your own sex."

At this, Michael pulled back and looked at Shinjirō. The daimyō's eyes held mirth and kindness. Michael was annoyed, but Shinjirō's expression stopped him.

"This is not to say that you did anything wrong. You were absolutely delightful."

The daimyō smiled. Michael became even more indignant. *He's treating me like... a girl.* Any further sense of outrage was shut down, though, when Shinjirō leaned forward and kissed him.

The kiss deepened, and Michael felt a pulse, a quickening down there again. *What is this?* Everything he considered "normal" had changed. He couldn't get enough of touching Shinjirō.

Everything in his world had just changed.

HE FOUND himself telling Lord Shinjirō about his early life, how his father had left the family early on, unable to cope with a rich, overbearing wife. How he had grown up alone, pursuing solitary interests, with few friends. How life at Berkeley had opened him up a little; he'd dated a few female students, including living with Ellen for six months before it all fell apart. How Ellen was still his closest friend. How he didn't know what he was going to do after he graduated.

The night took on a surreal feeling. He was in a hot springs in late-Edo-period Japan, with a samurai warlord with whom he'd just had sex.

But it felt more real to him than anything in his life ever had.

He stopped talking, suddenly aware that he'd been going on and on like a nervous party guest. "Sumimasen," he said.

"Not at all," Shinjirō assured him. "You interest me."

He began stroking Michael's hair, his large wet hand pulling the strands slightly. Michael's eyes closed again. What was it about the daimyō that affected him so? He felt as though he was falling under a spell....

Shinjirō kissed him again, deeply. Michael put his arms around the daimyō's neck, pulling him as close as humanly possible.

I want you.

He lifted a leg under the water, hooking it around Shinjirō's hip. Shinjirō, fast to respond, pulled Michael's other leg up, and Michael found himself against the daimyō's body, hard cock and balls up against the other man's privates. With his legs locked around Shinjirō's waist and their tongues deep in each other's mouths, the pressure and friction under the water did the rest. Michael cried out as he came again, throwing his head back against the night sky.

THE NEXT morning he awoke to the sounds of shouting in the castle.

He hurriedly threw on his yukata and went out in the hallway. The shouts seemed to be coming from the main hall of the castle, the large room where Shinjirō held meetings with his men.

Michael ran toward the room, remembering just in time that others who might not know about him could be there. He stopped in the hallway, keeping back from the doorway that was around the next corner. From here, he might be able to overhear what was going on.

A loud voice from one of Shinjirō's men. Something about houses... fires... the border between the Kaminishi and Shirakawa Han.

He heard Shinjirō issuing orders, and Tōru's voice raised in response, and then a number of men exited the room at a dead run.

Michael waited; then he cautiously approached the doorway and looked inside.

Lord Shinjirō stood alone in the center of the great room, his back to the doorway.

Michael entered the room. The daimyō seemed unaware of his presence. Given his warrior instincts, he had to have been incredibly preoccupied not to notice him.

When Shinjirō finally turned around, the look on his face startled Michael.

He was furious.

"Who are you?"

Michael's mouth hung open. "What?"

Shinjirō strode forward as Michael stood there dumbly, and suddenly the daimyō's hand was swinging toward his face.

Slap!

"I asked you, who are you?"

Michael stumbled back, then gained control of himself. "Sumimasen. I don't understand. What do you mean?"

Shinjirō glared at him. "The troubles continue with the Shirakawa clan. You were the one who went with Misako to the border against my orders. And now houses have been set afire along the borderlands." He advanced on Michael, who backed away. "I want to know *who you really are and why you have come into my life.*"

The two men stared at each other in silence.

Michael opened his mouth to speak. "I am from your future—"

And then everything went black.

HIS FACE was lying against something hard.

Michael lifted his head, blinking against the harsh artificial light.

He had been facedown on his book. He was seated at his desk.

He was back.

The TV was still on in the living room, tuned to CNN.

Michael slowly walked around his apartment. It was still nighttime. He thought of something and picked up his cell phone from the kitchen table.

It was 10:45 p.m. on the same day that he last recalled being... home.

He stood still in the middle of the living room, his mind a blank.

What... happened to me? What was all of that?

Was it a dream?

He went outside to the balcony. Looking at the night sky, at the Golden Gate Bridge in the distance, the cars passing on the street below, only one question was on his mind.

Was it all just a dream?

PART TWO
"THE LIFE I WAS MEANT TO LIVE"

CHAPTER FIVE

"SO... HE was a samurai warlord?"

There was more than simple disbelief in Ellen's voice—there was a touch of actual scorn.

Michael flinched.

"I know how it sounds—"

"Oh, I don't *think* so. Michael, have you been getting enough sleep? I know it's finals now, but—"

"Ellen." He sighed.

What did you expect? It was an unbelievable story. He wouldn't have believed her if she'd been telling it. *You're not even sure it happened.* But something had happened.

He looked down at his drawing of the samurai warlord. Late last night, he'd taken it down from the wall and fallen asleep with it in his hands; the last thing he remembered was staring at it.

There was no doubt in his mind. It was Shinjirō Kaminishi.

He had drawn a portrait of a samurai warlord from a dream, only to meet him in another dream.

Was it a dream? He had lived in the daimyō's castle—waking up each morning, going through his day, going to sleep at night, only to wake up again the next morning still in the castle. He had never heard of any dream feeling like it had gone on for weeks.

He'd checked his arm and back for scars from the whipping. Nothing. His skin was unmarked, and he had felt oddly... disappointed.

Did he *want* it to have been real?

He had been captured, imprisoned, abused, and initiated into sex with a man, something he wasn't sure he would have chosen had he stayed in this lifetime, living out his days as Michael Holden, a poor little rich boy, nice enough but with no particular aim in life.

He had lived a different life, one that felt more real than this one.

If he could choose which one to live, which would he choose?

"Michael? *Michael?*" Ellen sounded panicked. "Are you there?"

"Yes, yes, I'm still here."

"I'm coming over. You sound weird. Have you eaten breakfast?"

"Yes," Michael lied. "And I'm fine. You don't have to come over."

"You sound like you're losing it."

"I'm not."

"What are you doing the rest of today?"

"Studying, what else?"

"What about tonight? I can bring dinner. What do you want?"

"Are you going to give me another chance to explain this so you'll believe me?"

There was a silence on the other end and then a huge sigh.

"All right. Fine, then," Ellen said.

HE SHOWERED and put on jeans and a shirt, leaving it unbuttoned and his chest bare. Grabbing a beer from the fridge, he picked up the remote and clicked on the TV.

A movement reflected in the sliding glass door caught his eye; he turned to look.

No one there.

On edge, he set his beer down, walked to the sliding glass door, and pulled it open. He glanced around. No one on the balcony.

He turned.

A shimmering figure was standing in the middle of his living room.

Shinjirō.

He was dressed in his kimono, with the same long hair and gathered topknot at the back. But every cell seemed translucent, as if he were incorporeal or a ghost.

The look on his face was slightly stunned. He glanced up at the electric light; then he stared at the television for a long moment. Then his eyes lit upon Michael at last.

"Maikoru?"

"Yes." Michael stepped forward, not too quickly. He didn't want to spook the daimyō any more than he probably already was. "Shinjirō-sama. It's me, Michael."

"Where am I?"

"You're in my home," Michael replied.

Shinjirō looked around again with wonder on his face. "So it's true," he said. "What year is this?"

"It's 2010. This is Berkeley, in California. Across the bay is San Francisco."

He moved closer as Shinjirō merely watched him approach. Then he placed a hand on... and through... the daimyō's shoulder.

Shinjirō then raised his hand to rest, shimmering, on Michael's face. Michael felt the shock of a kind of pure energy on his cheek; the energy thrummed on his skin.

"Looks like sex is out of the question," he quipped.

Shinjirō raised his eyebrows, then snorted in a disbelieving laugh.

Michael laughed openly. This was so unexpected, this... visit or whatever it was, that he found himself completely in the moment, just enjoying it.

The daimyō turned his attention to the view outside, and Michael walked to the balcony, beckoning Shinjirō to join him.

Shinjirō stepped outside, looking up at the night sky and then down at the cars passing in the street below. "Those are cars—automobiles," Michael said. "I told you about them." He pointed across the bay. "And there's the Golden Gate Bridge. It's a little hard to make out with the fog, but it's there. See it?"

"Yes. It's beautiful."

"Much of modern-day Japan looks like this. The modern buildings, paved streets, cars. The people there live very well, like here."

Shinjirō said nothing.

Michael stared at the daimyō's fine features in profile, at his beautiful pale skin. The soft shimmer of his—ghost?—self just accentuated his splendor.

The daimyō turned to him then, his gaze softening. "I've missed you, Maikoru," he said. "It's been a month since you disappeared before my very eyes. I will never doubt you again."

Michael moved to embrace him and found himself holding only air.

"I wish this was real," he whispered.

The last thing he saw was the full moon over the daimyō's shoulder...

...And the next moment the full moon shone in the sky above, and Shinjirō was solid and real in his arms.

They were standing in the garden of the castle, just outside Shinjirō's receiving room.

And they were back in late-Edo Japan.

Startled, they pulled back to stare into each other's faces.

And then they laughed, their laughter echoing in the dark of the summer night.

CHAPTER SIX

THE DAIMYŌ'S skin was hot against his own.

Shinjirō's futon was covered with silk, and it moved against Michael's skin in a slippery caress.

The daimyō's hands were all over Michael's body, stroking, rubbing, taking possession, and it was all Michael could do to hold on to the daimyō's shoulders. If he let go of those muscled shoulders, he might be lost forever.

Sweat broke out on his forehead as Shinjirō mouthed his neck, nibbling and then biting. A sound came out of Michael's throat, needy and pleading. He was too far gone to even feel embarrassed. "My lord," he breathed.

Shinjirō loomed over him then, his big solid presence like a protective and dangerous animal. He lowered his hips down on Michael, bringing their groins together. Michael threw his head back, drawing his breath in sharply.

"Yes," he hissed.

The daimyō began slow, deliberate movements, pushing himself against Michael. Michael responded by pushing back with his hips, grinding their cocks together in a dance of pleasure. The back-and-forth pressure built and built until Michael grabbed Shinjirō's hips with both hands and pulled him down into his own upward thrusts, and he was getting closer... and closer—

Shinjirō reached down and pulled Michael's leg up, hooking it around his hip, and Michael instinctively did the same with his other leg until both legs were locked around the small of Shinjirō's back, bringing them into deeper contact with each other.

The daimyō grabbed hold of Michael's hair, holding him firmly in place, and plunged his tongue into his mouth, forcing Michael to open wide to him. Michael choked for a moment, then surrendered to it, allowing Shinjirō's tongue to push and roam as it would.

The heat and friction below threatened to drive him over the edge. He couldn't hold back any longer. A near-sob of frustration came out, muffled by Shinjirō's mouth, and he was sure he felt the daimyō *smile*. And then....

And then Shinjirō threw back his head and slammed his hips down into Michael's groin. Michael felt an explosion of pleasure where his body met the daimyō's. Above him, the daimyō gasped and drew in a ragged breath, then slowly let it out, his head lowering to rest next to Michael's.

Michael's eyes were closed. The daimyō's body was heavy on top of his own. He moved his hands up to hold Shinjirō lightly around the shoulders. He could feel the daimyō's heartbeat gradually slowing back to normal.

What surprised him wasn't that he'd had sex with a man, but that it seemed more natural than anything else in the world to have sex with *this* man.

THE NEXT morning Shinjirō was already gone when Michael woke up, but the elderly woman brought in his breakfast as if he were in his own room. So Michael assumed that from now on he would probably be staying in Shinjirō's room.

This was confirmed when he looked around and saw his clothing and personal items neatly stacked against the wall.

For being the daimyō's private chambers, this room was as spare as the others Michael had experienced while living in the castle—including his cell downstairs. But the few furnishings and personal items were exquisite, like the rosewood chest in one corner and the length of brocaded silk that hung over the simple bamboo screen behind which the daimyō changed his clothing.

Near the door that led out into the garden, there sat a short-legged desk for the daimyō to read or write on. Michael was looking at the garden from the opposite side now, as Shinjirō's room was on the other side of the garden from the receiving room.

He lay back on the futon, on the cool silk.

Shinjirō.

More than even the fact that he was somehow here again without explanation, just as the first time, Michael found himself thinking about the daimyō nonstop. His mind obsessed about what these changes between them meant.

He was having sex with a man.

Did this mean he was gay?

Or... Michael laughed. If this were a dream he was in, perhaps it didn't count.

He sat up and looked around Shinjirō's bedroom. If this were a dream, it had real rooms, with real furnishings, and a very real Japanese daimyō.

He closed his eyes.

I don't want to analyze this anymore.

He found that, strangely, he didn't really care whether this life were real or his other one, or if *neither* of them were real. Did it really matter, when....

When, for the first time... he was truly living his life?

IN THE afternoon, he wandered out to the garden and crouched by the small stream to gaze at the koi fishes. The sun wasn't as hot as he recalled. According to what Shinjirō said, it would now be mid to late July in 1851.

He crossed the garden to the other side, went around the corner to the secluded part of the courtyard, and slid open the door to his former room. The futon was gone. The wash bucket was gone as well. All of his personal items were in Shinjirō's room now.

Michael glanced around but felt nothing that resonated for him in the room anymore. Taking a last look, he stepped out into the hallway.

A hand closed around his throat, and he found himself with his back to the wall.

Tōru brought his face close to Michael's. "So it's true," he growled. "You're back."

"Yes." Michael struggled to breathe and remain calm.

"Don't think I'm not watching you. You're nothing but scum. Just one wrong step around Shinjirō-sama, and I'll drop you on the spot."

"Fine."

"If you betray Shinjirō-sama again like you did with Misako—"

"Interesting, isn't it? How you and your men were conveniently in the forest that night to find me and bring me back." Michael put his hand on Tōru's wrist, gripping hard. "A real coincidence."

Tōru stared at him, then drew his fist back. Michael braced himself—

—only to find Norio pulling the enraged Tōru off him. "Tōru-dono, oyame kudasai."

Tōru shook Norio off angrily. Then, after a last furious look at Michael, he turned and left.

Michael touched his throat gingerly. "Thank you," he said to Norio.

Norio blinked. "Iie," he said.

The look on his face said that he was still startled at hearing Japanese coming out of the gaijin's mouth. Michael smiled a little, trying to put him at ease. "I won't forget your kindness today."

SHINJIRŌ CALLED a meeting of his lieutenants, lower-ranking staff, and representatives of the various groups of samurai under his command. "I want you to attend this, Maikoru."

Michael was shocked. "My lord, are you sure?"

"Yes. Many who will be there today are not aware of your existence—and it would not be prudent to allow them to see you at this time. I will have you sit behind a screen."

"Hai, Shinjirō-sama."

The main hall was the largest room in the castle. It opened out onto yet another portion of the garden and had beautiful polished wood floors. Silkscreen prints covered several large screens at the head of the room, behind a slightly raised platform area where the daimyō would sit and head the meeting.

Michael was seated behind the screen that was to Shinjirō's right. He could only see the daimyō and a few of the samurai in the audience through a small opening between two of the screen's sections. But the acoustics in the hall were excellent, enabling him to hear everything that was said in the room.

Shinjirō began by reiterating the Shirakawa claim to the Kaminishi borderlands and recounting the incidents that had occurred in recent times along the border. Listening, Michael was surprised to hear how far back the dispute went. It had been going on for as long as both Shinjirō and the current head of the Shirakawa clan, Ryū, had been alive.

Ryū's father actually had begun the fight, claiming that the Kaminishi borderlands belonged to the Shirakawa clan. Indeed, he claimed that *all* of the Kaminishi lands actually belonged to his clan. Shinjirō's father had obtained legal documents from Kyoto that proved Kaminishi ownership of the lands extending all the way to the border. But this failed to appease the neighboring warlord.

The current situation was getting worse, with no obvious precipitator. Shinjirō and his men had done nothing to inflame the situation; they hadn't made raids into Shirakawa territory or provoked the other clan in any way.

The daimyō was exasperated and—unusual for a daimyō—was willing to listen to open discussion of the situation among his lieutenants. He asked his samurai for any information on persons or events that would shed light on the issue.

After a few moments of silence, discussion began among the samurai. They had all noticed the ramping up of hostilities along the border but could not pin down the reason for the increased level of disturbance. Some had relatives in Shirakawa territory; the border was open, after all, and a modest amount of trade even took place back and forth between the territories as a regular course of business.

Michael finally heard a voice suggesting that Shinjirō-sama and Ryū Shirakawa hold a summit meeting to resolve the issue. He recognized the voice as being Norio's. The soft-spoken head of castle security seemed to have the trust of the other men in the room, for the reaction Michael heard from behind the screen was a favorable murmur and voices raised in support of the idea.

Tōru then argued against the proposal, saying it would be interpreted as a sign of weakness on Shinjirō-sama's part to meet with Ryū. More voices were raised in the hall, and Tōru's voice became louder in opposition.

Finally Shinjirō spoke. He stated that he had considered all opinions that had been offered in the meeting. His conclusion was that the summit meeting idea would be presented to Lord Ryū and that it would be held for the purpose of resolving the border dispute once and for all.

Michael waited until all of the samurai had left the room before coming out from behind the screen.

Shinjirō was standing alone in the middle of the room, lost in thought.

"My lord," Michael said.

The daimyō turned, and his look of preoccupation softened. "So it is decided, then," he said. "We shall see what Lord Ryū has to say in person."

"I hope that all will go well."

"Yes," Shinjirō said. He regarded Michael with a glint in his eye. "Maikoru, if you would return to my room, please."

Michael gaped at him for a moment. Did that mean…?

"I will join you there shortly."

Oh.

HE DIDN'T know whether to be happy or annoyed.

The daimyō seemed to regard him as his personal property, seeing nothing wrong with ordering him to his bed in the middle of the day.

"I'm not a woman."

"I am aware of that fact."

"Not that women should be treated that way either... *Ah.*" Michael had just discovered how sensitive the nub of his left nipple was.

"Stop talking," Shinjirō said politely.

IT WAS hotter in August than it had been in July, with the added element of high humidity to top it off.

The vegetable garden was giving forth its gifts, and Michael enjoyed the time he spent assisting the gardener in his work. The small silent man had yet to say a single word to him, barely acknowledging his presence next to him in the garden.

One day the two finished their work early. Michael found himself sitting next to the gardener, who sat in the dirt wiping the sweat off his brow.

"Maikoru desu. Yoroshiku onegai shimasu."

The gardener didn't look at him.

Then, in a quiet yet deeply melodic voice, the man said, "Kanosuke desu."

"Your name is Kanosuke," Michael affirmed in Japanese.

"Hai." The gardener sat with his knees up and his hands resting lightly on them. He looked at his hands.

"Have you lived here in the castle for very long?"

"Yes, most of my life. I came here when I was thirteen." Kanosuke took a tool and stabbed at the dirt with it, then smoothed the dirt over.

"Have you always worked in the garden?"

"Iie," he said. He stopped digging. Then he looked at Michael.

Michael noticed for the first time how pretty the gardener's eyes were; they slanted upward, and he had long eyelashes, like a woman. The rest of his face had the same delicate look: high cheekbones, clear skin, and shapely lips.

"I was like you," Kanosuke said simply.

Michael blinked, not getting his meaning. Then he did.

"Oh.... I think you're mistaken.... I...."

Kanosuke merely gazed at him with soft humor in his eyes. "Shinjirō-sama's father," he said, leaving Michael to work it out on his own. "I was just a worker in the castle like everyone else, but when I grew older...." He fingered the dirt near his feet, his eyes taking on a faraway look. "He was a man unlike other men. He was like the Emperor himself. When he commanded you...."

A sudden lustful glint came into the gardener's eye, then disappeared as soon as it had appeared, replaced by the usual expression of mildness. "When Kenshirō-sama passed, Shinjirō-sama made me the caretaker of these gardens. Shinjirō-sama could have removed me from the castle, or even ended my life, but he did not. He understood that I had provided... relief and companionship for his chichiue."

"Did you love him?"

Kanosuke glanced at him, surprised. "It was my duty," he said. "My life belonged to Kenshirō-sama. Pleasing him was my only function." He looked away for a moment, then returned his gaze to Michael, smiling softly. "I loved him more than life itself."

HE LEARNED to turn off his mind during sex.

In the daimyō's bed, why he was here and what was going to happen next in this unpredictable dream/reality didn't matter.

Everything else faded away as his world was reduced to skin on skin, lips and tongues working, and the hot, hard reality of his cock and another man's cock. And feelings, and sensations, and *pressure—*

"Ahh!" he gasped.

Shinjirō had moved his finger inside Michael's ass.

Michael, lying on his stomach, felt the pushing halt, but the feeling of pressure remained. He lay there breathing in and out, trying to calm himself.

The last time someone had done this was not a pleasant memory.

The finger was withdrawn, and he heard Shinjirō pick up the small lacquer bowl that held the oil they used for massages. The next thing he knew, two oiled fingers were being inserted into him.

The stretching sensation was a little painful, but not too bad. He laid his hand down on the futon and pillowed his forehead on it, trying to relax.

"*Nghh!*" A sudden, sharp jolt of feeling coursed through him. He made a sighing exhalation of pleasure and heard the daimyō's accompanying chuckle. Michael moved back against the fingers, trying to get Shinjirō to hit his prostate again.

But instead, Shinjirō took them out.

Michael looked back over his shoulder. "What?"

The daimyō was placing oil on his ring finger. "Hush," he told Michael. Then he entered him with three fingers.

Michael grunted. He struggled to raise himself up on his knees, and Shinjirō helped him. Resting his elbows on the futon, he laid his forehead on his crossed hands and closed his eyes.

God, the feeling. He could stay like this forever, with sensations washing through him like waves. And the anticipation of more.

He had known this was coming. He was surprised the daimyō had been this patient. Michael was a little nervous but also curious. And he was as ready as he would ever be.

He gasped again as the daimyō touched his prostate gland. "Onegai shimasu!" Was he begging? Hell yes, he was begging.

More. Please.

The fingers were abruptly withdrawn, and he heard the daimyō preparing himself with oil. Michael's breathing shortened in anticipation. *Yes. Yes. I want this. God, how I want this.* He longed to stroke his cock but didn't want to interrupt Shinjirō's flow. So he waited.

He felt the tip of Shinjirō's cock rest against his anus and then slowly begin to penetrate the tight opening. Sweat broke out on his face, and he felt its warm glow envelop his arms and chest. This was definitely painful, but he kept breathing in and out, willing himself to relax.

Still... *it hurt.*

It wasn't a sharp pain, but more an intense, bulky pressure, unrelenting, opening him wide. It was the kind of pain that reminded one that this object was something that opening wasn't really made to accommodate.

After long, long seconds of hard discomfort, Michael felt his muscles start to relax. He could breathe more deeply. He wondered if Shinjirō was all the way in. His answer came in the next moment, as he felt the intruding cock go even deeper into his body, slowly filling him to the core. "Oh God," he breathed.

He couldn't take it, but he could and did.

He wanted it—more and more of it.

Shinjirō's hands were on his hips, holding him still as he worked his way in. Michael could hear the daimyō's heavy breathing as he controlled himself, pushing in slowly and gradually. Finally he was there.

The daimyō stopped, buried to the hilt inside him. For a long moment, the two of them just rested in their connection. And then Shinjirō began to move.

If he'd thought the sensations were overwhelming before, nothing had prepared him for *this*. Michael's breathing grew ragged. He panted through an open mouth. Only one word kept coming to him.

More. More. More.

The incredible sensations filled him to bursting. Each movement brought him to the brink of coming, then made it subside again.

Behind him, Shinjirō made noises of pleasure as he pushed and pulled out of him. He was gratified that Shinjirō was feeling this too, that they were sharing this together.

They moved in concert, wordlessly, the silence broken only by heavy breathing, sighs, and grunts.

Just as Michael thought of touching himself, the daimyō reached around and grasped his cock.

The feeling of being fucked while his cock was worked at the same time was too much. He clawed at the futon with his hands, incoherent sounds coming from his throat.

The daimyō responded by thrusting harder, driving Michael's face into the futon. A harsh cry ripped from his throat. He was about to come—

—and then the daimyō took his hand off his cock, returning it to Michael's right hip. With both hands holding his hips steady, Shinjirō pulled out.

And waited.

"Wh-what...?"

Silence from behind him.

"Shinjirō... sama...." He panted, trying to catch his breath. "Please... what...?"

Then Shinjirō—oh so slowly—began moving in and out again.

Long slow movements. He was fucking him, really fucking him now, controlling him, controlling his pleasure, forcing Michael to accede to his rhythms.

Demanding his surrender.

Michael groaned.

It was over.

Shinjirō. I'm yours.

He didn't say it aloud, but somehow the daimyō knew, and he felt Shinjirō take possession with greater abandon, moving inside him with deliberate intent, teasing and bringing him along—playing with him—all with the focus of making this unbelievably intense lovemaking last and last.

Sweat covered his body, covered both their bodies. He could feel the daimyō's hands growing damp against the skin of his hips. He felt drool trickling out of the corner of his mouth and didn't care. Michael's face fell onto the futon, where he buried sobs of... frustration? Passion? He didn't know. He grasped at the silk covering roughly, as if trying to tear it apart.

"Let me come," he pleaded in English. Tears flowed.

The movement behind him stopped. Shinjirō's hand returned to his cock. He began pumping Michael with his hand while slamming deeper and deeper into his ass.

Michael's arms began to shake, and then his knees; his muscles were seizing, and inarticulate noises came out of his mouth. "*Aaagh... nghh....*"

He came in waves, gasping raggedly as if emerging from drowning, hearing Shinjirō coming as well behind him. The daimyō's hand stayed on his cock until the last wave was finished; then he placed both hands on Michael's hips to withdraw himself from his body, expelling his breath harshly as Michael had, ending in a sort of groan.

He pulled Michael's legs out to lie flat before collapsing onto his back.

Lying sandwiched between the daimyō and the futon, Michael had never felt more deeply fulfilled.

LONG AUGUST nights in Shinjirō's bed led to hot days spent drowsing in the room or sitting in the garden next to the little stream.

In the afternoons Michael helped Kanosuke in the vegetable garden in the side courtyard. The pumpkin squashes and thin purple eggplants were full and ripe, and many other crops were now ready for harvesting.

Michael came to enjoy the quiet—almost silent, actually—hours working with the gardener in that patch of earth, the sun reaching them in elongated streaks as late afternoon approached the north side of the castle. He felt again that sense of timelessness during those long afternoons, he and Kanosuke working together, to the point where it began to feel like he'd always been here, like his life in California in the early twenty-first century had been a dream and this was actually the only reality he'd ever known.

The nights were lost in sexual pleasure with the daimyō.

He learned early on that Shinjirō was a master at prolonging sexual tension, both before the activity began and during the buildup to climax. The daimyō was a great masseur, pressing and kneading at the knots in Michael's back and shoulders with strength and precision, and Michael learned how to do this so he could give the same pleasure back to Shinjirō.

And so the nights would begin slowly, with massages or other simple tension releasers, such as bathing each other with towels wrung out in warm water, removing the perspiration of the sun-filled Kansai August from their skin. The hot, still night air would have them dry in minutes, and Michael would lie down on the silk-covered futon and wait for Shinjirō to join him.

He craved the daimyō's touch now. A simple stroking of fingers across his chest would leave him breathless, reaching for the man like a baby reaching for its mother. He didn't know how he had turned into this, a person who was addicted to the touch and feel of another, but somehow it had happened.

Shinjirō's hands and arms and lips on his own, every touch of the daimyō's body on his skin made him hot with desire. He surged his body against Shinjirō's, desperate to feel all of it against him.

Sometimes the daimyō allowed it, and sometimes he would pin Michael to the futon, holding his wrists down on either side of his head.

He would then lower his full weight onto Michael and move his hips against Michael's in a slow delicious grind, taking his time, making Michael squirm and try to rise upward in an effort to take control.

Shinjirō would nip at his neck with his teeth then, or discipline him in some other minor way until Michael subsided and let the daimyō take the reins again.

Sometimes there were... other things that they did, things that made him shut his eyes in embarrassment if he thought about them afterward. But one thing he was discovering was that if there was mutual acquiescence, nothing that brought pleasure could really be called perverse. It was all the play of their bodies on each other, with each other.

One night, after hours of pleasuring each other, Michael bathed them both with damp towels, and Shinjirō led him to the shōji door that opened to the garden.

He slid the shōji open. The little stream trickled and wended its way among the rocks and plants, the noise soothing to the ear. Above the roof of the castle, the night sky was filled with stars and the moon was eerily bright in its white light.

Shinjirō sat with his back against the doorframe and gently pulled Michael to lie against his chest. Together, they gazed at the garden and the stars.

Michael felt Shinjirō's strong heartbeat against his back. He felt like their bodies were connected, like they were one body with a single heart.

A warm feeling arose in his own heart then, like a door opening inside him. The feeling left him speechless with awe. A sense of other horizons came to him, other lives he had lived—or would live—and he was connected to them all.

He wished this moment could last forever.

"I SEE."

Tōru watched as the Shirakawa second-in-command thought over what he had said. *Fool*, he thought contemptuously. *I will enjoy turning on you when the time comes.*

Kenji pursed his lips, apparently deep in thought. "So, what do you expect Shinjirō to say at this summit meeting?"

"He will probably present the legal papers from Kyoto to show where the exact borderline is located. He will use logic and legal rights to try to convince Ryū."

The Shirakawa second was quiet for a moment. Then he said, not looking at Tōru, "Ryū-sama has reached a decision."

"About what?"

"He says that the borderlands will never be returned to the Shirakawa side unless... Shinjirō is out of the picture."

Tōru stared. "Meaning?"

"Meaning that Shinjirō must die."

A silence fell. Then it was broken by a solitary cricket's song. It was early evening in the bamboo grove.

"I see," Tōru said. He could feel Kenji staring at him. He turned toward the older man, the annoyance plain on his face. "What?"

Kenji lowered his eyes immediately. "My apologies, Tōru-dono," he said.

"What is it? Just say it."

"It is merely that, once Shinjirō passes and the borderlands are returned to Ryū-sama, the rest of the Kaminishi lands will need an administrator." Kenji cleared his throat nervously. "Shinjirō does not have a blood heir as yet. The lands would be in disarray upon his sudden... demise. It would fall to you, as his second-in-command, to take charge of the situation. And we—the Shirakawa Han—would fully support you. You would be able to do as you wished with the majority of these lands. We would not interfere with your governance."

There was a long silence.

"The problem with mere governance," Tōru said patiently, "is that it can always be taken away."

"If you were to agree to pay a certain percentage in tribute from the profits of those lands to the Shirakawa clan, then we would support your petition to Kyoto to obtain legal authority over the majority of the Kaminishi lands, independent from our rule."

Tōru mulled it over. Once the Emperor in Kyoto granted him legal rule, he would be free to do anything... including marshal his own forces and attack the Shirakawa clan for *their* lands. It was a gamble, but an excellent one.

"Yes. That would be acceptable."

MOONLIGHT STREAMED in through the open doorway to the garden.

"It will be time for tsukimi before too long," the daimyō said. He stood by the doorway, the light of the full moon shining across his tall, imposing frame.

The prospect of a harvest moon-viewing with Shinjirō-sama was very pleasant indeed. Michael smiled. "That would be wonderful, my lord," he said.

The daimyō turned, and Michael drew in his breath sharply. A soft breeze came in from the garden, moving through Shinjirō's long hair, framing his exquisite face.

Such a beautiful man.

From where he sat on the tatami mat near the futon, he felt he was looking at a god.

He reached out his arms to Shinjirō.

"Onegai shimasu."

MICHAEL HELD and caressed Shinjirō's hips as he sucked deeper.

The daimyō was standing, and Michael tried to concentrate on getting as much of Shinjirō's cock down his throat as he could.

It wasn't easy, but he had found that if he let the muscles of his jaw and mouth go slack a little, that seemed to help. He pulled back and fingered the foreskin, pulling it away so he could gently tongue the exposed head.

His reward was a soft gasp from above and a gentle gripping of his hair. The daimyō's other hand moved down his back, rubbing his skin in rhythmic movements. His long yukata surrounded Michael like a curtain as Michael focused all his attention on giving pleasure to this man who had suddenly become his main focus in life.

CHAPTER SEVEN

THWACK!

The arrow hit the right side of the target.

Michael exhaled. He was rusty—he'd last practiced archery in high school—but at least he'd hit the target.

The target was a bale of hay mounted on a pole to approximate the size and height of a man's torso. The arrows resembled Western arrows, down to the fletching at the tail end.

The bow was a different story. Straighter than most Western-style bows, it was long, more than five feet. It was wrapped in bamboo layers and was thin but felt incredibly sturdy in his grasp.

He set another arrow, then raised the bow and arrow as one and pulled the arrow back. As he aimed at the target, the tension set his shoulder to shaking slightly, and he released the arrow a little too soon. The arrow hit the top of the target on the left side.

"Kyūdō," said that beautiful voice behind him, "the way of the bow."

Michael turned.

The daimyō approached, smiling. He was wearing his customary daywear within the castle—a fine-thread silk-cotton kimono, light enough for the end of summer but warm enough for the evenings. The warmth and longing and familiarity caused by seeing him struck Michael hard. He was recognizing these days that he was literally addicted to Shinjirō, that his presence had become in some way essential to Michael's own existence.

"Shinjirō-sama."

"Your way of archery is very different."

"The Western way is not as contemplative. That is certain," Michael said, smiling.

He set another arrow, then raised it with the bow.

Thwack!

This time, the arrow hit close to the heart of the target.

"Good," Shinjirō said.

Michael grinned. "I'm out of practice."

The daimyō picked up his own bow, and Michael handed him an arrow. Shinjirō expertly set the arrow, then stopped and closed his eyes for a moment.

Michael watched as Shinjirō reopened his eyes and raised the bow high over his head. He made a slow, graceful, downward-arcing movement, coming to rest with his arrow poised toward the target.

The daimyō held the pose for a moment, then shot the arrow.

Thwack!

It hit directly in the heart of the target.

"Wow," Michael said.

"That was much too fast," Shinjirō said, frowning slightly. "This is an art. The way in which it is done is more important than whether you hit the target perfectly or not. You must be influencing me, Maikoru," he concluded wryly.

"Oh no."

"I would like to see your shot again."

Michael set another arrow and lined up the shot. *Thwack!* Even closer this time.

"Your speed would serve you well, were you on horseback in battle," the daimyō commented. "Kyūdō has developed in these many years of peace. It is more art than weapon now. But it is never advisable to lose the instinct for battle. One never knows when it will be needed again." He set an arrow, then looked at Michael.

Shinjirō raised the bow upward, Western style, with no formality, and released the shot.

It hit the heart again.

"Maikoru, let us both do it at once," Shinjirō said.

"Hai, my lord."

They set their arrows, then raised their bows as one.

"Hold," Shinjirō commanded. Michael started, losing his concentration momentarily. Then he refocused, found the target again, and held his bow steady.

They stood side by side for what seemed to Michael like an eternity.

"*Fire*," Shinjirō said, and they released the arrows.

Thwack! The two arrows hit the heart as one, just above Shinjirō's previous two hits.

Michael laughed. "We make a good team."

"Yes."

Shinjirō seemed preoccupied for a moment; then he nodded. "Maikoru, I have a question for you."

"Yes."

"You were reluctant to tell me about the future of Japan. I would like to know exactly what you were afraid would happen."

Michael opened his mouth to speak, then shut it. The daimyō stood without impatience, merely waiting until he felt prepared to open up.

"My lord, I don't know why I am here. Neither do you. Everything I've told you is true. Some of it you saw for yourself in my home, in the future." Shinjirō nodded. Michael glanced at him, then continued. "Since my purpose for being here in the past is unknown even to me, I cannot help but be afraid of changing something I'm not supposed to."

"What do you mean?"

Michael stopped. It would be hard to explain to a nineteenth-century samurai warlord that according to all the rules in science fiction, changing the past would be a bad thing. He closed his eyes. How to say it so it made sense.... "To me, as a person living in the twenty-first century, the past is something that can't be changed. It's complete, set in stone. It doesn't change—it's not supposed to change. But if I do something here and now in the past... that could change what takes place in the future. And I don't think I'm meant to do that."

The daimyō frowned, trying to grasp what he was saying. "So... if you did something...." Shinjirō blinked. "What if... not you. If you were not the one—"

"Shinjirō-sama—"

"Indeed, if you were not the one who changed the course of events, but if it were somebody else—"

"But that would be the same thing. It wouldn't matter who did it."

"No," Shinjirō said. The daimyō was suddenly excited by some possibility Michael didn't even want to imagine.

"This may be the reason why you were sent back in time. It was to inform me about Perry and his ships—so that I might bring forth actions to prevent their incursion onto our soil."

"No," Michael said desperately. "Forgive me, my lord, but that can't possibly be the meaning of my being here. Where I come from, it is an event that has already taken place. There is no changing it!"

"Why? Why can't it be changed?" The daimyō's eyes challenged him. "For what other reason would you be here telling me of these terrible things? I see no other reason."

Michael closed his eyes. *Please, let me convince him somehow.* "Shinjirō-sama, please reconsider. Think of what I said about Japan's recovery, and what it has become in my time. If you attempt to alter the course of history, Japan's future may be lost."

"Or Japan may never have to suffer in the first place."

"How could that be so?" Michael risked the daimyō's wrath. He had to be frank. "Are you the one who can determine that? Can you be certain that whatever path you take will be the correct one? What if this country winds up suffering even more than what I have told you? Why would you be the one who—"

"Enough," Shinjirō said. The command was curt and stopped Michael cold. "I have heard what you said and will consider it. But you have not convinced me that my choice would be incorrect."

He regarded Michael with a somber look, then turned and walked around the side of the courtyard and into the castle.

THE TEAHOUSE was located near the border on the Kaminishi side. It had seen any number of secret meetings, both political and romantic, in its fifty years of existence. Isolated in the midst of rice fields and the occasional grove of bamboo trees, it was considered the best place for an assignation in the two han.

But today's meeting was out in the open: Lord Ryū of the Shirakawa clan and Lord Shinjirō of the Kaminishi clan were to meet to discuss the situation of the borderlands.

Looking for signs of trouble, Norio gazed up at the second-story windows of the sprawling two-story building. There were stories of assassins who had thrown knives with deadly accuracy on moonless nights from those same windows. It was daytime, but that was no reason to relax one's guard.

Shinjirō-sama, on the horse in front of him, seemed calm and confident, as he always did. Whenever Norio had a momentary doubt, he knew he could look to his lord and be reassured. He set his back straight and slapped the reins on his horse lightly.

The teahouse proprietor, a wizened old man, was waiting in front, and as Shinjirō and his men approached, he came forward on rickety legs to greet them. Bowing very deeply, he stated that he was honored by Lord Shinjirō's presence and welcomed him inside.

After making sure several samurai were watching the horses—and in a position to raise the alarm in case of trouble—Norio entered the teahouse after Shinjirō.

The walls and flooring were made of some beautiful dark wood, and he stood admiring them for a moment before hurrying to catch up with the daimyō. Shinjirō-sama was of a one-point mind this day, a mood that had been apparent earlier when he'd told Norio to take extra care in watering and feeding the horses. In case of trouble, he had wanted to be sure all resources were prepared. Nothing was to be left to chance today.

Norio knew that this borderlands issue had been affecting the daimyō's concentration lately. He had been head of security for the castle and surrounding environs for four years and had been employed at the castle for a total of ten years, since he was sixteen. He had watched and observed Shinjirō-sama for all that time, seeing him gain stature throughout the Kaminishi domain as he gradually earned the trust of the people.

It wasn't just the borderlands, but the thing with the mysterious gaijin. He had appeared out of nowhere and had been a puzzle and a mystery for Shinjirō-sama. Then one day, he'd simply disappeared. The word was that he had vanished into thin air right before Shinjirō-sama's astonished eyes.

Was he a ghost or an oni? Norio didn't know what to think. Nobody knew. As the weeks passed, he had watched his lord turn quiet and introspective, as if he were trying to understand what the experience with the gaijin signified.

Then, once again, it happened—the gaijin reappeared! His return occurred on a night when Norio was on watch outside the castle. The next morning, the gaijin was there in Shinjirō-sama's room.

Where had he been for a month?

Norio shook his head even as he examined the security arrangements in the teahouse and made sure that Kaminishi men were posted at each entry and access point. The gaijin was a favorite topic of conversation among the denizens of the castle— though obviously out of earshot of the daimyō—and Norio had done his fair share of the speculating too.

There were oni that lived in nature and that haunted the living souls that walked the earth, but the gaijin was no oni. He was real flesh and blood—as Norio himself could attest to, having been the guard outside Shinjirō-sama's room the past few nights. He colored slightly, recalling the sounds that came from the room late at night.

Everything was in order. The meeting room was set up to accommodate each lord and three of his men, eight in the room in all. Two small low tables for tea for each lord. The men would be seated with no tables in front of them, with hands—and weapons—clearly visible at all times.

He had no reason to suspect that Lord Ryū would try anything that would bring serious consequences to himself or to his han. The daimyō of the Shirakawa Han had only been in power for two years, since his father had passed on. His power was not yet consolidated, and he had not yet gained the trust of his people. There were many reports of disruptions and lawlessness in Shirakawa territory. Norio was sure that Lord Ryū would tread carefully to avoid undermining his position any further.

And yet, Lord Ryū was the one who was constantly pushing this issue. Norio didn't understand it. It could be that, due to his inexperience in ruling, Lord Ryū didn't know how to pick his battles—that everything seemed important to him. But by causing disruptions along the border, he was weakening his own position. If he chose to wait and calmly seek negotiations with the Kaminishi Han, he would be more likely to win concessions from Shinjirō-sama. Not on the main points, but at least he would be making headway. This way, he was turning Shinjirō-sama against him, and unnecessarily so.

"Norio."

"Hai, my lord."

"Please ask Hikobei-san to come here."

"Yes, my lord."

Norio went to find the proprietor. The elderly man was instructing his staff in one of the inner hallways. "Shinjirō-sama would like to speak with you."

"Hai."

SHINJIRŌ-SAMA ASKED everyone to leave the room, except for Norio and the proprietor.

"Hikobei-san, it is my desire that the discussions between myself and Lord Ryū proceed smoothly today."

"Hai, Shinjirō-sama."

"To that end, I would appreciate it if you could assure me that there will be no surprises from any areas of this building, particularly the basement and subground levels."

Hikobei looked confused. "Shinjirō-sama... sumimasen.... I don't understand—"

"The underground levels lead to passageways and to doors that open onto this floor. This is no secret. It is something that everyone knows. I do not wish to be surprised in any way during this meeting. Do I have your understanding on this?" Shinjirō-sama said sternly.

"Hai, my lord." The proprietor's assent was immediate.

Shinjirō-sama tended to have that effect on people.

The underground levels and passageways were part of the teahouse's unique structure. Not only had they been used for escape in the past, but also ambush—and assassinations. Shinjirō-sama's statement to Hikobei, with Norio as witness, ensured that Hikobei couldn't feign ignorance later should something occur. And that there would be consequences, even if Norio had to carry them out over Shinjirō-sama's dead body.

LORD RYŪ looked even younger than Norio expected.

Only in his twenties, he was a handsome young man with a round face and smooth skin. His eyes were the focal point of his face; they were narrow but striking.

Norio watched as Lord Ryū argued how the borderlands traditionally belonged to the Shirakawa side, how the land went back for generations, and how the bureaucrats and paper-pushers in Kyoto had made a grave error in their determination of the actual borderline between the two domains.

Shinjirō-sama stated his side of the case based on the documents from the Imperial Court in Kyoto, which clearly showed the disputed territory to be Kaminishi land. He added that the farmers who lived in that area identified themselves as being part of the Kaminishi Han and not the Shirakawa Han. That sentiment, Shinjirō-sama asserted, even more than the legal verification, meant to him that the land belonged to the Kaminishi clan.

As he listened to the two daimyō speak, Norio could see that Shinjirō-sama was actually being somewhat easy on Lord Ryū, when in reality he had no need to be conciliatory whatsoever. The legal right, and as Shinjirō-sama noted, the moral right as well, was clearly on their side, and yet Lord Shinjirō was speaking to Lord Ryū with the utmost respect, as if they were two equals in a discussion where the disputed issue weighed equally in favor of either side. Norio realized that this was Shinjirō-sama's way of recognizing that the other daimyō, though young and inexperienced, was in all likelihood going to be in power next door for some time, and that treating him better than he actually deserved was insurance that would make future dealings with the Shirakawa clan go more smoothly. Lord Ryū's fiery, youthful impetuousness had not been Shinjirō-sama's way when he himself had been that age, but it was hardly unusual behavior from young men in power. And Shinjirō-sama had been around men in power all his life.

The meeting stretched on interminably as Shinjirō-sama engaged in every formality in a show of reassurance to his young counterpart that his views were being taken seriously. Norio noted how his lord was managing to do this without the slightest hint of patronization toward the younger man. *Shinjirō-sama is truly gifted in negotiation*, he thought. Not that there was any negotiating going on today. Given the strong feelings of the farmers in the borderlands—who had no desire to be part of the Shirakawa Han, particularly given its current state of chaos—his lord was not about to relinquish control of a single bit of that land.

He turned his attention to the three men who sat opposite him, Lord Ryū's lieutenants. Like the daimyō, they were young. It wasn't difficult to imagine how the daimyō and his youthful lieutenants probably inflamed each other's passions, reacting to each event with the fervor that only the young possessed. Norio himself wasn't much older than they were, but then he had always had a steady disposition.

Raised voices filled the room. Norio's attention swung sharply back to the meeting. Lord Ryū was loudly proclaiming that he was prepared to see something through to the end. The men rose from their seated positions, and Norio and his two samurai followed suit.

He looked to Shinjirō-sama, whose face showed the same masklike countenance it had the whole day. The daimyō curtly nodded. Norio walked out of the room, down the hallway, and into the main entrance hall before exiting the teahouse through the front door and down its steps.

Watching for signs of trouble, Norio glanced around and down the road in either direction. Lord Ryū and his men must have left their horses around the side of the building, as they were nowhere to be seen.

Their own horses were in front. Norio gestured to the samurai who had been watching them to get them ready for departure.

Shouting interrupted his movement. It came from the side of the teahouse. Norio took off at a dead run, followed by Shinjirō-sama and the other two samurai.

Coming around the corner, the first thing he saw was one of their men, bloodied, being supported by another samurai who had his arm around the injured man's shoulder. "Hidenori," Norio said. "What happened?"

Before Hidenori could respond, there was further yelling from somewhere under the teahouse and then, emerging from below a recessed area in the structure, several of the Shirakawa samurai came flying out, swords drawn and brandished.

Norio's was also out in an instant. Behind him he could hear Shinjirō-sama and the other samurai similarly unsheathing in a flash. He ran forward, placing himself between Hidenori and the Shirakawa men. "Stop! What is going on here?"

Lord Ryū and his three men who had been in the meeting room appeared.

Then Shinjirō-sama was at Norio's side. The look on his face was deadly, and Norio held his breath.

"What is the meaning of this?" Shinjirō-sama's voice was deceptively soft. He turned his full attention to Lord Ryū.

Lord Ryū's face was impassive. "Lord Shinjirō, I assure you that I am, like you, completely at a loss about this. Fumio, what is this?" he asked, turning to one of his men.

The samurai he addressed said, "Ryū-sama, the two men you see there were lurking in the passageways beneath the meeting room. We were able to surprise and rout them, as you can see."

"And your own purpose for being in the passageways was what, exactly?" Shinjirō-sama acidly inquired.

Lord Ryū said smoothly, "My men were instructed to guard the passageways under the meeting room—"

"As were my own men," Shinjirō-sama said. "And yet, one of my men is injured, while none of your men are. I believe that would show who attacked whom."

"There is no evidence as to who attacked first. The fact that it is one of your men who was injured may only show who was the least competent in fighting skills." Lord Ryū smirked.

Norio froze. *Lord Ryū is very, very unwise.* He scarcely dared to breathe, not wanting to look at Shinjirō-sama's reaction.

His grasp on his sword tightened.

"Lord Ryū," Shinjirō-sama said. His voice was soft, but no one present could mistake the deadliness behind the quiet tone. "You would be wise not to try my patience in this matter. I consider any wounding of my men to be a serious incident."

The two daimyō stared at each other implacably.

Norio's hand twitched on his sword.

Then Lord Ryū backed off first. "Lord Shinjirō, my apologies. It was certainly not my intention to have a violent outcome here today."

Shinjirō-sama nodded shortly. Then, without further ado, he turned and walked back to the horses, Norio and the others making haste to keep up with him.

The thing that lingered in Norio's mind was the grim expression on Shinjirō-sama's face as they made their way back to the castle.

SEPTEMBER ARRIVED, and with it a moon that was waxing and bright.

From Michael's vantage point inside Shinjirō's room, the moon's left side was in shadow. Its reflection in the small pool in the garden outside glittered on the surface of the water.

It was beautiful beyond description.

"Tomorrow night will be the matsuri."

He turned to Shinjirō, who had joined him in the doorway to the garden after advising his guards they were not to be disturbed. Shinjirō sat down and leaned back against the doorframe, and Michael poured sake into his bowl.

"That is the festival to celebrate the harvest, right?"

"Yes." Shinjirō smiled, bringing the sake bowl to his lips.

"That's wonderful." Michael sipped at his sake pensively. How he would love to go out into the town and see the festival himself!

Shinjirō regarded him somberly. "You realize, Maikoru, that festivals are not something you can attend."

Michael glanced at him. "I know that, Shinjirō-sama," he said, a little too quickly.

"That is—under normal circumstances."

Michael stared at the daimyō, who now looked as though he were stifling a smile. "My lord...?"

The daimyō laughed then, looking younger than his responsibilities usually permitted. "It is a custom in this han to wear masks for the harvest festival." He took another sip of his sake, raising his eyebrows slightly.

The realization dawned slowly on Michael, and when it did, he almost dropped his sake bowl. "Does that mean... I can... go *outside in the town* tomorrow?" He waited, holding his breath.

Shinjirō smiled. "Yes. I think it would be wise to wait until evening, when it is harder to distinguish features and when much sake has been consumed and people are less observant. Your hair will also have to be covered," he noted, gazing at Michael's light brown hair. "What?"

Michael couldn't stop the silly grin he knew was on his face. "Thank you," he said. "I'm so happy.... Thank you."

The daimyō stared at him, then burst out laughing. After calming down, he said, "I am pleased that you are pleased, Maikoru." He wiped a tear from his eye. "I find you so... refreshing in your own way. I—" His next word was stopped by Michael's mouth on his.

His sake bowl clattered to the floor as Michael seized his face between his hands and kissed him. He straddled Shinjirō's lap, feeling his arousal and pressing his own against it.

The daimyō embraced him, pulling him close and holding him tight.

THE NEXT day, Shinjirō petitioned both the Imperial Court in Kyoto and the Shogun in Edo regarding the Shirakawa-Kaminishi border dispute. But, as he told Michael, he did not expect much in the way of resolution from either authority.

It would be left up to the two clans to settle the matter—with bloodshed if need be.

CHAPTER EIGHT

THE HARVEST festival carried on with raucous merrymaking in the streets of the castle town, and throughout the day Michael listened to the noise coming from the streets and prepared himself mentally for going out that evening.

He would be wearing a piece of cloth tied about his head to cover his gaijin hair and a simple cloth mask with a face painted on it. A long cloak over peasant clothing would complete the look.

After a simple meal of fish, eggs and rice, and miso soup, some hot sake was brought in by the elderly woman for Shinjirō and himself. Michael poured the sake into the bowls, and he and the daimyō drank their fill.

"My lord, will you also be wearing a mask this evening?"

"Yes. I have performed all official duties already this day. In the evening, it is traditional for the daimyō to be masked and walk among the people as one of them."

"Did Kenshirō-sama do this also?"

Shinjirō looked startled. "How do you know my father's name?"

"The gardener, Kanosuke-san, told me," Michael replied, realizing belatedly that perhaps he shouldn't have divulged this.

But the daimyō didn't look upset. "Ah," he said. "Yes, I've seen you helping Kanosuke in the garden. He was one of my father's favorites." Shinjirō sipped his sake calmly, watching Michael.

Michael knew that sex with young men and boys was actually common among the samurai and considered to be part of the culture. But still, it startled him that it was such an ordinary thing, not worth being surprised over.

"There seems to be a need to categorize everything in the time you come from," Shinjirō said. "I think that life flows however it does, and we simply live it as we see fit. Desire is a part of that. It does not need to be named as anything." He turned to look out the doorway to the garden, up at the sky. It would soon be dark.

"Let us get ready."

NORIO LED Michael out through the underground passage, and Michael began the long walk around the castle, which included traversing a small wooded area.

It had been agreed that Shinjirō would exit by the main door of the castle as normal, while Michael would enter the town surreptitiously, making his way along the small river that ran behind the back of the town buildings and using an alley or passageway to enter the main street.

This was the third time Michael had been outside the castle, but the other times he had gone through the woods to other destinations. He had never seen the castle town itself, the main street he had been dragged through with his head covered by Tōru and his men.

He made his way swiftly through the wooded area, excitement growing in him. He hadn't dreamed he would get this opportunity to see history in the flesh, an actual late-Edo-period castle town in Japan's Kansai region.

The sounds of the festival were louder now, beckoning him on, and Michael tripped lightly along the gravelly shore of the small river, the back of the town's buildings to his right above a small upslope. He wanted to gain distance from the castle before entering the town, trying to avoid causing trouble for Shinjirō.

When he felt he'd gone far enough, Michael made his way up the slope and found a dark passageway between two wooden buildings. He stopped to check his head covering and his mask, adjusted his cloak, and prepared to join the festival.

THE FIRST thing he saw was a fire.

The fires were lit at intervals down the main street of the town, and as Michael emerged from the passageway, he saw people wearing masks and colorful kimonos dancing unevenly down the street.

He saw wooden buildings up and down the street in either direction. It looked like some of the back streets he'd seen in Kyoto when he'd visited there a few years ago. Sugoi, he thought in Japanese. *Amazing.*

And the *people.* He knew Shinjirō was an anomaly with his height, but all the people he observed seemed to be around five feet tall or just a little above. Tōru was taller than most of them. A number of them had rickety legs and bowed backs, indicating poor nutrition and osteoporosis.

Some of them had forgone masks, and Michael, through the slits in his mask, struggled to make out their features. *These are Japanese faces from the nineteenth century.* His heart pounded in his ears.

The night sky, the fires, the laughter and shouts, the people in their masks and kimonos…. It was all surreal. And yet, he was really here.

Music filled his ears—was that a shakuhachi flute?—and the deep, noisy beat of taiko drums resounded throughout his body.

With a start, Michael recalled himself and began walking down the street. Just standing there watching made him look suspicious; he needed to blend in as much as possible. He slouched and bowed his head slightly, aware that he still looked too tall.

People were dancing near the taiko drums. Others drank sake and stood around, swaying a little.

Guess street festivals are kind of the same everywhere. He smiled behind his mask.

He turned and looked up the street and saw the castle. For the first time, he was viewing it from the outside.

It was impressive. Not as large and magnificent as the one that had survived in Himeji, certainly, but the Kaminishi castle was impressive. A number of steps led up to it, ending at a set of ornate double doors. The main structure looked to be two stories high. But he knew there were several subfloors, and now he clearly saw how that was so. The castle was on a foothill, with its back to the mountain.

Mountains, actually. The entire town was located at the base of a range of mountains.

Was he looking east? Or west? Or north or south—he had no way of knowing. He knew that Kyoto was a half-day trek to the east on horseback. Was Kyoto directly over those mountains?

A roar from the crowd interrupted his thoughts; he turned to see Shinjirō, dressed modestly in a regular samurai's clothing with his swords and wearing a porcelain mask of a smiling kami. Apparently the townspeople recognized him despite the getup. There was bowing and nodding, but generally Shinjirō was not being made too much a fuss of, considering who he was. Michael guessed that what Shinjirō had said was true: this night, they could treat him more or less as one of them.

Shinjirō made his way through the crowds and walked in Michael's direction. Michael decided to walk past him and toward the castle. He was curious to see it up close. The two of them had decided that they were not to stand together or even to acknowledge each other. It would be safer that way.

He hunched over a little more, pulling the cloak tighter around him as he passed the daimyō. But he knew Shinjirō saw him, and the thought made him feel warm inside.

He felt... something more than that. Something that had been building up for a long time now....

LATE IN the evening, a kyōgen pantomime was taking place by one of the fires, and Michael wandered over for a moment to watch. The performers, wearing hard-shelled masks, were acting out an errant husband and an angry wife. The crowd gathered around was in peals of laughter, the women covering their mouths, the men downing more sake.

A movement in the corner of his eye caught Michael's attention. He turned to look. A dark figure was disappearing down one of the alleyways.

Michael hurried to the alley and stared down its impenetrable depths. He could see nothing, so he walked between the buildings, senses alert for any sign of trouble.

He reached the end of the alley and poked his head around the corner, looking one way and then the other. *There.* The figure glanced at him, then began walking quickly down the path behind the buildings.

Michael followed, picking up the pace. The river was to their left down the slope. He felt nervous. Here, there were no witnesses. The two of them were alone in the dark night.

Was the man leading him somewhere specific? Perhaps he had cohorts waiting somewhere, ready to jump him. That was a scary thought, even more so if they were able to unmask him. Maybe he should return to the main street—

Suddenly the man stopped.

Michael stopped too. And realized why he'd been following the man.

He was wearing contemporary twenty-first-century clothing.

MICHAEL STARED.

The man was wearing black trousers and a three-quarter-length black coat. He was standing about a hundred feet up ahead with his back to Michael.

Michael cautiously moved toward him.

A sense of dread came over Michael as he got closer and it became clear that this person was from his own time.

Who was he?

When he was twenty feet away, the man made a small movement, as if he were about to turn around. For some reason this made Michael stop.

He could see now that the man had almost shoulder-length hair in a layered style. His hair was black. He was tall, maybe Michael's height. And his coat was black leather.

"Dare da?"

Michael wasn't sure if he expected an answer. The man appeared Japanese, but he tried it again in English anyway. "Who are you?"

The man understood, in whichever language. Because he turned around.

The clothing was different, the hair was different, but the face was the same.

Shinjirō.

Michael could only stare in amazement.

The man who was Shinjirō from his own time gazed at him, an indecipherable expression on his face.

A chill ran down Michael's spine. He opened his mouth, but nothing came out.

Please—

He forced himself to move and took a few steps toward the man. "Shinjirō-sama," he said.

The man stared at him.

Michael ripped off his mask, revealing his face. "*Shinjirō-sama.*"

The man with Shinjirō's face blinked. He shook his head, eyes widening by the moment. "Don't follow me," he said.

A helpless feeling overtook Michael. He was afraid to spook him by coming closer, but he had to reach him. He *had* to.

But the man with Shinjirō's face turned and ran.

Michael followed him. "Matte kudasai!" he shouted. "Please wait! Shinjirō-sama!"

The man turned right and ran down one of the alleys that led back to the main street.

Michael was desperate to reach the alleyway. He ran with all the speed he had.

But when he got there, Shinjirō was gone.

He had run into the alley and disappeared.

MICHAEL HASTILY put his mask back on and continued down the alley to the main street.

He had to find Shinjirō—the Shinjirō of this time and place.

If *this* Shinjirō had vanished....

Michael moved through the crowds, now thinning out. It was late at night, and most of the festivities were winding down.

Where was he?

He went quickly down the main street, dodging drunks and merchants steering their carts home, growing increasingly desperate the more he searched.

The castle. He had to have returned to the castle. It had been dark for hours, and the festival was virtually over.

He hastily made his way back to the path behind the buildings, hurrying as fast as he could along the river and through the forest to the hidden entrance.

Michael ran through the dark passageway. He tore off his mask, throwing it down as he ran.

Shinjirō. Please be there.

Finally he reached the main floor. He hurried past the garden and down the hallway that led to Shinjirō's room.

The paper door was softly illuminated; there was lantern light within.

He opened the door, breathing hard.

Shinjirō—in his normal nineteenth-century yukata—was sitting on the floor. He looked up at Michael. "Maikoru, you are back." His smile vanished when he saw Michael's expression.

Michael knew he probably had a dumb look on his face, but he couldn't help himself. He smiled in relief. "I thought—"

"Thought what?"

"I—" Michael stopped. He suddenly realized he didn't want to tell Shinjirō about his double. Enough strangeness had happened around him, and the daimyō was likely to begin doubting him again if he kept telling him more.

"Maikoru." Shinjirō sounded a little stern. "Please tell me."

He sighed then and sat down across from Shinjirō. "I saw someone who looked like you," he said. "But he was wearing modern clothing, like what I wore when I was first brought here and when you saw me in my apartment."

The daimyō's reaction surprised Michael; he merely laughed lightly. He leaned forward and took Michael's face between his hands. "It never stops with you, does it, Maikoru?" And then he kissed him.

He's a little drunk... good, Michael concluded. *Maybe he won't remember us talking about his double.*

"Why didn't you invite him here?" Shinjirō continued, straight-faced. "Then the two of us could have enjoyed you."

Michael was indignant, but Shinjirō just laughed. "Come here."

HE PUT his mask on Michael's face, and Michael played along as Shinjirō stalked him around the room.

"Who are you?" the daimyō asked playfully. He reached for Michael, who backed away, cocking his head to the side.

"Who are *you*?" Michael responded. Through the slits in the mask, he watched Shinjirō as he approached.

"I am the daimyō of this domain. You are a stranger here, I see."

"Yes, a stranger."

"Where do you come from?"

"I come from a faraway land, my lord."

"Ah. Yes." Shinjirō walked around him slowly, as if examining him, making a full circle. "And what can you tell me about these faraway lands, stranger?"

"There are many people there, and tall buildings, and machines that transport things and animals and people." *I think he's not the only one who's drunk, actually.* Michael smiled behind his mask. He was enjoying this playacting now. He was also getting hard. "I can tell you a secret."

Shinjirō's eyes glittered. "A secret."

"Yes. But you must promise not to tell anybody."

"I promise."

Michael stepped closer and whispered in Shinjirō's ear. "I love you."

Shinjirō fell still. "Do you, now?"

"Yes." He pulled back to gaze at Shinjirō's face.

The daimyō raised his eyebrows. "I see." Then, almost imperceptibly, he began moving Michael back toward the wall, using only the touch of his fingertips on his chest. "But you are a stranger to me. There is still much I do not know about you."

Michael swallowed his disappointment and said, "But in time, you will get to know me more. And you will see that what I am saying is true." His back hit the wall with an abrupt bump. "If it takes time for me to prove it... I can only pray that we will have the time." *Why did I say that?* Michael thought bemusedly. He almost felt like someone else had said it through him.

He had no time to ponder it, though, as Shinjirō unexpectedly took both his wrists in his left hand and held them against the wall, above his head.

"There is time," he told Michael. "Tonight... we have all the time in the world."

He fingered the mask at the hairline; then he slowly pulled it down, revealing Michael's face inch by inch.

When his face was fully revealed, Michael lifted his chin. "Do you like what you see?" he asked, still playing the part of the siren stranger. His wrists being restrained made him harder, and he strained against the hold, feeling Shinjirō tighten his grasp. His cock jumped. *God, this feels amazing.*

"Oh, yes. You please me greatly." The daimyō's fingers traced his jawline, moving down to his neck. His right hand grasped his neck lightly. Michael lifted his chin again, turning away, inviting kisses on the side of his face.

Shinjirō seemed amused at his surrender and indulged him, kissing where his ear met his face, lingering over his cheek, and nipping at his jawline. Michael breathed harder, little noises beginning to come from his throat.

The daimyō's tongue left a warm, wet trail down his neck, and Michael's arousal intensified. He panted, beginning to plead. "My lord...."

Shinjirō placed his hand on Michael's groin, and Michael moaned. "Is this what you want, stranger?" he asked, resuming the charade. "Tell me."

"Yes."

"Yes... what?"

"Yes, this is... what I want." He was unable to keep still. His body undulated, and his head moved restlessly back and forth. "Please."

Shinjirō worked Michael's cock through the rough cloth kimono with slow, deliberate movements.

"*Aaahh*," Michael gasped, then began breathing raggedly in and out. Noises were coming from his throat. He couldn't stop them. It was as if the daimyō knew exactly how to manipulate his cock to elicit from him an aroused sound or a helpless sound. He was totally under Shinjirō's control.

"*Unhh... aah....*"

The daimyō suddenly let go of his wrists, using both hands to fling open Michael's kimono. He tore at the layer beneath, finally reaching his fundoshi.

Ripping it away, he grasped Michael's fully erect cock, wringing a cry out of Michael's throat. Slick with precum now, it slid underneath the daimyō's experienced hand as he stroked it up and down. He used his other arm to pull Michael closer.

The two men stood like that for some moments, with Shinjirō working his cock. Michael placed his hands lightly on the daimyō's shoulders, hesitating. Then he moved them to the daimyō's hips, beckoning him closer.

Shinjirō grabbed him and slammed their bodies together. The resulting friction was heaven.

The daimyō pulled the kimono off Michael's shoulders, and the underlayer as well, dropping both to the floor and leaving him naked. Michael reached for Shinjirō's clothing, but Shinjirō himself impatiently pulled off most of it.

Even just clad in a fundoshi, the daimyō was magnificent.

Michael drew in a breath, then exhaled. The daimyō's hands were cupping his face and he was being kissed again. The hands moved down to his ass and squeezed. Michael didn't know where to put his hands first, but he wanted to touch every inch of the daimyō's body.

Somehow they made their way to the silk-covered futon, and the rest of their clothing was dispensed with shortly thereafter.

"Shinjirō-sama...." Michael's voice trailed off plaintively. He wanted all of the man, all at once, every inch of that fine strong body in his hands *now*. He reached out, enfolding the daimyō in his arms and sinking down onto the futon.

Being on the bottom, though, wasn't really what he wanted... for now. He flipped them over, with a surprised Shinjirō winding up on his back.

But he didn't do it to dominate the daimyō—just the opposite.

Michael began lavishing attention on the daimyō's body, kissing his face, his neck, tonguing his nipples—earning a few moans—and back up to bite his collarbone mischievously. His hands didn't lie idle either; they roamed every inch of the daimyō that he could reach.

When he finally began sucking Shinjirō's cock, the daimyō was primed and more than ready for it. He groaned, and his hands moved through Michael's hair. Michael moved down to suckle his balls and then the area between there and the anus.

Shinjirō writhed in reaction, his legs twitching involuntarily. He emitted soft moans.

Michael returned to Shinjirō's cock then and laved the underside with his tongue, tasting precum. He moved the foreskin back gently with his fingers and softly tongued the tip of the head. The daimyō was making vulnerable noises from deep in his throat, and Michael was pleased that he was causing the daimyō to react that way, that he was getting good at this. He wanted to become fantastic at doing this, to please Shinjirō.

Every cell in his body wanted to please the daimyō, to fulfill him, to be the one by his side forever.

He was in love.

A hand on his head urged him wordlessly to *stop*, and then the daimyō reached for the bowl of oil. Michael moved to accommodate him, then lay on his back on the silk futon.

He drew up his knees as Shinjirō blinked. "Do it this way," he urged the daimyō. "I want to see your face... when we...."

The daimyō nodded, then coated his fingers with the oil.

He began with one finger, then soon added a second. Michael writhed, moving his lower body, trying to help Shinjirō find the suddenly elusive spot. "Stay still," Shinjirō said, the sake and perhaps the sight of Michael wriggling about combining to amuse the daimyō.

The grimace on Michael's face also seemed to amuse him.

At that moment, Shinjirō's fingers found the spot.

"*Aaaah... haa... aaaaahh!*" Michael cried out.

Shinjirō jabbed the spot again, prompting the same ecstatic reaction, then withdrew in order to add a third finger.

Within a few seconds, Michael was panting, hands hitting the futon, trying to control himself. "Please," he said. "Do it now. *Please*."

The daimyō oiled himself and set his cock at the entrance. He began to push in as Michael strained to keep his knees up and spread apart. This position was difficult, but something about the tension in his muscles added to the arousal building in his entire genital area.

He felt sweat break out all over his body and was feverishly hot everywhere: his groin, his face, and every inch of his skin.

He touched Shinjirō's face, and Shinjirō leaned down, pushing his knees into his chest, going in deeper. Michael let out a choked noise. It felt like every part of his body was being invaded and occupied. It was so intense a sensation that he could barely draw breath.

The lack of air brought him closer to the edge; combined with the muscle tension and stretched-to-the-limit feeling in his lower body, he was on overload. Something had to break. At that moment Shinjirō pushed his knees into his chest even more and stabbed him deep, deep within.

Michael threw his head back and came in a series of choking gasps, the jolt of pleasure in his groin so strong that he thought he would black out.

The daimyō also came at that moment, that last thrust enough to do it. He was more vocal in his release, and dimly, through a semiconscious haze, Michael could hear the hoarse cries torn from his throat.

MICHAEL FOUND Shinjirō in the garden the next morning.

The morning air was soft and refreshingly cool. Autumn was descending on the Kansai region; the leaves were just beginning to turn.

"Shinjirō-sama."

The daimyō turned, smiling. "Ohayō, Maikoru," he replied. "You are awake early." His eyes were crinkled in amusement.

Michael started, then glared at the daimyō. "You mean, early considering...."

"Considering our activities last night. They did go on for a significant length of time, did they not?"

Michael looked away, annoyed, while the daimyō laughed.

"Sumanai," Shinjirō said unexpectedly.

Michael glanced at him, startled; he'd never heard the daimyō apologize for anything. "I know you're not laughing at me," he said quickly. "It's just that...."

He didn't know how to say it. What they did together was incredibly exciting, but at the same time, private and embarrassing. Or it was for *him*, at least. The daimyō seemed to have no difficulty with it.

"You are a true delight, Maikoru," Shinjirō said gently. "I am always surprised, however, at your modesty in these matters." He moved closer to Michael and gently traced a finger down the side of his face. "Sex, our bodies, it is all part of life. None of it is anything to be ashamed of."

Michael heard birds chirping. The wind gently moved through their hair. Shinjirō's eyes were clear, and his gaze at Michael was direct and inviting. The quiet beauty of the garden and the soft sunlight on his skin lulled Michael into a state of heightened reality that made him realize something important.

"This is the life I was meant to live," he said.

The daimyō gazed at him mildly. "Really," he replied.

"Yes," Michael said quietly. He looked at Shinjirō. "I'm supposed to be with you. That's why I came to this time, this place."

Shinjirō blinked, then looked amused again. "That is the ultimate meaning you ascribe to this event? I would have thought that an occurrence this profoundly mysterious might have more world-changing significance."

"I'm serious."

Shinjirō stared at him soberly. "I am serious as well, Maikoru."

Michael placed a hand on the daimyō's handsome face. "If the time travel gods permit it, I want to stay with you for the rest of my life."

"Could you be happy remaining a veritable prisoner of this castle? You will not be able to go outside."

"But that won't remain the case for long. Remember, my lord, Japan will open to trade with foreign nations soon. The sight of a blue-eyed gaijin will not be so unusual."

The daimyō turned and walked a few steps away from Michael.

Too late, Michael realized he'd reminded the daimyō of *that* issue. "Shinjirō-sama," he said softly. The daimyō's back was turned to him.

"Shinjirō-sama, it will be as I told you. You saw what the future was like. It is the same for your country. In the end, things will turn out well for Japan. And it is something that has already happened where I come from. You cannot change it, and there is no need for you to try. You would be risking your life for a pointless cause."

Michael went to stand in front of the daimyō. Shinjirō's face was turned to the side, his expression unreadable.

He waited, but Shinjirō made no response.

"Shinjirō-sama, please."

"It is my duty to try to stop this Perry from entering my country," Shinjirō said at last. "I am becoming more convinced that this is so as I consider the matter."

Michael opened his mouth to say something but held his tongue. What more could he say to convince him?

Suddenly there was shouting from the main entry hall. Both Shinjirō and Michael turned to see Norio running toward them.

"Shinjirō-sama," Norio said, out of breath. "There is violence at the border." Several samurai came in behind him, similarly winded.

The daimyō muttered under his breath.

He barked out commands to Norio, who nodded and ordered the others to retrieve weapons from the armory. "I'll assemble everyone," Norio said, bowing to the daimyō before taking his leave.

Shinjirō gave a last order to one of the samurai to get the horses ready.

Five minutes later, in full armor, the daimyō strode down the hallway toward the main doors. As he passed Michael, he ordered, "Stay here."

Michael started to speak, but the daimyō's look quelled him.

Shinjirō turned and walked to the main doors, flanked by his lieutenants.

A shout rose up from the ranks as the samurai waiting on the steps outside cheered their daimyō. Then the main doors were pulled shut.

In frustration, Michael could only watch Shinjirō leave.

CHAPTER NINE

THE BORDER was in chaos.

Norio stared as Shirakawa men dragged farmers and their families out of their homes. Children were screaming. Several dwellings were on fire.

Shinjirō-sama was shouting commands, pulling his horse up and unsheathing his long sword in one movement.

Norio unsheathed as well, as did the other samurai. This was no small skirmish. The Shirakawa samurai had destroyed property and manhandled Kaminishi civilians. This clearly called for bloodshed.

He narrowed his eyes and clutched his sword tightly.

THE WARLORD was like a whirlwind, slicing through the enemy samurai with a deadly swiftness.

Norio was nearly as efficient, if not as fast—or as graceful. There was a sinuousness to Shinjirō-sama's fighting that was unique to the daimyō. His father, Kenshirō-sama, had also possessed power, but not such grace.

Norio turned to his left, sensing danger, and swung his katana at the neck of the charging samurai. Blood spattered across his chest; he felt it as it *thwapped* against his breastplate.

The next one came at him from the rear. Norio pulled his horse around, intending to trample him, but the samurai wielded a naginata. The long lance with a blade attached to the end made for a deadly weapon against a warrior on horseback, and Norio parried the deathblow just in time.

He pulled the reins, forcing his horse to rear up and balance on its hind legs, intending once again to trample his attacker. But the samurai instead went for the horse, piercing it squarely in the chest while Norio was aloft and unable to maneuver the horse out of danger.

The horse screamed and collapsed, sending Norio sprawling to the ground. He rolled to avoid being crushed by the still-bellowing horse and found his feet, at the same moment bringing his long sword up to parry the naginata's next blow.

The naginata-user was a skilled one, but in the end, Norio's own training and expertise won the fight. It was over in twenty seconds.

Norio pulled his sword out of the naginata-user's neck and turned to survey the scene.

Farmers were picking up fallen weapons and taking up defensive stances against the Shirakawa samurai. Everywhere he looked, the fires were spreading. His fellow samurai were waging deadly fights all around him.

Norio unsheathed his wakizashi and wielded the shorter sword in his left hand as he lunged with his katana toward an enemy samurai.

The next few minutes will decide this fight.

DOWN THE road, another naginata-wielder was on the attack.

His prey merely laughed.

Shinjirō deflected the long blade, knocking it upward with his katana as he leapt off his horse. He parried the naginata with a deft blow, then knocked it out of the stunned samurai's hands.

The daimyō's katana made an arc through the air. The blood spray followed a second later.

BODIES WERE lying on the ground everywhere.

Norio leapt over one, landing lightly and breaking into a dead run toward one of the houses. He'd seen two Shirakawa samurai chasing a farmer and his wife into it.

Out of the corner of his eye, he noticed Shinjirō-sama engaged with an enemy samurai, their katana flashing in the sun.

As he ran, he saw the glint of something in the bushes nearby. At the same time, his hearing picked up the sound of horse's hooves approaching.

Norio's mind couldn't piece it together in analytical terms, but in some general, encompassing sense, he knew what was happening.

And that everything would be all right.

He charged into the house, blood pounding in his ears.

SHINJIRŌ HAD to exert more of his strength and skill on this one than the others.

He relished it. Every cell in his body was engaged in this deadly back-and-forth game of life and death.

He never felt more alive than when fighting.

His hearing registered the sound of a horse approaching at a fast clip. It was far enough in the distance that he didn't need to move out of its way yet. He also felt a vague sense of threat coming from behind him on the right side, but the enemy in front of him was too skilled for him to attempt to maneuver him around so the threat would be to his enemy's rear and not to his own.

Shinjirō managed to draw blood, wounding the samurai's right hand.

One more blow.

THE MASKED ninja seized the moment.

The Kaminishi warlord was going for the kill on the opponent in front of him, and all of his focus and concentration would be on delivering the final blow.

He leapt out of the bushes, drawing his ninja straight blade. He saw only the target—the daimyō's back. He didn't hear the arrow flying through the air that would seal his fate.

SHINJIRŌ WITHDREW his katana from the enemy's body and whirled around at the sound of a cry.

A ninja lay at his feet, struggling to rise.

An arrow had pierced his right shoulder from the back.

The warlord glanced up to see a masked man on horseback, carrying a longbow.

The man dismounted a bit clumsily and pulled his hood farther down over his face, covering the eye slits on the mask that looked quite familiar.

Shinjirō watched impassively as the man approached and then dropped to his knees before him, placing his hands on the ground and bowing his head.

Several of Shinjirō's men ran up and secured the ninja, who was making as if to escape.

Shinjirō stared at the bowed figure on the ground for a long moment. "You may rise," the daimyō said.

The man stood up and quietly retreated to stand about twenty feet back from Shinjirō and his men.

Norio walked out of the house he'd run into. "Secure," he called to the warlord.

Shinjirō nodded, then surveyed the area. The action was winding down. His men had won the day.

He gave orders to several samurai to finish up and then check the perimeter beyond the buildings to ensure that calm was fully restored.

And then he returned his attention to the ninja being restrained in front of him.

MICHAEL HAD managed to convince the master of horses that Shinjirō-sama had ordered him to bring up the rear of the assault, and he had been given a horse to ride.

It had been years since he'd ridden, and he was well out of practice. But the cold trickle of fear that he'd felt ever since Norio came running in to report the violence at the border made him take risk after risk. He *knew* he had to get to Shinjirō.

Something horrible was about to happen.

Michael rode toward the border, going by instinct and memories of the night with Misako.

Once he spotted the smoke from the fires, he sped toward it, urging the horse on. His hand that grasped the longbow grew numb, but he rode on.

Fortunately his approach brought him to the edge of the border village, where he could ride up to the action without being seen. He slowed the horse down, taking it on a path through a small grove of trees.

As he neared the village, he heard shouts and screaming and what could only be called war cries. His heart pounded, but he continued on.

A queasy feeling of *danger, danger* alerted his senses as the village came into view. He urged the horse to pick up the pace again.

The first thing he saw was Shinjirō fighting an enemy samurai. His back was to Michael, and though it looked like he was prevailing in the fight, Michael's heart leapt in his chest.

For the next thing he saw was the black-clad ninja speeding toward Shinjirō.

Without thinking, he lifted the longbow and set an arrow in one motion.

And shot it.

MICHAEL SHUT his eyes behind the mask.

The screaming had been going on for some time. First a Kaminishi samurai had twisted the arrow in the ninja's shoulder. The ninja somehow remained silent through that treatment, but then other samurai surrounded him as he lay prone and restrained on the ground. One of them took out his wakizashi and went to work on the rest of the ninja's body.

The ninja was encircled by Kaminishi samurai so Michael couldn't see what they were doing to him, but he could guess. He willed himself not to move an inch, to stand there as unmoved as the other samurai as the horrible screams continued.

He opened his eyes and viewed the surrounding witnesses through the mask's eye slits. The farmers and their families were present to see this, including the children. The little boys and girls watched, their eyes huge. It sickened him.

He turned his attention to Shinjirō, who merely stood off to the side and waited. The daimyō's face was impassive. Norio came up and gave him a report on the area in a quiet voice, and Shinjirō nodded.

At length, the ninja began screaming words. Shinjirō gestured for his men to halt. They parted to allow the daimyō to approach.

Michael stepped closer to try to hear what the ninja was saying. He could make out Shirakawa and another name... Tōru.

The samurai surrounding the ninja stepped back in shock. Shinjirō, crouching over the ninja, exchanged several more words with him before standing up.

He nodded curtly to one of his men, who finished off the ninja by plunging his katana through the man's throat.

"Find Tōru and bring him here," the warlord said.

SHINJIRŌ'S SECOND-IN-COMMAND had carried out his duties with his usual competence, to all outward appearances.

He had led the samurai into the village with Shinjirō and directed much of the action. He'd taken out a good number of Shirakawa samurai single-handedly, as was to be expected of someone of his training and experience.

The entire episode had been planned to succeed on two fronts: first, to display the intent of Lord Ryū to thoroughly subjugate the farmers living in the borderlands to Shirakawa rule; and second, of course, to take out Shinjirō Kaminishi.

To the first end, Lord Ryū had intended Tōru to play his part as the loyal Kaminishi lieutenant; that is, to kill Shirakawa samurai in his role as Shinjirō's second. It didn't matter to the young daimyō that some of his men would die. If they died in a mere village skirmish such as this, then clearly they hadn't been true Shirakawa samurai to begin with.

But the most important part by far was to kill Shinjirō.

And in this, Tōru had now failed.

SHINJIRŌ'S FACE was impassive as Tōru was brought to him.

Michael stared as the second-in-command stood before Shinjirō, meeting the daimyō's eyes evenly, stone-faced and silent.

The daimyō stared at him for a long moment. Then he asked, "This man said you hired him to kill me. Is this true?"

Tōru didn't bother to look at the dead ninja on the ground. He continued returning Shinjirō's stare, saying nothing.

Shinjirō approached him, never breaking his gaze. "You served me for ten years. I am ordering you to answer me. By our code and on your honor, you will answer me."

Shouts and calls came from nearby. Another man was being brought before Shinjirō.

Michael saw Tōru start slightly, a flicker in his eyes.

It was one of the Shirakawa men, and judging from his dress, a high-ranking one. "It's Futawara Kenji-dono," said one samurai. From what Michael was able to glean from the samurai muttering around him, Kenji was the second-in-command to Lord Ryū. He held the equivalent position to Tōru's for the Shirakawa clan.

He was older than Tōru, in his thirties. There was a badly bleeding gash on his right forearm, and blood on his face from a flesh wound on his forehead. But he looked Shinjirō calmly in the eye, notwithstanding that he knew his execution would take place within a few minutes at the most.

"Shinjirō-sama." Kenji bowed formally.

"Kenji-dono ka?"

"Hai, Shinjirō-sama."

"What was the intent behind today's fight? Is it Lord Ryū's intention to take the borderlands by force?"

"These lands belong to the Shirakawa clan," Kenji responded politely, stating his clan's party line.

Michael watched as Shinjirō said to Kenji, not looking at Tōru, "Was there any other purpose to today's activities?"

And then Kenji smiled.

"Hai, Shinjirō-sama. It was to bring about your death. Tōru-dono was the one responsible for seeing to that. But as he has failed, he is of no further use to us now."

A roar went up among the Kaminishi samurai, and multiple katana and wakizashi were at Tōru's throat instantly.

"Tōru."

Everyone fell silent.

"Is this true?" Shinjirō asked.

Tōru stared back at him.

Then, almost imperceptibly, the daimyō's shoulders slumped. Anger and sadness competed in his face before the implacable mask returned.

He turned to Kenji. "I am returning you to your lord," he said.

Kenji was startled. "Shinjirō-sama?"

"Tell Lord Ryū what you have seen here today. The people of the borderlands fought for the Kaminishi Han, and some gave their lives for it. They will not bend to Shirakawa rule, not now and not ever. Tell him to abandon his claim on the borderlands. For this purpose, I spare your life today."

Kenji gaped at him. "Hai, Shinjirō-sama," he said finally. He turned and ran toward the eastern forest and the border beyond.

Shinjirō assigned several men for protection should any Shirakawa men come back, and then he ordered the rest to return to the castle.

He did not look at Tōru again.

MICHAEL LIFTED the wet cloth again to the daimyō's shoulders and rubbed at the skin while blood ran down the bare back.

The water in the wash bucket was steaming hot, and Michael wrung out the cloth again and again, turning the water red.

The daimyō stood patiently, naked, in the small but deep wooden tub as Michael returned to his task. The blood spatter had gotten under the armor, under the vestments beneath, soaking completely through all the layers and sticking to Shinjirō's skin like body paint.

Shinjirō himself had sustained no wounds. *Thank God*, Michael thought. He squeezed out the washcloth again and began using the second bucket of hot water that had been brought to the bathing room.

He finished washing the daimyō's back and moved to the front to start on his torso and arms.

The two men were silent as Michael worked the cloth over the daimyō's skin, and he was glad for it. His nerves were at their limit after all that he had witnessed today, the blood and screams and people lying in literal pieces on the ground.

He took a deep breath, trying to calm himself.

The horror of samurai fighting had been brought home to him today in real time, in flesh and living color. The difference between reading about it in books and eyewitnessing the real thing was not even describable in words. He had known that bushido, the samurai code dictating actions and ethics, while making sense within its own context, was an extraordinarily brutal code by modern standards. Everyone romanticized the samurai; he himself did, though intellectually he knew better. But today's carnage proved a point to him.

The samurai had needed to cease existing.

Michael closed his eyes. Was that really true? Had there been no other way to go, in historical terms? Could samurai culture have survived the enormous changes in Japanese society and political history that occurred after Perry's arrival?

What if history could be changed?

If it could be changed, *should* it be changed?

No. Don't go there. The way it happened is the way it needed to happen.

Suddenly he recalled where he was, standing in front of the daimyō. His eyes flew open, and he found Shinjirō regarding him somberly.

And then the daimyō's hand was on the back of his head, pulling him close. He laid his face against Shinjirō's shoulder.

IN THE morning, Tōru was led out from the same basement cell Michael had been kept in and brought to one of the side courtyards.

Shinjirō had insisted Michael be present, and Michael had assented. His gaijin identity was obscured with the same clothing and mask he had worn the day before.

Tōru had not said a word since being restrained and placed in the cell. But Michael could put two and two together. It was obvious Tōru had promised to betray Shinjirō in return for control of the Kaminishi lands after they had been conquered by the Shirakawa clan.

The daimyō's face was as impassive as always, and Michael wondered what Shinjirō was thinking. A betrayal of this magnitude had to be a huge blow. Tōru had served under Shinjirō for all those years. Michael couldn't imagine what that would feel like.

That's because you've never been that close to anyone for that long.

Michael's mouth quirked bitterly behind the mask. That was certainly true. He tended to get along with people while keeping them at a safe distance.

His thoughts were flitting here and there because he was nervous. He didn't want to witness what was about to happen, so his brain was trying to keep his mind off it. He supposed he could close his eyes when the moment came and no one would be the wiser, as he was masked, but somehow he thought that would be betraying Shinjirō. Shinjirō had wanted him to be present. He could just as easily have ordered him to remain in their room while the execution took place.

He would bear witness then, as Shinjirō had wished.

Tōru's hands and feet were not restrained. When Shinjirō had asked him if he wanted to commit seppuku, as opposed to simply being beheaded, Tōru had nodded his assent. The daimyō was being gracious in this respect, as Tōru was literally the worst kind of criminal: a snake-in-the-grass betrayer of a leader's trust. To have offered the choice was magnanimous of the daimyō.

He observed the daimyō from behind his mask. Shinjirō was the perfect late-Edo-period samurai warlord: strong, extraordinarily skilled in the fighting arts, honorable. And beautiful. He was a man's man, and yet he was beautiful. Michael felt a quickening pulse down below and grimaced. This was not the time and place for that.

And yet... life and death were connected with each other. He'd read somewhere that people often wanted sex after a funeral or after someone had died, as sacrilegious as it might seem.

Michael came to, as Shinjirō was now standing behind Tōru, who was seated on the ground in seiza position with his knees tucked under him. Norio was kneeling and appeared to be pouring water on Shinjirō's katana.

There were four samurai whom he recognized as castle guards standing at four points in the courtyard, creating a perimeter. Along with himself, Shinjirō, and Norio, they were the only witnesses present.

Tōru secured the ends of his obi under his knees, which were spread open now. A short knife lay on a white cloth in front of him. He adjusted his white kimono to open the area that was covering the abdomen.

Shinjirō had taken a position behind and to the left of the sitting man. He had shaken off the water from the katana with a slice through the air. He now stood waiting.

Tōru removed the short knife from its scabbard and laid the scabbard back down on the white cloth. He held the knife and bowed his head slightly.

Then suddenly he turned his face toward Michael.

"This is how a true samurai dies. Remember this, gaijin."

He plunged the knife into the left side of his abdomen and began pulling it across to the right side.

Michael watched Shinjirō make a sweeping movement with his katana—before everything went black.

MICHAEL STOOD on the wooden walkway just outside Shinjirō's room, gazing at the garden. The soft, soothing sounds of the trickling water were comforting to his ears.

It was evening, and Michael had only been conscious again for an hour or so. When he'd woken up, he was in Shinjirō's room, lying on the silk-covered futon. Embarrassingly enough, he had fainted at the moment when Tōru's head had been cut off.

He must have been carried back to the room and allowed to awaken naturally. He had been naked when he awoke, so Shinjirō or someone else must have removed his clothing.

The disorientation had worn off, and Michael was feeling better now. He adjusted his yukata and was about to walk out into the garden when he heard Shinjirō behind him.

"Daijōbu ka?"

"Hai, my lord," Michael replied. He turned to greet the daimyō. "I'm fine now."

"Good," Shinjirō said.

There was a pause. "I'm sorry," Michael said. "For... blacking out like that."

The daimyō smiled slightly. "It's all right," he said. "I was concerned that it might be too much for you. I don't expect you've ever seen an event such as that in the time you come from."

"Hai."

The two men stood silently side by side in the quiet evening, each alone with his own thoughts.

Michael didn't know what to say about the events of that day or the day before. He had never been exposed to such violence. But if he was going to stay with Shinjirō, there would be times like these.

And he very much wanted to stay with Shinjirō.

"Maikoru, I will be leaving for Edo tomorrow morning."

Michael started. "What?"

"I am going to request an audience with the Shogun. I want to warn him about Perry."

"No."

The daimyō ignored the interruption. "There are two years before Perry's arrival. If the Shogun can bring the daimyō and their samurai legions together on this, there will be two years to prepare to win this fight. We can keep the gaikokujin out of Japan."

"My lord, please reconsider your words. This can only lead to bloodshed and grief, and it will not bring you the result you seek." *Nor what I seek*, he thought privately. "Shinjirō-sama."

"This is something that I must do."

Michael moved to Shinjirō, placing his hands on the daimyō's shoulders. "I want to spend the rest of my life with you." He embraced the other man, head resting on his shoulder. "Don't do this."

He felt he was in a dream as he looked at the crescent moon over Shinjirō's shoulder.

The last thing he heard was the daimyō's soft voice.

"I am sorry...."

GODDAMN THIS fucking hill.

She trudged up the asphalted slope, cursing for the thousandth time the steep hill that led students off the campus and toward Berkeley's Northside neighborhood.

At least Michael was doing the food; all she had to do was stop at the little market at the corner of Ridge Road and pick up a six-pack. With the way he was zoning out right now, he was probably out of beer and didn't even notice. She snorted.

Ellen bought Heineken, tortilla chips, and canned salsa at the store and reached Michael's apartment building around eight o'clock.

She couldn't believe her name was still on the mailbox.

He is such a space cadet.

She walked up the staircase and knocked on the door.

No answer.

She rang the doorbell, waited, and then rang a second time. "Michael. *Michael.*"

Fine. She still had her old key.

MICHAEL STILL didn't answer when she entered, so she went to the kitchen to put the beer in the fridge and then walked around the apartment looking for him.

A strange sound came to her ears. The sliding door to the balcony was open.

Ellen walked to the open doorway and looked outside.

Michael was crouched in the far corner of the balcony, face in his hands, crying.

She went to him, getting down and putting her arms around him.

He murmured something, so softly she wasn't sure she heard him correctly.

"He's gone."

Part Three
End of the Dream

CHAPTER TEN

"SO WHAT are you going to do?"

Ellen prided herself on being pragmatic. She didn't know if Michael had really time-traveled to nineteenth-century Japan, and she didn't care if he had fallen in love with a samurai warlord. What was he going to do next?

"Do?" Michael looked down at his hands.

They were sitting on the couch together. Michael had no appetite, but Ellen had eaten her chips and salsa and was now sitting with her beer, trying to piece her former boyfriend back together again.

"What can I do? Every time this happens, it's out of my control. I can't predict when I'll go back, and I can't make myself go back."

He looked a wreck. There were dark circles under his eyes. His hair was a mess.

Ellen sighed.

Michael glanced at her. "You don't believe me, do you?"

"I have no idea," Ellen said. "I'm sure there's a lot of psychic phenomena or whatever that can't be explained in this world. I believe that you believe it, and that... *something* happened to you. I know you. You wouldn't pull my leg like this."

She put a hand on Michael's shoulder. "I'm just concerned about you. You look like shit. Seriously, like you haven't slept for days. Are you sure you don't want something to eat?"

"No. I'm fine." He turned to look at her and tried to smile. "Really. Thanks."

Ellen snorted. "It's even worse when you smile."

They laughed a little at that, and then there was silence.

"Do you want me to stay overnight?"

Michael looked at her.

"Just to sleep, I mean. *Geez.* You look like maybe you shouldn't be alone tonight."

"No, thank you. I'll be all right."

"Don't you have a paper due tomorrow?"

He closed his eyes. "I worked on it last week. It's nearly finished. I can always take an incomplete if I can't get it done by tomorrow."

He looked so miserable that Ellen leaned forward and put her arms around his neck.

They stayed like that for a long moment; then she sat back and picked up her beer.

"Get some rest tonight, however you can. And call me if you need me."

EVERYTHING WAS white.

He was in a haze of white fog. Stepping through it cautiously, he began to see a light in the distance.

White light....

And in the midst of it... a figure.

The figure was tall, with long black hair. He wore a white kimono and obi sash. His face was beautiful and austere.

He ran toward the figure, but his feet were like lead. He struggled to reach the other man.

The figure smiled at him—a smile of peaceful acceptance.

Then the figure turned and walked away until he disappeared into the distance.

HE WAS reaching for the figure... reaching... and then—

Thud!

Michael woke up.

He was lying on his side—on hard ground.

It was night, and he was outdoors.

He lay there for a moment, collecting himself. Rolling onto his back, he gazed up at the moon.

He was back in Japan.

Slowly he sat up, feeling the chill. He was naked.

He stood up, looking around. It took a moment, but he realized he was at the back of Kaminishi Castle, not far from the hidden entrance.

The passageway was dark and dank, and Michael was careful to slow down. He couldn't risk an injury now, but time was precious.

Finally he emerged into the lower level of the castle. He ran into one of the guards—fortunately one who remembered him. The samurai stared, and Michael covered his privates with his hands as he asked him to find Norio.

Norio didn't seem surprised to see him. He hustled him above to the main level and into Shinjirō's room as quickly as possible. He gave Michael some clothes, then began assembling a pack for him, already assuming he wouldn't be staying overnight.

"Shinjirō-sama—doko desu ka?"

"He left around two weeks ago," Norio replied. "For Edo."

Edo. Tokyo. The capital city.

"How long does it take to reach there on foot?"

The head of security pursed his lips and considered. "Six or seven days, if you take time to rest—and you'll need to, if you're walking all the way. There's a single main road to Edo—the Tōkaidō road—once you've made it through the mountains to Kyoto. A lot of merchants travel that road to Edo with their goods. Try to get into the back of a wagon if you can without anyone seeing you. Travel by night and sleep by day, off the main road if you have to walk."

He continued to give Michael instructions on how to enter Edo without papers and how to bypass the security patrols, and further details on how to reach Shinjirō's home in the Yamanote district.

Michael stood by as Norio sent the elderly woman off to the kitchen, telling her to put together food and supplies for a long journey on foot.

"You know why he's gone to Edo."

"Yes," Norio said. "He's going to seek an audience with the Shogun about what you told him."

"Do you agree with his decision?" Michael asked. He respected Norio and was curious as to his views.

"No. I do not," Norio said unexpectedly. "This is a difficult time right now, with the Shirakawa clan breathing down our necks. We've had to place a lot of men on the border to ensure the security of the farmers. It is not the time to make plans for something that may or may not occur two years from now." He looked down, troubled. "And there is no guarantee that the Shogun will be receptive to what he will say. He may lose his life for this, for an imaginary future event. I do not agree with this at all."

Michael stared. It was quite a speech from the quiet head of security.

"That is why," Norio continued, "I am hoping you will reach him safely and be able to change his mind. I do not feel I can lead this han as a true leader. Shinjirō-sama places more faith in my abilities than I deserve."

He looked Michael in the eye. "Please. Do all that you can to change his mind."

WITHIN A few minutes of his final conversation with Norio, he left the castle.

The night sky was clear. The stars were out. He checked that the pack was secure on his back as he walked through the dark field, making his way toward the mountains.

He wore a cloth half mask over the lower part of his face. It was not uncommon to see peasants protecting themselves from dust and insects this way, or from germs from sick people. The second part of his disguise was a conical peasant's hat with some cloth strips that hung down from its rim, which many people in this period used to keep insects out of their faces. Finally he had begrimed his entire face with dirt dampened by water from a stream, wiping off the excess with his sleeve and letting it dry before bringing up the half mask.

This way, if he kept his face lowered, it would be nearly impossible to notice his gaijin eyes or anything else unusual about his face. Here in the nineteenth century, in the countryside, people's faces were tanned by the sun. The darkened tone from the dirt should help there.

The only remaining problem was his height. At five feet ten, he was taller than nearly everyone he came across. He couldn't think of anything he could do about that, except to walk slightly crouched over.

The rest of his clothing was a rough kimono and multiple layers of covering wraps, one of them literally a blanket.

The way east through the mountains was a bit treacherous, but it was the only way to avoid traveling through Shirakawa territory. There was a path, but it was narrow in parts with a sheer drop on one side, meaning there would be no cover. He would have to make haste at night and somehow find a place to hide during the day.

Once in Kyoto, as Norio had said, there would be a main road to travel alongside of, or—even better—he might be able to secretly hitch a ride in the back of somebody's wagon.

The cold night air made his lungs ache, but his sense of urgency and the long journey ahead of him made him keep moving.

Shinjirō. Wait for me.

I'm coming.

HE WALKED up into the mountains and along the path until the sun began to lighten the skies ahead of him. The path, fortunately, did have its sections where a small flat area existed between the path and the mountain. He would have to look for one of those areas soon.

There had been no one else on the path all night. Though he could not see it, Michael heard rushing water from somewhere below. As the sun began to rise, he saw it was a river, over a hundred feet down.

Dawn was soft and beautiful, shining gradually over the mountaintops and illuminating the scene before Michael's eyes like a painting being slowly revealed.

The mountains had gorges and rivers and streams in between the peaks. Looking down, here and there he saw small suspension bridges made of ropes and planks hanging over some of the rivers. The path he was on fluctuated in its width: in some parts it was twenty feet wide, in some only ten.

Now that the sun was coming up, he would have to leave the path and seek shelter where he could sleep undetected. The night had been cold, dropping to perhaps fifty degrees, but his constant movement and sheer adrenaline had kept him from being too affected. He was tired, though, and that and becoming visible with the daylight made him feel vulnerable.

As he came around the side of the mountain, he saw a small temple-like structure on the side of the path. It wasn't an enclosed structure but was made of stone, with a wooden overhang.

What really caught Michael's attention was the small copse of trees up against the mountainside, about twenty feet behind the temple. There was a fair amount of brush and other foliage at the base of the trees, dense enough for him to roll himself in his outerwear and the blanket from the pack and be hidden from view.

He quickly unpacked the blanket and made a bed on the ground behind the biggest tree and some bushes. The adrenaline high was pretty much gone by now, and he needed to get some sleep as soon as possible.

Michael settled himself into the most comfortable position he could manage and closed his eyes.

He had walked, by his estimate, somewhere between five and six miles last night. It was a short mountain range, so he was within a few miles of reaching the foothills on the eastern side. Another few miles after that, and he would be in Kyoto.

He fell asleep in less than a minute.

When he awoke, the sun had just come off its midday peak and was starting to head toward the western sky. It looked like it was midafternoon.

Michael spent the time before sunset checking his supplies and using some water from his leather pouch to wash up a little. He then closed his eyes and rested again, trying to let his body recover from the long overnight walk.

Around sunset he took out some food for dinner: onigiri rice balls with pickled plum, and a kind of dried fish jerky. He decided to save the cooked yaki-imo sweet potato for later. The fish jerky was tough and stringy, but wetting it down with water helped a little.

Throughout the afternoon he'd only heard one person pass by; the man had briefly stopped to pray at the temple, then continued on his way west.

He waited until evening had set in, then placed the pack on his back and set out on the path again. It was all downslope from here. He would be coming out of the mountains before dawn.

AS THE sun rose, Michael came down into the foothills west of Kyoto.

This was an area he was somewhat familiar with. During his last trip to Japan, between his second and third years at Berkeley, he'd spent several days in Kyoto and had visited a famous bamboo grove and temple in this area. He tried to recall what the general layout of the area was as he'd seen it from the train.

First he would need to seek shelter again, somewhere hidden from view. He was out of the mountains now, in civilization again—though rural and nineteenth century—and he would have to be careful.

It frustrated him to lose another day just because he couldn't travel in the open, but there was nothing to be done about it. He would have to hope he could sneak into the back of a wagon heading to Edo that evening.

He covered his face with the half mask again and brought the hat down over his eyes.

He found a small grove of trees and made his makeshift bed as far away from open ground as he could.

Sleep was difficult this time. It was hard not to be anxious thinking about the next part of the journey. He would have to find the main road heading east out of Kyoto and get into someone's wagon undetected. The risk of something going wrong was high.

Michael closed his eyes. He was lying in his blanket behind a bush, and the early morning sun streaked through the bush's leaves. The soft rays of light played across his face as he finally fell asleep.

HE MUST have been more tired than he thought, because he awoke when the sun was going down.

He sat up abruptly, feeling disoriented. He checked around him for his pack items. All was in order.

Taking a deep breath, he calmed himself. The next part was tough, but he could do it. He had to do it.

Or he would never see Shinjirō again.

He ate some of the fish jerky, softening it with water, and some dried mountain vegetables. Kanosuke had told him that Shinjirō-sama's grandfather—Kenshirō-sama's father—had once been involved in a siege situation. That experience had taught him to preserve foodstuffs, which the Kaminishi daimyō continued to do to this day. Before finding a place to sleep that morning, Michael had also come across an apple tree and taken some of the fruit. The fresh apple tasted good after the dehydrated foods.

Michael prepared his face with dirt again and brought the half mask up to cover the lower part of his face. He put the pack on his back and placed the hat carefully on his head.

He walked through a field about a hundred feet from the road, paralleling the road but walking behind trees as much as he could. He was trying to look like an itinerant worker, a peasant who felt more comfortable walking off the road than on.

More dwellings and other wooden buildings came into view.

A large forest of bamboo trees soon appeared on his left; it looked like the famous bamboo grove he'd visited before. He took a deep breath and walked steadily on, trying not to get too excited.

He was only a mile from Kyoto.

THE BUILDINGS on the western edge of Kyoto came into view. Michael had to fight to keep his head lowered as he walked along.

This was living history, Kyoto in 1851. The scholar in him wanted to see it. But the rest of him had a greater agenda. He had to keep moving.

Since it was night now, he could progress more freely. He had passed few people on the road, and his disguise held up well in the darkness.

The density of buildings increased, and Michael found himself walking through what was a good-sized city for the nineteenth century. It looked like the pictures he'd seen of this period of Kyoto's history: rows of wooden buildings and unpaved roads, and in the distance, looming above the smaller buildings, temple-like structures here and there. He wondered if one of them was Nijō Castle.

He kept walking on the northern side of town, as Norio had told him the main road to Edo ran along there. Norio said there were teahouses and brothels and small shops that serviced the main road. Michael thought that sounded like the frontage roads in America, the ones that ran alongside highways with their offerings of gas stations and fast-food restaurants. Behind the half mask, his mouth quirked in a little smile.

He found the main road with surprising ease, and as Norio had said, it was lined on both sides with the aforementioned establishments.

His walk down this street was something he would never forget. The food stands in the streets selling yaki-imo sweet potatoes and roasted chestnuts; the women in kimonos with painted faces standing in front of brothels; and everywhere the people of pre-Meiji-era Kyoto going about their everyday lives in what was, for Michael, a living panorama of history.

The smell of the yaki-imo, the hot cooked sweet potatoes, tempted him. Norio had included some mon coins in his pack. He decided he could pull it off.

The yaki-imo seller was a small old man, and as Michael approached his stand—pulling his hat farther down—he didn't even look at Michael's face as Michael silently handed him the coins.

Taking the wrapped, hot yaki-imo into the nearest alley, Michael sat down and began to eat it. It was so good it brought tears to his eyes. How he could ever have doubted that this experience was real, that he was really here in the past.... He knew the memory of this physical experience of eating this delicious food would always remind him it had all been real.

After he finished eating, he resumed walking eastward down the main road. The buildings began to get sparser, and he noticed more wagons parked with their loads in front of the buildings. Michael eyed each one, looking for those that had their loads covered by a cloth over the back of the wagon. He needed to get in undetected and stay undetected. Spying one that looked promising—a single man as driver, with a load of what looked like kabocha pumpkins in baskets in the back covered by a burlap cloth—Michael darted into a nearby alleyway and watched as the man checked his load, then walked to the front.

As the man climbed into the driver's seat, Michael emerged from the alley. He quickly looked around, seeing no one in the near vicinity.

He crept to the back of the wagon and carefully climbed in.

He held his breath as the wagon pulled out and began heading east.

SOMETIME DURING the night, the man pulled the wagon off the road a little ways, apparently to sleep for a while.

Michael waited. Finally, when he could reasonably assume the man had fallen asleep, he lifted the burlap cover and got down from the wagon.

Looking around, he saw the wagon was about fifty feet off the main road. The driver, wrapped in a blanket, was asleep, sprawled out across the bench seat.

The night sky was full of stars. There was a small copse of trees, and Michael went there and relieved himself. When he came out, he took a moment to look at the stars.

Since leaving the castle, he had had much time on his own to think. The night walk through the mountains and then the walk as he entered Kyoto had cleared his mind of any doubts.

He knew he loved Shinjirō, and he knew he was meant to be by his side for the rest of his life.

He didn't know if he would be able to, given that his travels through time to the Kaminishi Han hadn't been instigated by himself. He hadn't controlled either going there or returning to his normal life in Berkeley. He had thought about it over and over, picking the time travel events apart, trying to see if there was any pattern that could account for them.

The first time he'd traveled to the Kaminishi Han, he'd been studying at his desk at night. What had occurred just before he'd returned was the confrontation with Shinjirō. Shinjirō had hit him, reacting to the recent events with Misako and the trouble at the border. He had told Shinjirō he was from his future. Then everything had gone black.

The next time, Shinjirō had come to him in his apartment. He had told the daimyō that he "wished this was real," and then they were both back in the nineteenth century.

The last time, he had embraced the daimyō and implored him not to see the Shogun, and then he had found himself sitting on the balcony of his apartment.

Could it be that his own wishes somehow controlled the timing of his travels back and forth between the centuries?

Michael wanted to believe it, because then he might be able to control it. But then why had he returned to the twenty-first century the last time? He had been pleading with Shinjirō not to go to Edo to see the Shogun. Shouldn't that have forced him to remain there with Shinjirō? His feelings were very strong in that moment; he had wanted to stay with the daimyō to try and change his mind.

He sighed. It was impossible. If there was a pattern that explained everything, he was incapable of discerning it.

Michael gazed at the moon and starry sky. It was a beautiful night. In the distance, he could see a mountain range. Around him were fields of grass and of rice, the ubiquitous rice paddies that would still be here a century and a half from now.

In the interim, this country would go through several cataclysms, triumphs, and disasters, and two appalling moments that would literally change the world's view of war forever. If there was some way that Japan could be spared all of that while still becoming the peaceful and prosperous nation it was in the twenty-first century—

But that way lay madness. Michael had considered it again and again, and he still couldn't see any way that a country's history could be changed without the results being changed as well.

This nation had recreated itself from the ashes of World War II. If World War II never happened the way it had, Japan wouldn't be what it was today.

Or rather... the way it will be in the future.

Michael shook his head. No. He had been the one who came back to the past, who put those facts and those images in Shinjirō's head. That was the reason why Shinjirō had gone to Edo to see the Shogun. And that was why he had to stop him.

Because if he couldn't stop him, whatever happened to Shinjirō would be his fault.

THE DAY wore on.

After the man had slept a few hours, he started back on the road again. Michael had already settled himself back in his place behind one of the baskets of pumpkins and slept himself.

When he awoke, he crept to the opening at the back of the moving wagon and lifted the burlap to peek out. It looked like it was late afternoon. He must've slept through the man taking another break, because the oxen didn't seem fatigued. Both the driver and the oxen must have rested for a while that day. Michael was grateful that the driver hadn't thought to check his load.

It was getting on toward nightfall when Michael felt the driver slow the oxen. After they came to a full halt, Michael heard the driver get down from his seat.

Unexpectedly he heard the driver conversing with another man; then the voices came closer to the back of the wagon.

Michael froze. He was behind one of the baskets closest to the driver's seat, so it wouldn't be one of the first baskets they would see. But they would see him eventually, especially if they took the burlap off.

He held his breath.

The two men lifted the burlap at the back of the wagon, and the setting sun's rays lit the baskets in streaks. Michael huddled behind his basket, sitting with his knees up to make himself as invisible as possible.

"...mon da," one man was saying. It must have been the driver, as he was quoting a price.

"Taka sugiru," the other man countered. Apparently he didn't find the price to be too fair.

The two went back and forth as Michael shut his eyes and prayed for the buyer to buy a kabocha or two and just leave.

Finally the two men agreed on a price, and the basket closest to the back end of the wagon was lifted out and placed on the ground. Michael snuck a look from behind his basket.

Both men were peasants by their dress: they wore the same loose coverings as Michael did for warmth. The driver looked to be around forty years old, while the buyer was younger.

The driver placed pumpkins into the other man's sack; then money changed hands. Michael drew his head back quickly as the driver put the basket in the wagon, and then threw the burlap over the back of the wagon again.

He let out the breath he'd been holding.

Safe again—for now.

NOT TOO long after that, the driver pulled off the main road. It was evening now. Michael had a feeling the driver would be sleeping through the night tonight. He'd only gotten a few hours' sleep the night before, after all, and the oxen needed rest too.

Michael heard the driver get down from his seat and begin walking somewhere. He moved to the back of the wagon as quietly as he could, then looked out from under the burlap.

The driver was going into a small forested area, presumably to take a leak.

This was his chance.

Michael watched as the driver disappeared into the trees, then got down off the wagon with his belongings. He walked around the blind side of the wagon, away from where the driver might look back and see him, then made for the trees about fifty yards from where the driver had entered the forest.

He set up camp in the woods. If possible, he would try to sneak back into the wagon before dawn came and the driver took off.

If that didn't happen... he would be walking again.

HE WOKE up just before dawn.

Hurriedly disassembling his camp, Michael gathered his things into the pack and then quickly made his way back toward the wagon.

When the wagon came into view, he saw the driver was sleeping next to a still-smoldering campfire.

Yes.... Michael thanked his lucky stars.

The next stop would be Edo.

Chapter Eleven

It was late afternoon when Michael heard the wagon stop and the driver being questioned by guards.

They had reached the outskirts of Edo.

He crept behind the basket that was the farthest from the back of the wagon as he could get; he was basically sitting right behind the driver, unbeknownst to said driver.

He heard the driver speaking to the guard, but their voices were muffled. Eventually the voices traveled toward the back of the wagon, as Michael had expected they would.

He held his breath as the burlap was thrown far back, exposing most of the baskets of pumpkins in the wagon. The burlap still concealed him, though the area a mere foot in front of him was fully exposed to view.

The late-afternoon sun helped, since it was autumn and not the full glare of summer. The thin streaks of sunlight barely reached into the section of the wagon where Michael was, as the wagon's back was facing at an angle to the waning afternoon sun.

He stared at the small patch of sunlight in front of him illuminating the wagon's floor, waiting for it to be over.

Finally the burlap was thrown back over the wagon bed, and he heard the driver walk around to the front of the wagon.

He didn't breathe easily until they had entered the city of Edo.

He knew it wouldn't be long before the driver stopped again, either to eat somewhere or else to drop his load at his destination.

He had to make his move soon.

It was evening. Michael could hear the sounds of people going about their business in the streets of Edo: conversations, other wagons passing, and the footsteps of pedestrians.

He quietly made his way to the back of the wagon, dragging his pack along the wagon bed. The sound of the oxen's hooves drowned out the noise he was making, but he still needed to be careful.

At length, the wagon turned and was traveling on a street that seemed less crowded than the ones it had been on.

Night was falling quickly. It was already dark in the streets.

Michael neared the edge of the wagon's back end and lifted the burlap from above his head, then flipped it over.

It was indeed a dark street, with few people.

He took a deep breath.

It was now or never.

He jumped off the wagon.

MICHAEL LANDED in the street, sprawling awkwardly on all fours.

His pack fell off his shoulders, hitting the ground.

He stood up, placed his hat back on, then picked up his pack.

He couldn't resist turning to watch the kabocha seller and his wagon as they drove off into the distance. *Thank you*, he thought.

A quick look around revealed that no one had seen him come off the wagon, or if they had, they couldn't be bothered to care about it. He walked to the side of the road and stopped to take his bearings.

He was on a slight upslope, which gave him a view not only of the street he was on but of the streets directly below. Edo was as much of a maze as its contemporary counterpart, only its nineteenth-century version was populated with wooden buildings instead of glass skyscrapers. The streets were winding, like in any old-world city. Michael realized how much he made assumptions whenever he traveled outside America. In America, most cities had been constructed by city engineers and urban planners in an orderly grid pattern. In the rest of the world, the cities had grown organically, and the streets were more circular, winding and unpredictable.

He peered between the cloth strips hanging in his face from the hat, trying to see if he could make out the Imperial Palace in the maze of buildings in the distance. Norio had given him precise directions to Shinjirō's Edo home from the Imperial Palace, one of the buildings that Michael could recognize from the twenty-first century.

He was unable to identify any of the buildings where he stood now, but he knew he was on the outer edge of the city. If he traveled on the main, populated streets and made his way toward the central area, he could see from here, he would surely reach the center of the city and the Imperial Palace.

It was night, and he could risk being in the open.

Michael took a deep breath and began walking.

SHINJIRŌ'S HOME, as were the homes of the other daimyō, was located in the Marunouchi area of the Yamanote district. Yamanote was literally the "high ground" of Edo for feudal lords and their samurai, while Shitamachi, the lowlands, was home to the merchants and all other manner of Edo denizens.

He knew that Asakusa was northeast of Edo Castle, and that the Kanei-ji Temple would be close to where the Ueno train station was in modern-day Tokyo. The famed Yoshiwara pleasure district would be located north of Asakusa in the Shitamachi.

The largely horizontal skyline, filled in all directions that he could see with one-story or two-story wooden buildings, was broken up here and there by tall tower-like structures. He realized that these were fire watchtowers. A ladder led up the middle of the stem of the structure, which ended in a guard box at the top. He passed close by one of them, and looking up he could see a metal object in the guard box, either a bell or something similar that was used to alert the public of fires spotted from that high perch.

As he walked along, Michael observed the clothing and demeanor of the people of Edo. Like the people in the Kaminishi Han, the people were short, most of them barely over five feet tall, though there were exceptions. Most wore kimonos with the same kind of simple, layered outerwear as he himself wore, which he was grateful to see. He already stood out—he'd had a few curious glances tossed his way—due to his height. He didn't need different clothing to add to his odd look.

Fortunately the hat with its cloth strips and the grime on his skin, along with his lowered face and the dark of night, were keeping his gaijin identity hidden.

He began to encounter streets that were more crowded with people, meaning he was getting closer to the city's central area. He tried to keep to higher ground and look for the moats of water surrounding the Imperial Castle—or rather Edo Castle—which would be in the center of the city.

A structure in the near distance caught his eye. It looked like a temple of some sort and was three stories high. Michael pulled his outer wrap more tightly around himself and hurried toward it.

As he reached the end of the street, he saw water.

It was one of the outer moats of Edo Castle.

THE THREE-STORY structure was Fujimi-yagura, as he'd suspected. One of the keeps of Honmaru—the Shogun's palace within the castle grounds—it had similar styling on each of its four sides, giving it a distinctive look.

Michael picked up his pace. He knew Fujimi-yagura was located at the southeast corner of Honmaru. With this landmark, he now knew where he was.

And he knew how to reach Shinjirō's home from here.

The wind turned cold as he made his way through the dark streets. People hurried toward their destinations, and no one was looking at him as he walked quickly around the southern side of Edo Castle toward the Marunouchi district.

This district was where all the daimyō built their Edo homes. The daimyō were required by the Shogunate to spend every other year in Edo, a system of control called "alternate residence," and they also had to spend most of their domain's income to maintain a lifestyle that was in keeping with their elevated station.

Norio had given Michael every detail of Shinjirō's Edo home, from where the guards would be doing their rounds to the location of Shinjirō's meditation room, which was where the daimyō was likely to be in the evening hours.

Unable to suppress his excitement, he made his way down the street that would bring him to Shinjirō.

Finally he saw it—a large and imposing traditional home, in keeping with the style of its neighbors. In the Marunouchi district, there was distance between each daimyō's home. So he was able to carefully make his way around the side of the house undetected, knowing the guards' routines.

Unexpectedly he saw something he wished he hadn't.

One of the shōji doors on the first floor was open, and Michael caught a brief glimpse of a beautiful woman with two small girls in the sitting room. The woman was seated in seiza, watching the girls as they played with toys or dolls Michael was too far away to see.

A servant then came and shut the door.

But he knew he'd just seen Shinjirō's wife and daughters.

SHINJIRŌ'S MEDITATION room was on the far side of the house on the second floor, and Michael had to wait until one of the guards finished making his rounds before moving to stand on the ground below the room.

The shōji was open by one or two inches, and it opened out onto the sort of paneled walkway that bordered the courtyard garden in Kaminishi Castle. Since it was on the second floor, this served as a kind of balcony.

Michael stared up at the room. It was lit by lantern light, so he knew Shinjirō was inside.

I've made it. I'm here.

Shinjirō....

He had a few minutes before the guard made his rounds again.

Picking up a small pebble, he lobbed it at the paper shōji.

Immediately a shadow moved inside the room, illuminated against the screen.

The shōji slid open, and Shinjirō stepped outside.

He looked at Michael, impassively staring down at him.

Michael then remembered. He took his hat off and brought the half mask down from his face.

The daimyō's eyes widened; then he made a gesture to be quiet.

In the next minute, Shinjirō was outside and hurrying toward him. He pulled Michael by the arm, dragging him into the shadows. Again he made the gesture to keep silent.

The guard passed by on his rounds again. When he turned the corner of the mansion, Michael could wait no longer.

He grabbed Shinjirō and kissed him with everything he had in him. Shinjirō just stood there. Finally he returned the kiss, eventually breaking it off and gently setting Michael back. Still holding him by the shoulders, he gazed into Michael's eyes.

"I thought I would never see you again," he said at length.

"Aren't you glad to see me?"

"Yes and no," Shinjirō said honestly. "This is unexpected."

Michael blinked; then he smiled. He couldn't help it. He was with Shinjirō again. He couldn't feel anything but ecstatic.

Shinjirō's eyes crinkled, and a ghost of a smile appeared on his beautiful face. "Maikoru," he said. Then he became stern. "You can't stay here. But there is somewhere I can send you to. Wait here."

HE WAITED as Shinjirō entered the house and apparently sent the guards away on some pretext or other.

Shinjirō returned, all business now. "This is where you will go tonight," he said. Without further preamble, he told Michael a precise set of directions to a place in the Yoshiwara. Then he gave him some money and further instructions as to how much to bribe the guards at the entrance to the pleasure district.

Finally the daimyō said he would send word to Michael the next day, and until then Michael was to wait. "Do you understand?"

"Hai, my lord."

Michael must have looked forlorn, because Shinjirō laughed softly. He placed a hand on Michael's face. "I will tell you more tomorrow, don't fear."

"Shinjirō-sama, have you met with the Shogun yet?"

There was a pause, and Shinjirō's face was impassive.

"Not yet."

"When are you—"

"I will speak with you tomorrow," Shinjirō cut him off. Then he softened a little, taking Michael in his arms in a hard hug. "Be well."

HE STOOD staring at the big golden dragon in front of the establishment.

The walk to the Yoshiwara had been thankfully uneventful. The official pleasure quarter of Edo was north of Asakusa, and visitors wishing to enter were monitored at a great central gate.

He kept his head down, letting the cloth strips fall over his face as he silently passed coins to the guard for entry.

He was let in without any trouble.

The quarter was laid out in a neat grid pattern. Michael recalled reading that the quarter had been relocated to this area following one of Edo's great fires in 1657. So, as a created district, its planners had laid out the streets in an easy-to-follow pattern.

As in Kyoto, Michael felt like he had stepped inside of a living history diorama. The streets were unpaved and lined on either side with wooden buildings with long, wide-open windows. At the windows, the women of the Yoshiwara sat in full dress, with perfectly coiffed hair and elaborate makeup. The streets were filled with men of different stations in life, from daimyō and their samurai to those of the merchant class.

Michael found the place easily. As Shinjirō had told him, it was the only pleasure house that had a big golden dragon statue in front. It was a two-story wooden building, with the same baked-tile roof that covered most of the machiya buildings in Edo.

He stood there for a long moment, for some reason not wanting to go inside, though that had been Shinjirō's instruction. The daimyō hadn't told him what he would find in the room he'd been given directions to, just that this would be where he would be safe for the next few days.

Michael set his shoulders, took a deep breath, then let it out.

He walked up the steps to the front door.

A man stopped him at the door, and Michael passed him some money and uttered a code word Shinjirō had given him. The man bowed and stepped aside, leaving Michael free to enter the house.

Michael nodded to an older woman in a deep blue flowered kimono, who bowed back to him. She was probably the senior prostitute in the establishment, or possibly its madam.

He saw the stairs and started up them.

At the top of the stairs, turn to your right. The room will be the last door on the left.

Michael walked up the steps, then turned right. He saw a long dark hallway with many doors on both sides.

He walked down the hallway and stopped at the last door on the left.

"Ojama shimasu."

"Irasshaimase," a young woman's voice said.

She was seated with her back to Michael on a futon on the floor of this sparsely furnished room.

She turned her head to look at him.

It was Misako.

CHAPTER TWELVE

MISAKO STARED at him.

Michael was similarly slack-jawed. Recovering, he walked to the futon and knelt down. "Misako. I am glad to see you well."

She was dressed in a red silk kimono with nothing on underneath, and her face was made up with something that made her skin look white and powdery. Her eyes were ringed with a line of black dye, making them stand out in a smoky, mysterious way.

Her lips were tinted in an odd orange-red color. Despite the crude layer of artifice, she was still as delicately beautiful as when Michael had known her at the castle. Whatever else she had lived through since then had not dimmed that in her.

"Oh... gomen nasai. It is you, Maikoru-san." Misako continued to stare at him, but the look in her eyes softened.

Michael remembered something. He dug around in the small bag tied at his waist. "This must be for you," he said, handing her the rest of the money Shinjirō had given him. "Shinjirō-sama requests that you give me shelter for the next day or two. He will send further word tomorrow," Michael added, removing his hat and half mask.

Misako took the money and nodded, not meeting his eyes. "Dōmo arigatō."

"Dō itashimashite. You are helping me very greatly, Misako-san."

She nodded again, head lowered.

He was puzzled at her demeanor; then he remembered. "Misako-san.... Something happened between you and Tōru-san, didn't it?"

She didn't look at him.

"He blackmailed you," Michael continued. "He was there in the forest when I tried to return to the castle. He set you up, didn't he?"

Misako began to cry, putting a fist to her mouth and shaking her head.

"It's all right. I was taken back to the castle. Shinjirō-sama was angry with me for a while, but it was all right eventually. As you can see, I'm fine. There was no harm done by it."

"Please forgive me," Misako whispered. "I did a terrible thing."

"No," Michael replied firmly. "You were under pressure from someone who was threatening you. I would have helped you that night regardless of any deception that went on. There's nothing to forgive you for, Misako."

He reached out and touched her hand. "Shinjirō told me what happened to you after you returned home. I'm sorry that things didn't work out for you."

She wiped her tears with her hand.

There was nothing more he could say, so he just sat with her as she calmed herself. *It's so unfair*, he thought. He couldn't help but compare Misako's situation with Ellen's. Though Ellen was American, not Japanese, she was of Japanese origin and could have been the sister of the woman sitting in front of him. Ellen was a brash, confident feminist, sure she could achieve anything in life, while Misako's options were limited to those few allowed by men in a restricted, caste-based society.

And yet, this is the society that you would be a part of—to be with Shinjirō. He recognized the irony and his own hypocrisy.

Eventually Misako settled herself and offered to send someone for tea. He gratefully accepted her offer and asked if she could procure a bath for him. He had only been able to scrub his skin with river water and a rough cloth since leaving the castle and knew he smelled pretty bad at this point.

Misako took him to the bathing room, where he spent a luxuriant few minutes scrubbing himself down with soap and hot water. As he rinsed off, he noted with disgust that his washing off made the water in the tub a dark gray.

When he returned to Misako's room, there was rice with fish and pickled radish and warmed sake to drink. He was famished, having not eaten anything since that morning, when he'd consumed the last of the fish jerky. The whole day he'd been going on adrenaline alone, especially while walking the streets of Edo on the way to Shinjirō's home.

When he finished eating, Misako left the tray outside in the hallway, then shut the door.

Michael suddenly realized he was meant to literally stay in this room overnight—and there was only one futon. "Gomen," he said hastily, moving off the futon. "I'll sleep against the wall." Sleeping on a solid wooden floor was actually a luxury after several nights spent on the hard ground in the cold outdoors.

"Iie," Misako said. "We can both sleep on the futon. You must be very tired after your journey." He stared at her until she turned away and began undoing the obi sash to her kimono. Realizing he had no other choice, he began undressing as Misako moved to blow out the lamp.

SHINJIRŌ WAS standing in front of him.

This time, he was wearing the white kimono Michael had drawn him in, in the sketch he'd taped above his desk. He was... shimmering slightly, like he had been in Michael's apartment. But his eyes were clear and bright—and he gazed at Michael with a kind of fond affection.

Then he faded out entirely.

Michael awoke with the feeling of someone caressing his shoulder.

He opened his eyes. The room was still dark. It took a moment to remember exactly where he was—in Misako's room in a Yoshiwara brothel.

The hand—soft and small—gripped his skin tighter now. He turned to meet Misako's eyes.

He opened his mouth to say something, but she put a finger to her lips. Her delicate hand snaked around his head and pulled him close, and the next thing he knew she was kissing him.

Still half-asleep, his mind struggling to come to grips with this, he allowed her to take his hand and place it on her breast. The warmth of her skin suddenly made it all real to him, and he gasped.

"Misako-san."

"Don't," she said, keeping his hand there. Her other hand took on a life of its own, traveling down to lightly touch his member.

He knew he should stop her, but her touches and whispers put him in a trancelike state. *This isn't what I want. This isn't really what you want either, Misako... Misako....* "Misako."

His voice rang out loudly in the darkened room, and she stopped then.

He placed his hands on her shoulders. "Please. This isn't good for either of us. You are truly beautiful, Misako-san, but I... can't do this. I'm sorry."

Her face lowered, and her eyes did not meet his. Then she turned to lie on her side, facing away from him.

Michael watched her sadly. He wasn't turning her down because he had some notion that Shinjirō would be upset if he found out; the daimyō probably wouldn't mind at all. It was just that it didn't feel right... though a certain part of him was disputing that.

He closed his eyes, waiting it out. When his erection softened and he felt more under control, he spoke again. "Shinjirō-sama is all that I can see, Misako-san," he said softly into the darkness. "The failing is mine alone. No man in his right mind would turn you down."

"I never loved him." Misako's voice came through clearly. "He was kind, but I didn't want to be there. And yet, no one has ever treated me better than he did." She paused, then went on. "He is still looking after me, though he won't visit my bed. The reason he took me from my home no longer exists, and yet he is still taking care of my needs. I don't understand," she finished, her voice trailing off.

Michael didn't say anything. Relationships were incomprehensible to him much of the time; his experiences here in historical Japan notwithstanding, he still didn't understand the ebb and flow of how people related to each other, particularly in intimate relations.

Why people broke up and got back together again; how they forgave each other; what was underlying these intimate bonds—Michael hadn't had much experience in that regard. Ellen would probably scoff, saying it was all dysfunction and codependence. But he knew there were mysteries in the realm of relationships that he hadn't yet experienced in life.

And his feelings for Shinjirō were at the heart of those mysteries. He wasn't lying to Misako; he could only see Shinjirō before him. No one else even registered in his consciousness.

"I don't understand why I love him," he said aloud, more for his own sake than Misako's. "I just know that I do."

A YOUNG boy arrived the next morning with word from the daimyō.

Shinjirō requested that Michael meet with him in Misako's room that evening.

Michael spent the day in the room while Misako went out on some errands. He tried to remain calm, eat his meals, drink his tea—and wait.

Misako returned as the sun was going down, and they ate dinner together in silence. It wasn't an awkward silence; they had spoken earlier in the day before she had gone out. Nothing had been said about her advances the previous night. But it seemed there was simply nothing left to say at this point.

After dinner, he lay down to rest awhile as Misako went downstairs to help the staff with refreshments for a private party on the first floor. He was tired from the stress of waiting all day. Still, he wanted to prepare himself at least mentally for what he wanted to say to Shinjirō. But instead—incredibly—he fell asleep.

He was awakened by the sound of the door opening. He sat up on the futon, blinking, trying to orient himself as he saw Misako go to the door and open it.

Shinjirō entered the room then, removing his cloak. He wore a very simple kimono made of a rougher and more natural cloth than Michael had seen him in. But nothing could make him look like anything other than what he was. The aura of the warrior-aristocrat still surrounded him, as if radiating from his body.

Michael watched as Shinjirō spoke in a soft voice to Misako; she nodded and left the room.

Shinjirō shut the door, then turned to face Michael, who was groggily getting to his feet. Shinjirō's eyes held a glint of amusement. "Did I wake you, Maikoru?"

"Forgive me, my lord. I was more tired than I thought, I guess." Now standing, Michael gazed at Shinjirō, who was regarding him with a contemplative look.

He was standing about ten feet away. Michael wanted to remember the way he looked right now forever; he was that perfect, that beautiful. He walked toward the daimyō. "Shinjirō—"

And then he was in Shinjirō's arms, and he wanted to just stay there forever.

"THERE IS not much time, I'm afraid," Shinjirō said. His hand was making slow circles on Michael's back. "I have been granted an audience with the Shogun tomorrow morning."

Michael pulled back, staring into Shinjirō's eyes. The daimyō's expression was calm and serious.

He disengaged himself gently from Michael and stepped away to gain a little distance from him. "I am very anxious to speak with him. I am very fortunate that he has agreed to see me."

Michael said nothing.

"This is still not as you would have me do, I take it."

"No, my lord. I believe what you are doing is the wrong course of action to take. Nothing can come of this, except placing yourself in danger."

"I see," Shinjirō said.

He turned away from Michael, walking into the room. Michael followed him. "My lord."

"Yes?"

"I don't understand why you are choosing to do this."

The daimyō was silent for a few moments. "I am doing what I believe is right. Are you saying I need further reason than that?"

Michael opened his mouth to reply but found that there was no intelligent reply to be made. Shinjirō's answer caught him in a bind. He had been all ready to argue, but the daimyō's question and the way it was framed stopped him cold.

He lowered his head, feeling defeated.

Shinjirō gently set his hand on Michael's head, caressing his hair, then pulled him close. "I'm sorry," he said. "But we have had this conversation already. I understand what you are saying. I know that you are... distressed about this." Shinjirō tightened his arm around Michael, who relaxed against his chest. He laid his head on the daimyō's shoulder and closed his eyes. "I don't know if our concept of duty is the same or not. But I'm a patriot, and I see it as my duty to use the information I have learned to try to save my people from suffering in the future."

"You know it's unlikely that the Shogun will believe you."

"Yes," Shinjirō said.

"You'll be condemned as unfit to lead, or even be branded as a traitor."

"That's possible," the daimyō said. He gazed into Michael's eyes fondly. "I regret that this is painful for you."

Michael stared at Shinjirō's face, that beautiful face that had haunted him from the moment he'd drawn that picture, long before he'd had his first experience in mid-nineteenth-century Japan. It was a face he'd known before he ever saw it.

"I know there's nothing further I can say to convince you," he said quietly. "I just can't believe this is the result of my telling you about the future." He looked at Shinjirō. "I can't believe that this would be the reason why I came to the past, to Japan in this era. It seems so... pointless."

"But you don't know that," Shinjirō said kindly. "You don't know what the outcome will be. It may be as you say, or it may turn out quite differently. You are too concerned with outcomes, Maikoru. No one can say what the outcome will be of any action we take. If that were the case, no one would act." The edges of Shinjirō's mouth quirked a bit, as if he was suppressing a smile.

Michael found he was blinking back tears. He opened his mouth to say something, anything, but no words came out.

The daimyō embraced him again, tightening his hold as he whispered in his ear. "I'll send word after it's done."

He could only watch as Shinjirō left the room and softly closed the door behind him.

THE MOMENT the daimyō walked into the cell, and he saw him for the first time in the flesh.

The moment he realized that Shinjirō was beautiful.

The moment he saw the look of desire in Shinjirō's eye....

He turned restlessly to lie on his side again. Images and words rose in his mind, playing themselves out, bringing to mind everything that had happened between him and Shinjirō.

Over and over the scenes came to him. His wonder at being in late-Edo Japan. His discovery of so many things. The long quiet evenings at the castle, first in his cell and then in Shinjirō's bed.

He felt his face grow warm as Misako, on the other side of the futon, moved in her sleep.

He couldn't deny what Shinjirō meant to him anymore.

Shinjirō was the reason why he lived.

"This is the life I was meant to live," he had told Shinjirō. *"I am supposed to be with you."*

What he hadn't said was something he had not realized until this moment.

You are the reason I am here.

I was meant to be with you.

Without you, I have no purpose for my life.

CHAPTER THIRTEEN

AUTUMN HAD finally arrived in Edo.

The man stood at the edge of one of the gardens, watching a butterfly flit in the sunlight between the red-leafed maple trees. The light glinted off the creature's wings as it hurried on its way, and the man thought of the transience of life and the death of all things.

The garden he stood in was surrounded by a palace and outbuildings, an inner citadel that itself was surrounded by a moat. Around this inner moat were yet other structures, an armory and stables, administrative buildings. Surrounding all of that was yet another system of moats and keeps, watchtowers, gates, and drawbridges.

Between where this man stood and where the million citizens of one of the largest cities on earth, Edo, lived and worked and went about their business stood a gigantic circular gated city eight miles in circumference. The number of armed guards, bureaucrats, and servants within this city numbered over twenty thousand.

The sole purpose of those twenty thousand was to protect him.

And to support him in his rule over the city of Edo—and the nation of Japan.

He was Ieyoshi Tokugawa, the twelfth Shogun, and his was the bakufu—the Shogunate—that ruled over this nation.

He was fifty-eight years old and had ruled this nation for fourteen years. In that time he had instigated the Tenpō Reforms that reestablished dominance over the daimyō and their many han. The centuries of peace had been threatened in recent decades by rebellions in outlying domains and some domains uncomfortably close to Edo itself.

Change appeared to be forthcoming. But the Shogun preferred not to acknowledge this. Foreigners had always attempted to enter Japan, and the nation had always been able to keep them out.

Though the world outside Japan's borders was evolving in some ways, or so the reports said, the Shogun would ensure that the nation would remain as it had always been.

The butterfly he had been watching flew up higher and higher, eventually disappearing into the sky.

He watched it fly away without emotion.

HONMARU PALACE, the Shogun's residence at the heart of Edo Castle, was divided into three sections. The innermost chambers were the Shogun's private living quarters. Then there was a secondary area where he received family members, high-ranking daimyō, and other significant officials. The outermost section was for meeting with important members of the public.

The meeting with Shinjirō Kaminishi, daimyō of a small but long-standing domain west of Kyoto in the Kansai region, would be held in one of the private rooms in the secondary meeting area. Though the Kaminishi Han was not of any great political importance, it had been loyal to the Shogunate for its two hundred years of existence. The Shogun concluded that this alone should dictate the meeting take place in a room that denoted respect.

That, and....

An assistant approached, bowing, to inform him that Lord Shinjirō of the Kaminishi Han had arrived for their meeting.

ONCE THE Shogun had settled himself in the appointed room, he nodded to the assistant.

Moments later, Shinjirō Kaminishi, daimyō of the Kaminishi Han west of Kyoto, entered and prostrated himself on the floor in a deep bow.

After the daimyō finished his formal greeting to the Shogun, the Shogun bid him to raise his head. Lord Shinjirō sat in perfect seiza as the Shogun asked for a status report about the han. The daimyō responded with a detailed account of the domain's crop yields and financial solvency while the Shogun sat and reflected on death and only half listened.

His report finished, the daimyō stopped speaking and politely inclined his head slightly down, awaiting the Shogun's next question or statement.

The Shogun regarded Lord Shinjirō with an impassive face. The lord of the Kaminishi domain was unusually tall and cut an impressive figure indeed. He had only spoken to him briefly on previous occasions of state, but his overall impression of the man was that he had integrity and did not abuse his position as ruler of his domain. In a nation where domain lords increasingly misused their power over their feudal serfs while simultaneously seeking to hide income from the Shogunate and defraud their superiors over taxes, this daimyō was one of the exceptions.

The topic turned next to Lord Shinjirō's petition regarding the border dispute with the Shirakawa Han. The Shogun sat patiently as the case for the Kaminishi side was outlined, then indicated that this matter would be determined at a future time.

The Kaminishi daimyō nodded his acceptance, his eyes respectfully lowered.

There was a silence.

The Shogun waited.

"Is there another matter that you wished to present?" he asked finally.

"Osorenagara, gozaimasu," Lord Shinjirō said.

HE LISTENED as the Kaminishi daimyō told of a future event two years hence that would change the nation forever. A fleet of black ships with terrible cannons, greater than any Japan had produced, and at the head, an American naval commander named

"Perry." Failed negotiations, and eventually a treaty that would open Japan's borders to trade on less than equal terms. The loss of pride and tradition. The threat to the Shogunate and its authority over the nation and its people. The terrible wars in the future that would be the result of opening its borders to the world.

He continued to listen as Lord Shinjirō urged that the Shogun bring all the daimyō together, that all armies be consolidated and knowledge be obtained from the Dutch traders at Nagasaki on modern weapons. That modernization of weaponry would be needed to face and defeat the threat. That the enemy could be repelled and the nation and its unique ways could be preserved....

He listened until there was no point in listening further.

"You may stop."

Lord Shinjirō looked surprised—though he covered it well—and nodded.

The Shogun paused. He had reflected on this matter for some time before Lord Shinjirō had arrived for today's meeting. Had the daimyō refrained from telling this story of these black ships, the Shogun might have considered waiting and observing the Kaminishi lord for some months. But now, there was really only one outcome for this situation. Only one decision that could be made.

It always came down to death, after all.

"I would ask from where you received this information," the Shogun inquired.

Lord Shinjirō blinked once, then stared at the Shogun.

There was a silence in the room; then, with a heavy air—because it was autumn and the sky was still blue, and the Shogun was not immune to life and its possibilities and how the end of even one existence somehow affected everything else—he sighed before he opened his mouth to say the following words.

"There has been a report from Lord Ryū Shirakawa of a gaijin that has been seen at Kaminishi Castle...."

MICHAEL DIDN'T think he'd be able to stand the wait, but oddly enough, the morning passed quickly.

Michael had managed to get a little sleep toward dawn after a night of tossing and turning. When he awoke, the morning was already underway, and he could smell fish cooking downstairs.

He sat up on the futon, blinking. Misako was gone. She had left already for the meeting place in Asakusa where she would receive the news of how Shinjirō's meeting with the Shogun had gone.

He ate a light breakfast of fish and rice and miso soup. It was a meal he'd had hundreds of times since his first time in late-Edo Japan, but today he really seemed to taste it, and it was delicious.

The things he had done by rote during the days he'd spent in 1851 Japan all seemed highlighted this morning by a kind of extrasensory awareness. He was aware of every minute detail of his morning ritual of eating, toilet functions, washing, getting dressed. A brief flash of intuition made him think that this would be the last time he would ever do these things.

That thought made him pause a moment.

Then he… shrugged. *If that's the case… I'll deal with it.*

He would see Shinjirō today, no matter what happened. He would be with Shinjirō. Nothing else mattered.

It was early afternoon when Misako returned. He looked up from where he sat on the futon as Misako entered the room and shut the door behind her. He could tell from the look on her face that it was bad.

"Maikoru," Misako said, then stopped.

He watched as she stood with silent tears rolling down her cheeks.

EVEN WITH the news, Michael didn't panic or give in to despair.

The Shogun had relieved Shinjirō of leadership over the Kaminishi Han and had—albeit in an indirect way, with words that were intimating rather than direct—ordered him to commit seppuku, or ritual suicide, at the hour of dawn the next day.

Michael had felt only a momentary shock when Misako said this, and then his nerves settled into a kind of twilight numbness. *Okay*, he thought. *This was as expected. But Shinjirō is still alive. Something else might still happen.* Whether there could be intervening circumstances, or the Shogun might clarify or retract the order, or possibly he might be able to convince Shinjirō that it would be better for him to disobey the order and flee from Edo... he didn't know. But as long as Shinjirō was alive and breathing and free from custody, all things were still possible.

He wouldn't consider that he was in denial.

From far away, he heard Misako saying something about Shinjirō requesting his presence at his residence that evening, and from far away he heard his own voice responding that, yes, he would be there.

SURPRISINGLY SHINJIRŌ had sent a palanquin to take him to his house.

The palanquin was a small boxlike carriage made to fit just one passenger, which was carried along by a bearer in front and a second bearer in the rear. The bearers bore the weight by holding the ends of long poles that supported the carriage section.

Though he still wore the hat with its cloth threads hanging down to hide his Caucasian face, Michael was able to relax somewhat within the dark confines of the carriage. He gazed out the windows, watching the street scenes of Edo play out in the dark cool night.

He wondered vaguely if he would see Shinjirō's wife and daughters at the house.

Soon enough they arrived. Michael exited the carriage and—after hesitating a moment—walked up to the front doors of the house. There were two guards on duty; they opened the double doors and silently bid him enter.

In the foyer a manservant, a middle-aged gentleman, greeted him with a bow and indicated that they should walk to the right and down a long hallway. Michael kept his head lowered as he walked, with the cloth strips hanging in front of his eyes, mindful that he didn't know who might be at Shinjirō's house this of all nights; it was better to be careful.

Even here at the end.

He couldn't see much beyond the cloth strips, but as he and the manservant walked on, he noted that Shinjirō's mansion was furnished in an ascetic yet beautiful way. A small bit of hysteria welled up at that thought. *Yes, nice house. I don't think that matters, actually, anymore.*

They reached a room, and the manservant directed him to enter. Michael glanced around, seeing only a small table with a stack of neatly folded clothing on top of it. After closing the shōji, the manservant went to the clothing and picked up the first item. He turned and looked Michael directly in the eye for the first time and nodded.

Michael took this to mean that he was to undress and the manservant would help dress him in the proffered clothing. He removed his hat, noting that the manservant took a peek at his face and hid his shock fairly well.

One by one the pieces of a formal samurai kimono were placed on his body: light cotton kimono, dress kimono, obi, kataginu, hakama.

Finally the manservant walked behind him, and Michael felt a light hand on his shoulder push down slightly. He went onto his knees on the tatami mat, settling into seiza position. The manservant sat behind him and began to comb his hair and draw it back into a facsimile of a samurai's topknot.

He shut his eyes. It was as if he were being costumed for a play. The formality—and what it might mean—disturbed him.

Suddenly he felt as though he couldn't breathe.

When the manservant finished his hair, the same light touch on his shoulder bid him rise, and Michael stood up.

He turned to face the manservant and bowed. "Arigatō gozaimasu," he said formally.

The manservant blinked, nodded, then bowed in return. "Dōzo," he said as he opened the shōji and indicated that Michael should enter the hallway.

Several hallways later, they were at a doorway. The manservant opened the door and disappeared inside for a few moments.

When he emerged, he gestured for Michael to enter the room.

Michael walked into a room with one wall made up of enormous sliding screens decorated with painted nature scenes.

Shinjirō stood in the middle of the room, dressed in a starkly formal ceremonial kimono suited for the highest occasion.

He smiled at Michael, holding out his hand. "Maikoru."

Michael went to him, feeling his heart start to pound and then open wide to this man. *Shinjirō.* He laid his hands on Shinjirō's upper arms as the daimyō held him gently around the waist.

He opened his mouth to speak, but Shinjirō shook his head. "Later," he said. "We will have time later. For now, there is something I would ask you to do for me."

MICHAEL SAT in seiza behind the screen on the far right, and he watched as two of the sliding screens were pulled across the room.

A large hall was revealed, much like the hall in Kaminishi Castle, and around fifty samurai in formal dress, each with their two swords—long and short—sat in seiza position on tatami mats.

All their eyes were on Shinjirō, who was seated in the middle of what had been the room Michael had entered a few minutes ago. It was like a stage now, with Shinjirō as the main actor and the samurai as the audience.

From where he sat with head slightly bowed, Michael could see some of the samurai in the front on the far left of the hall at an angle. Which meant that they could see him, but their focus right now was on their lord.

Shinjirō nodded to the samurai who were positioned at the doors, and at once all the doors slid shut.

"This morning," Shinjirō said, "I met with the Shogun. The outcome of this meeting is that I am to end my life at dawn tomorrow morning."

There was a stunned silence.

"The reason for this order is that I have received information about the future of our country. I have received this information from this man."

The last screen began to slide slowly to the right, revealing Michael where he sat. A murmur arose in the hall, and several samurai put their hands on their katanas.

"Silence," Shinjirō said. The hall fell silent.

He turned to look at Michael, who met his eyes, then slowly got to his feet.

The samurai received a second shock as Michael addressed them in Japanese. "Warriors of the Kaminishi Han," he began. "What I am going to share with you are events that will take place in the future. I do not know if the future can be changed or not," he added, glancing at Shinjirō. "But I offer these facts to you freely, for your own consideration and possible use."

He recounted everything that he had told Shinjirō before. The atmosphere was surreal to him. He was a twenty-first-century American man speaking before a hall full of nineteenth-century samurai warriors in 1851. Of all that he had experienced in late-Edo-period Japan, this moment was the most psychically jarring.

He didn't know how long he spoke, but he made sure to tell everything important he could remember about the next one hundred and sixty years for Japan. When he finished, he fell silent and looked to Shinjirō.

Shinjirō nodded, then gave his final address to his men. "The Shogun has given permission for Norio to assume leadership of our land," he said. "I will leave it to each of you to decide whether to continue under Norio's leadership or to go your own way, having heard what you have heard here tonight."

A cry rose up from the back of the room; Michael couldn't make out what had been shouted, but others soon took up the cry.

Shinjirō smiled a little, then held up his hand. The hall fell silent again. "I thank you for your offer. You honor me more than I deserve. But I feel that it is my duty, and my duty alone, to end my life. I would prefer to see each of you continue to live and to make decisions for yourselves with what you now know."

MICHAEL WATCHED as Shinjirō bid each samurai who had served under him farewell with a brief personal conversation. One by one, each took his leave, until only Shinjirō and he remained.

Shinjirō turned to him and held out his arms. His face looked as calm as always, despite the events of the past twelve hours—and of the next twelve hours to come. "Maikoru," he said.

Michael went to him and allowed himself to be embraced. He laid his head on the daimyō's shoulder. "What do you need me to do?" he mumbled into the fine-woven fabric. "Tell me what you need from me." He felt beyond helpless in this situation. All he could offer was to give himself to Shinjirō for whatever the daimyō might need in this moment. Michael closed his eyes, swaying against him.

"There is one more thing you can do for me—tomorrow morning," Shinjirō said gently. "Until then, simply be with me. I would appreciate that."

A thought occurred to Michael. "Where is... where are your wife and children?"

"They left several hours ago," Shinjirō said.

"Where did they go?"

"Nagasaki."

He stared, and the daimyō explained. "My wife and daughters were allowed to go free by the Shogun. I said I would send them to Hokkaido, which is where my wife is originally from. However...." Shinjirō's lips tightened. "I am not certain their safety is completely assured."

"Do you think the Shogun would come after them?"

"I don't believe so. But I want to be careful. They are on their way to my sister's home in Nagasaki."

Michael stared. "You have a sister who lives in Nagasaki?"

"Yes. She is a Christian."

"Isn't that... illegal?"

"She practices her faith in secret. Due to her religious beliefs, she was disowned by my family. They all believed she died years ago. But I've kept in touch with her. My wife and daughters will be safe with her." The daimyō's eyes held a faraway look. "I gave my wife a note to give to her. The note says that my grandchildren and her grandchildren must leave Nagasaki before the year 1945. I will not take any chances of their coming to harm should the future that you have told me come to pass."

A small smile quirked the corner of Shinjirō's mouth. "I am glad you are here with me, Maikoru," he said. "I would appreciate your company tonight."

CHAPTER FOURTEEN

SHINJIRŌ'S MOUTH was hot on his, and he clutched at the daimyō's hips, pushing his own hips up to grind against Shinjirō's.

"*Aaah*," he moaned. Shinjirō ground himself slowly into Michael's cock, rubbing their groins together in a circular motion. He felt sensations he'd never felt before. He was almost frantically aroused.

The daimyō's hand was raising his left leg, and Michael lifted both legs and circled them around the small of Shinjirō's back, bringing them more tightly together. No space remained between their bodies; Michael felt sweat break out on his chest, on Shinjirō's chest, and he threw his head back on the small flat pillow. He wanted control, he wanted to climb inside Shinjirō's body and never leave it, he wanted....

Shinjirō bit down on his collarbone. A sound Michael had never heard himself make before came from his throat. Precum was leaking between their bodies, and he reached in to get some of it. "My lord," he breathed, and Shinjirō pulled back a little to allow him to spread the liquid near his hole.

He couldn't quite reach all the way down there, so Shinjirō swept some precum from Michael's abdomen and did the job himself, plunging two fingers and then three into him as Michael gasped sharply.

The daimyō pulled out his fingers. Michael spread his knees wider apart as Shinjirō positioned himself at the entrance.

He clutched at Shinjirō's arm.

"*Do it.*"

THEY PLUNDERED each other's bodies, giving and taking until the lines blurred and Michael was unsure where his body left off and Shinjirō's body began.

The hours passed.

At one point Michael lay on top of Shinjirō, just feeling the man's form beneath him. Trying to memorize every line and curve, every muscle, every inch of skin on this beloved body.

I can't let this go.

He kissed Shinjirō, gnawing at his mouth, his jaw, trying to take him into himself piece by piece. *It can't be true that this will disappear*, he thought, the concept more unreal to him than the fact that he was here in the past. He'd never asked to be here, and yet he'd found his life here. It couldn't be that it would be taken away from him.

Not when he'd only just found it.

You are my reason for living. I can't give you up.

Somebody, help us.

It can't be meant to end here.

He'd never felt as alive as he did now.

SHINJIRŌ REQUESTED a bath, and Michael prepared the deep tub with hot water and rough sea salts.

They sat in the steaming water, relaxing in the quiet of the predawn hours.

Michael wanted to speak, but something about the daimyō's demeanor bid him remain silent. Shinjirō was lying back against the tub's wall, his eyes closed. The expression on his face was placid, and his brow was unfurrowed. He didn't know how the daimyō could relax at this moment, but relaxed he was. Michael restrained his own selfish need to communicate with him.

As if sensing Michael's mood, Shinjirō reached out and took Michael's hand in his own. He opened his eyes and gazed at him with such frank and open affection that Michael caught his breath.

How can you look at me like that...

...when I am the one who brought you to your death?

HE DRIED Shinjirō's body with the towel as they both stood there naked.

"Maikoru," Shinjirō said. "I would appreciate it if you would serve as my second."

Michael stopped a moment, then resumed with the towel. "Hai, my lord."

He had assumed this would be his duty. After everything he had been responsible for, it was only right that he be here for the end.

They helped each other to dress in formal kimono once again. Shinjirō's kimono was pure white.

As it had been in Michael's drawing.

The traditional Japanese color of death.

The sky outside had slowly begun to lighten, and Michael's fingers trembled as he combed Shinjirō's long hair and pinned the upper portion back to form the topknot. He had barely gotten any sleep the two nights before and had had none this night. He tried to steady his arms and complete Shinjirō's hair and dress. There wasn't much time left.

He cleared his throat. "My lord, may I speak?"

"Yes."

Michael stood behind Shinjirō and laid his hands gently on the daimyō's shoulders. "Ever since I came here—to Japan, to the past—I have only brought you trouble and sorrow. I wish to apologize for that."

The daimyō expulsed breath softly—was he smiling? "There is no need."

"But—"

"You were unaware of why you were sent here to the past. I expect that everything you have done here was exactly what you were meant to do." Shinjirō turned his head to gaze at him. "I am satisfied with your actions."

A helpless desire rose in Michael, and he suddenly embraced Shinjirō, his cheek against the daimyō's cheek. "I have brought you to your death. I can't express my grief sufficiently in words.... Please forgive me." He whispered the last, clutching Shinjirō's body tightly.

"Our meeting in this lifetime was guided by fate." The daimyō stood quietly in Michael's embrace. "All of life is ultimately mysterious. Wouldn't you agree?" Michael could feel Shinjirō smile.

"I don't blame you for anything. I thank you for the unexpected gift of your presence in my life and for the opportunity you presented me to do what I could for my country."

THE FIRST rays of sunrise softly lit Shinjirō's meditation room.

Michael followed Shinjirō as the daimyō slid one of the shōji doors open. The early dawn light streamed inside.

Shinjirō gazed out at the cityscape of Edo, and gentle light illuminated his form, framing him against the open doorway to the outside.

Michael waited.

Finally Shinjirō turned and slid the shōji shut behind him. He smiled at Michael. "This may be difficult for you, but I am certain you will do well. This is how we will proceed. It is a simple process."

He outlined in basic steps what was to occur next as Michael listened and nodded.

Shinjirō walked to where his attendant had set the small wooden table. On top lay the daimyō's short knife.

Michael went to Shinjirō's katana and picked it up.

The daimyō settled himself in seiza position on the floor, the small table in front of him. "Maikoru."

Michael came to stand behind Shinjirō and to his left. Shinjirō adjusted his long hair, pinning it on top of his head underneath the topknot. Michael focused on the now-exposed back of Shinjirō's neck as the daimyō picked up the knife from the table.

With graceful movements, the daimyō eased the top part of his outermost kimono off, leaving a solid white kimono with a silk undergarment beneath, which he opened to the bare skin. Taking the knife in his right hand, he picked up the small table and placed it behind him, using it as a seat, forcing his body to lean forward slightly.

Michael turned and set himself at an angle, both hands gripping the long sword's handle.

"It's been a privilege to know you," Shinjirō said.

Only the feeling that all of this was surreal enabled Michael to respond. "Yes. It's been a privilege to know you as well, Shinjirō-sama."

He could almost feel the daimyō smile. *I love you*, Michael thought.

"Please prepare yourself," Shinjirō said.

The next moment took on the hazy feel of a dream. He saw the quick movement of Shinjirō's arms tensing and heard him grunt slightly; then a slower, deep drawing in of breath. Then silence.

"Now, Maikoru" was the next thing he heard.

He felt his own arms raising the long sword.

"My lord," he whispered. Then he brought the sword down in a long arcing swing across.

Blood misted in front of him and he saw an object tumble to the floor to his lower left.

Then all was darkness.

MICHAEL WAS lying on a cold hardwood floor.

A muted sound reached his ear: traffic. He was naked but wrapped in a bedsheet. He opened his eyes. It was dark—night. He was lying on the floor next to his bed.

He was back.

THE APPROACHING sunrise from the east stained the dark sky with a faint orange glimmer.

The waters off the Berkeley marina lapped quietly at the pier's wood pilings.

The air was still.

Michael sat on the pier and watched as the morning sky slowly brightened with the dawn, the sun rising to illuminate the Golden Gate Bridge in the distance.

CHAPTER FIFTEEN

ELLEN HEARD Michael's end of the conversation going on in the next room and tried not to eavesdrop, but.... Well, she couldn't help it if she was *curious*.

He was on the phone for a while; that was unusual when it was his mother on the other end of the line. Michael's mother was notorious for brief phone calls. It was as if anything taking place in her life was more important than a phone call from her son. Today's call, however, seemed different.

Well, he is quitting school to move to Japan.... Guess that's worth a slightly longer phone call.

She smirked.

Finally Michael entered the living room. "How was it?" Ellen asked him bluntly. Patience and decorum were never her strong suits.

"Okay. Once I told her I'd taken incompletes in all my classes, she relaxed about it. She thinks this means I can come back and pick up where I left off, so it's no big deal." Michael lifted a stack of books and placed them into the box he'd been packing.

"But you don't think you'll be coming back."

"No."

"Why not?"

He didn't answer her.

She put a hand on his arm. "Michael."

When he didn't respond, she pulled him over to the sofa and sat him down. She took a deep breath, then let it out.

"Do you really think he's there?"

HE'D ONLY looked slightly shell-shocked when she came over after he'd called her yesterday morning.

It had just happened—whatever *it* was—the death of the samurai warlord and Michael's return to the present. They had sat at the kitchen table and he'd told her everything, all that had happened during this time he'd gone back. The journey on foot to old Kyoto and the ride in the wagon all the way to Tokyo. Seeing Shinjirō in his home, staying at the brothel with Misako, the Shogun's seppuku order.

Shinjirō's death.

"I've felt him," he'd told her at the end. "He's in Japan now. I have to see him again."

Ellen closed her eyes. She wanted to help him. She had an open mind but didn't know whether there was any truth, in reality, about what he'd told her; she just didn't want him going off on a wild goose chase if at the end, all he would be was hurt.

A soft touch on her hand surprised her eyes open.

"It's all right. Don't worry. I'm going to be busy for the first few months. I'm going to do some research in Tokyo and Kyoto first, and then I'm going west of Kyoto to try and find where the Kaminishi Han was located. If all else fails, I can go to Nagasaki and see if he left any surviving descendants." Michael smiled at her. "I'll be too exhausted to go off the deep end and lose my mind. Unless, of course, that's already happened."

He laughed, looking as cheerful as he used to when they'd first gotten together.

"What if he's not there?"

Her former boyfriend stopped smiling, then turned to her with an oddly gentle, open expression on his face. "Thank you," he said unexpectedly. "You are a wonderful person to care so much. I've never had that."

"Michael."

"But you don't have to worry," he continued. The look in his eye startled her. "*Because I know that I will find him.*"

BOOK TWO
THE LONG JOURNEY

PROLOGUE

Two months later
Kameoka, Kansai Region, Japan

THE GRAVEYARD was overgrown in the hot August sun.

Michael stayed on his knees as he moved from one stone monument to the next, comparing the kanji characters on each marker to the list he'd obtained from the local historical society.

The kanji markings were remarkably clear for being over a hundred years old. He wondered offhandedly if the humidity in the Kansai air had something to do with the engraved parts being so well preserved.

The graveyard was nestled between a few trees on a steep hillside. He had been through most of the markers that were pre-Meiji era and could cross this graveyard off his list soon.

It was unlikely, given the way things had ended one hundred and sixty years ago, that any sign of the Kaminishi name would be found in a Kansai graveyard, but he had to investigate all the ones local to this area west of Kyoto just to be sure. He used a cigarette lighter to light any incense that remained at each marker out of respect for the dead.

The late afternoon sun was still blazing when Michael finished his task. He sat on the smooth ground and took out the bottle of lemon water he'd purchased from a vending machine in town. Taking a swig, he leaned back against the low wall that encircled the graveyard and closed his eyes against the heat.

TOKYO HAD been a whirlwind of activity. He'd started doing research from the moment his feet hit the ground at Narita, searching at libraries and government offices for any trace of the Kaminishi Han and the Kaminishi family line.

Nothing had turned up. He'd walked the streets of Shinjuku and Shibuya at night, alone in the crowds, returning late to the gaijin house he shared with expatriate students and English teachers. More than once he'd gone to gaze at the Imperial Palace along with hordes of tourists. He'd looked for Shinjirō's home in the nearby Marunouchi district but found only office buildings, stores, and restaurants where the daimyō's mansions used to be.

Similarly the Yoshiwara pleasure quarter where he'd stayed with Misako had been built over and was now an ordinary commercial district, just one of hundreds in the Tokyo metropolitan area. Nothing remained of the blocks of brothels and teahouses, the dark alleys full of secret enticements.

It was one hundred and sixty years later. Nearly everywhere he'd been, everything that had touched his life in 1851, had vanished.

At night he wandered through the streets and the parks, looking for glimpses of the past. One night the sight of a yaki-imo seller selling hot sweet potatoes strangely out of season—it was July and meltingly hot and humid, even at night—brought tears to Michael's eyes. He bought a potato from the seller despite the heat, remembering the yaki-imo he'd bought from the stand in Kyoto before he'd snuck into the back of the pumpkin seller's wagon. How delicious that potato had tasted.

He checked his e-mail at local Internet cafes. Ellen's e-mails were carefully worded, containing updates on what she was doing and questions on how he was coming along in his research. In between the lines, Michael read that she was still worried about him.

Obviously he couldn't blame her. He knew how he must've sounded before he left America—like a madman. *I know I'll find him*, he'd told her. Shinjirō had been dead for a century and a half. She probably thought he'd finally gone over the edge.

But Michael was certain of one thing and one thing only: Shinjirō was definitely here. He knew it as solidly as he knew his own name.

He only needed to find him again.

CHAPTER ONE

KAMEOKA WAS now the name of the area that had once been the Kaminishi and Shirakawa domains in this part of the Kansai region of Japan.

It was approximately nine miles west of Kyoto, through the same mountains Michael had traversed on foot from the castle. He knew he'd be able to find the approximate location of the Kaminishi Han, given that the topography and the landscape wouldn't have changed, but the issue was how much the area had been built up in the meantime.

He'd left Tokyo in late July, taking the shinkansen, the bullet train, to Kyoto. He'd found a small ryokan near Kyoto Station and settled in for what he expected would be the remainder of the summer.

Summers in Kansai were hot; he certainly remembered that part well. Some things didn't change in one hundred and sixty years.

He escaped the stickiness and the heat by hanging out in Kyoto Station in the evenings, and Porta, the huge underground shopping mall whose entrance was a few steps outside the station's front doors. The massive train station also contained a large number of restaurants and stores, its large glass atrium soaring into the Kyoto night skyline like a modern interloper among the old traditional machiya wood-framed buildings.

Kyoto had always been a dreamlike city to him. Its quiet, elegant beauty and the traditional buildings and temples lingered in his memory. When he'd experienced it again that evening in the fall of 1851, it stole his heart once more as the ideal old Japanese city.

He continued his research in Kyoto, but most of the public records of old family names were in Tokyo and he had already reviewed them there. In Kyoto he had hoped to uncover more information about the Kaminishi Han itself, but virtually nothing came to light. The Shirakawa Han pre-1868 was mapped as including nearly all the Kameoka valley, meaning the Kaminishi Han had been taken over at some point after Shinjirō's death.

So he had destroyed not only Shinjirō's life but his family's domain as well.

All of the history of the region west of Kyoto that he'd hoped to find was nonexistent. He had one last resource to contact in Kyoto the next morning before moving his search to Nagasaki.

THAT NIGHT he went to a sushi restaurant he'd discovered his first night in town, in July.

It was a small family-owned place, blocks off the beaten tourist track near the station, with a TV on above the sushi bar and a tropical fish tank in one corner of the room.

Michael was greeted by the owner and took a seat at the bar. He ordered yellowtail and sea eel and watched as the sushi chef took the fish in hand and began to prepare his dinner.

Two men seated themselves to his left, setting smartphones down on the counter next to their hashi. Kyoto businessmen, as formal as Tokyo businessmen but somewhat less harried. Michael supposed no place in Kansai could simulate the mad rush that was Tokyo city life.

The chef lifted Michael's plate of yellowtail, and Michael took it and set it down. The hamachi was fresh and nearly melted on his tongue. "Oishii," he told the chef, smiling.

The local news was on, and the report was about some yakuza gang war in the Kansai region. Michael glanced up for a moment to look. A number of grim-faced men in business suits were getting in and out of numerous Mercedes on some street in Osaka. The Japanese news anchor was using the careful language and tone of voice they frequently used when discussing the yakuza underworld.

He chewed his fish and rice, thinking about yakuza and samurai. Supposedly the yakuza weren't descended from the samurai, but from the defenders of village citizens against ronin samurai in the mid-Edo period during the isolation; the yakuza were actually the underdogs who fought against the samurai. He hadn't studied the yakuza much. He wondered what Shinjirō would think of them.

What Shinjirō *had* thought of them. They'd existed back in his day, after all.

Michael finished his meal and paid up, then thanked the chef and the owner on his way out.

The streets of Kyoto in 2010 were full of shoppers and tourists and cars. Stores and restaurants were full; it was the height of tourist season.

He was suddenly tired and decided to make an early night of it.

THE FUTON on the floor of his room in the small family-run ryokan was hard. Not as hard as the one in his cell in the lowest level of the castle, but still hard.

Michael opened his eyes in the dark room and turned his gaze to the faint city lights coming in through the gauze-curtained window.

I know you're out there.

Feeling foolish and a little melodramatic, he dragged the futon over and laid it down just under the window. He wanted to lie as close as he could to the streets of Kyoto, where his lover was. Somewhere out there.

What are you doing right now? Are you sleeping or out on the town? I hope you're not with somebody else... though I suppose I have no right to say anything about it.

He sat up on the futon and leaned his shoulder against the windowsill.

Ellen had asked him how he knew Shinjirō was in Kyoto; he'd replied that it was a strong feeling, more a knowing than anything else. "Then why are you going to Tokyo first?" Ellen had demanded, in her usual way.

He smiled, remembering. He'd told her that he needed to research the Kaminishi family name, most of which could only be done in Tokyo, that it made sense to do that first. "Besides, I'm not sure I'm quite ready to see him yet," he'd added. "I think I need to build up to it."

She'd nodded soberly, but Michael hadn't been fooled. *She thinks I've completely, utterly lost it. In grief and in denial—not facing reality.*

"I said this before, but you know... call me anytime."

"I know."

"Even if you get the time difference wrong, just wake me up."

Michael grinned at her. "You can call me too." He wanted her to feel confident about him, that he wasn't falling apart, that she didn't need to save him. He was saving himself.

He moved the filmy gauze aside to look at the Kyoto night scene. The ryokan was on a side street south of the train station, still in a commercial district but quieter than the area north of the station.

He knew this could be a fantasy about Shinjirō, and he also knew that it wasn't. He felt Shinjirō was closer now than ever before.

He lay back down on the futon and touched himself, feeling his member pulse to life, thinking of Shinjirō's face, his hair and skin, his body. *Shinjirō-sama.* Michael fingered the underside of his cock, remembering the daimyō's first exploration of his circumcised member, his curiosity and concern—he thought Michael had been mutilated, perhaps tortured.

A gentle laugh escaped his lips, and then he palmed himself in earnest, shutting his eyes, fingers wrapping around his length. *Shinjirō.* His warmth and the immediacy of his overwhelming presence. Shinjirō was nearby. Michael knew this. He *knew* it.

He rode that knowing to orgasm, then slept.

CHAPTER TWO

SEIICHI TAMAGUCHI was eighty years old and had spent summers in Kameoka in his youth. He was also Ellen's great-uncle, whom Ellen had met once on a family vacation to Hawaii when she was a child.

Tamaguchi had traveled some, but never to California, so he grilled Michael with interest for about an hour on the Golden State.

They were sitting in Tamaguchi's small living room in his house in suburban Kyoto. It was a bright, sunny morning.

"I can tell you what my obāchan told me about the Kaminishi family," Tamaguchi finally said. "I'm afraid it will be secondhand knowledge, since she herself was born long after the Shirakawa family took over that region."

"Kameoka is where the Kaminishi Han was located, am I right?"

"Yes." The old man pushed his glasses up on his nose; they kept threatening to slide off. "West of Kyoto, just on the other side of the mountains."

"What happened between the Kaminishi and Shirakawa clans?"

"Well, it's a little unclear. But it appears that the Shirakawas took over not long after the opening to the West."

Michael grimaced.

"The Kaminishi family had been the dominant family in the Kameoka valley for hundreds of years. They were a small clan but had a reputation for being fierce fighters when called for. They were in the northern part of the valley while the Shirakawas covered the southern part." Tamaguchi took a sip of his green tea before continuing. "According to my grandmother, there was a shift in power in the valley sometime before the fall of the Shogunate—before 1868, in other words. The Shirakawa clan took over the entire valley. That's all I know, I'm afraid."

"Was she familiar with any of the Kaminishi family by name? Did she ever hear of a Shinjirō Kaminishi who was head of the clan?"

Tamaguchi thought for a moment, then shook his head. "I don't recall that she knew any of their given names. I'm sorry."

Michael spent some additional time with Tamaguchi but failed to glean any further useful information from him. After exchanging some concluding pleasantries, he took his leave.

HE HAD now researched the Kaminishi clan and name thoroughly both in Tokyo and Kyoto. Shinjirō had told him on that last night that the Shogun had ordered the clan's name be stricken from the official registry of family names; this appeared to have been carried out. Aside from Tamaguchi's statements and some references in first-person accounts from that era, the Kaminishi name had fallen out of historical record.

There was no further research to be done in Kyoto. The next place would be Nagasaki.

Shinjirō had sent his wife and children there. Somewhere in the historical records of Nagasaki there might be some confirmation that they had been there. There might even be descendants still living there. Not everyone in Nagasaki had died in the atomic bomb attack, after all.

Michael still felt Shinjirō's presence in Kyoto, so much so that he found it difficult to make plans to leave. He had packed his things and paid his bill at the ryokan that morning, leaving his bag there. He would be back to pick it up before going to Kyoto Station to catch the late-night local train to Nagasaki. The train would arrive just before dawn in that city far to the south.

It was early afternoon. There was still one more place he needed to go.

THE SAGANO Scenic Railway, or "Romantic Train," was a bit of a tourist trap, but a pleasant one.

It was a sightseeing train that traveled from the Saga-Arashiyama station on the western outskirts of Kyoto through the mountains to Kameoka.

The old-style wooden train cars shook on the tracks as tourists leaned out the open windows to take pictures. Michael had taken the modern Japan Rail train to Kameoka on his previous graveyard-hunting excursions. This was the first time he'd taken the Romantic Train.

The Romantic Train moved on a less-developed path through the mountain range, veering around steep mountainsides and over rattletrap wooden bridges that spanned flowing rivers and creeks below. Every now and again, the train traveled alongside a footpath high on the slope, the waters moving far below, and Michael was jolted by the remembrance of walking through the night on what could very well have been the same path.

Lost in the past, he sat among the tourists taking pictures and videos.

THE SCENIC railway stopped in Kameoka, but at a different station than the regular JR line did.

The Romantic Train's end point in the Kameoka valley was in a somewhat isolated area. The tiny station was surrounded by open fields with the mountain range close by.

Michael alighted from the train and walked past the souvenir booth and down the wooden steps. He was alone as he left the train station; most tourists simply waited at the station to take the same train back to Saga-Arashiyama, where they would then transfer to a regular JR train to return to Kyoto's city center.

He walked through the fields toward the mountains. It was another hot day in the region. He had brought some bottled water and energy bars that he'd purchased at Kyoto Station.

He began to get an eerie feeling as he crossed a small stream near a copse of trees, stepping on the rocks to go across without getting wet. There were tall grasses, and the banks of the stream were muddy....

He stopped. This was where....

This was where he—

"I WILL always think of you as having come from that stream," Shinjirō had said softly as they bathed in the hot water together that last night. "One moment everything was as it had always been, and the next moment... there you were."

THE NIGHT air surrounding Kyoto Station was hot and fetid.

He stood numbly on the escalator that led to the rooftop viewing area ten floors up from the station's main floor, with his backpack on his back.

The view from the roof was a 360-degree view of the entire city. Kyoto Tower and the surrounding buildings glittered in the bright lights of the downtown city center.

His mind was a blank. He'd been drinking since returning from Kameoka, first at one tourist trap bar and then the next.

There were couples standing around him enjoying the romantic view, looking out at the night sky. He felt like he couldn't breathe.

Shinjirō... I'm sorry.

THE TRAIN to Nagasaki was leaving in five minutes.

Michael walked briskly toward the turnstiles, taking his ticket from his pocket. The amount of alcohol he'd drunk made the scene of the line of travelers in front of him take on a surreal, too-lit glare.

A slight prickling on the back of his neck stopped him.

He stood stock-still as waves of Japanese travelers and foreign tourists moved around him.

He blinked.

Shinjirō.

HE TURNED and scanned the crowd milling around the vast lobby area of Kyoto Station.

It was the usual August mix in Kyoto: Japanese salarymen heading home after a very long day's work, Western tourists on holiday, young people out for a summer night on the town.

His eyes darted from person to person, looking for him.

Three Japanese men dressed in dark clothing suddenly stood out as if a beacon had highlighted them in the crowd. Two of them wore their shirts unbuttoned halfway down their chests. The third one was neatly coiffed with almost shoulder-length hair and a conservative tie. He stood in profile to where Michael was, but Michael watched as the man suddenly stilled.

The two men with him were puzzled. One of them laughed, covering up the awkward moment.

Michael stared, mentally willing the third man to turn toward him.

He could see the man set his shoulders, as if steeling himself to face something difficult. And then he turned to face Michael.

Shinjirō.

From the moment their eyes locked, even with the modern dress and hairstyle, Michael knew. It was, beyond any doubt, the man he had fallen in love with one hundred and sixty years ago.

"Shinjirō."

He was twenty feet from Michael, but Michael knew he'd heard. The two men with him were likewise frozen in place, waiting for Shinjirō's reaction to determine theirs.

The expression on Shinjirō's face was one of shock, and then a neutral expression came over him. He shook his head slightly, then turned to his companions, placing a hand on the shoulder of one of them.

The three men headed toward the front doors of Kyoto Station.

Michael quickly followed.

The men picked up their pace, almost breaking into a run. Michael began to run after them, weaving around people, muttering apologies.

The warm night air hit him in the face as he exited the front doors. Out of the corner of his eye, he saw three dark figures moving quickly toward a waiting Mercedes. He dashed into the lanes in front of the station where people were being dropped off or picked up, causing several drivers to slam on their brakes.

He got to within fifteen feet of the Mercedes, memorizing the license plate number as it drove off.

The man he knew as Shinjirō Kaminishi stared at him through the back window as the car pulled away into the night.

CHAPTER THREE

THE OFFICER at the police kōban the next morning was less than helpful.

Michael gave him the Mercedes's license plate number and explained that the car had hit his bicycle the night before and done some damage. He was an American tourist, had rented the bicycle, and was upset that he would be charged for it. He only wanted to contact the Mercedes owner to see if his insurance would cover the cost. Could the police officer help him by checking the plate number and giving him the owner's contact information?

He felt a little bad for lying, especially to a police officer, but he needed to get the address and didn't know any other way to do it.

The officer hemmed and hawed in that very polite way of the Japanese. Michael persisted and used even more formal language until the officer finally gave in and looked up the license plate number.

Michael watched as the color drained from the officer's face.

OF COURSE Michael had known even before the information came back that Shinjirō was a yakuza.

The black Mercedes, Shinjirō's suit, the clothing and appearance of his two colleagues—it all added up to the Japanese underworld. The officer's reaction just confirmed it.

Michael walked down the narrow, winding street that led out of Kyoto's city center, looking at the map in his hand. His destination was another two miles or so in this direction.

The blocks became less commercial and more residential as he went farther on. There were fewer apartment buildings and more houses.

Gradually the houses were getting bigger, approaching mansion size, or what passed for it in densely populated and overcrowded Japan. The streets became broader.

At last Michael entered what appeared to be an exclusive neighborhood with large houses hidden behind ivy-covered walls and gated entrances for cars. Shinjirō's home was on the next street.

He didn't know if Shinjirō's house would be hidden behind a wall or out in the open. He suspected it would be behind a wall.

He turned the corner.

The houses on this street were large, traditional Japanese-style homes. With a sudden wave of nostalgia, Michael recalled Shinjirō's house in Edo in 1851. He guessed that Shinjirō could be considered another kind of warlord these days. With a wry smile, he put the map in his pocket.

The house was behind a wall and a gate. Michael thought over his options. There was an intercom system where he could speak and identify himself. That was one way to try to see Shinjirō.

He was in a neighborhood where he clearly stood out. One advantage to that was that he could always pretend to be a tourist who'd gotten lost on the way to the Golden Pavilion, one who spoke no Japanese. On the other hand....

On the other hand, he'd seen the look in Shinjirō's eyes at Kyoto Station. Shinjirō had recognized him. He had no doubt about that. There had been a spark of recognition of some kind on that beautiful face, and Michael wanted to see that again if it was the last thing he did.

While he'd been pondering all this, his feet had unconsciously taken him right up to the gate of Shinjirō's house. He stopped. What was he thinking?

Just then, the gate began to open.

Michael jumped behind the narrow bushes that ran along the wall, hitting the dirt with a thud. He lay flat on the ground, heart pounding, as the gate finished opening and there was a short silence.

A black Mercedes emerged from the gate. Michael lay still, waiting for the car to continue on into the street. Instead, it stopped halfway through the gate.

He held his breath.

The rear passenger door on the driver's side opened, and Shinjirō stepped out.

He was standing not ten feet from where Michael lay hidden behind the bushes. A man came out to the car from the house.

It was an older gentleman in a formal yukata. He approached Shinjirō deferentially and spoke to him in a soft voice.

Michael strained to hear Shinjirō's response.

The only word he could make out was "Osaka."

The older man bowed, then turned and left. Shinjirō got back in the Mercedes, and the car pulled into the street and drove off.

THE TRAIN to Osaka was less than half-full.

It was early afternoon on a weekday in August. Michael supposed that not many tourists would be taking the train between Kyoto and Osaka in the middle of the day, but he was still a little surprised.

It made a certain task easier, however. He took out his rented Japanese cell phone and called a number.

Tamaguchi was surprised to hear from him, but even more surprised to hear what his request was. "I must say, I'm not familiar with yakuza hangouts in Osaka. Let me ask someone who might know. I'll call you back."

The landscape between Kyoto and Osaka alternated between suburban tracts and empty fields. Michael stared at the neat rows of houses and apartment buildings, the empty lots unmarred by trash or rubbish, the blue skies over everything.

Japan was a peaceful, prosperous place, just as he'd told Shinjirō. Whatever Michael had done in 1851, and whatever had happened after Shinjirō's death, the future had been left unchanged.

He was grateful for that. His guilt over what had happened to Shinjirō was more than he could bear already. If Japan itself had been affected as well, he didn't think he could live with himself.

Shinjirō....

He was so lost in thought, he almost didn't hear his phone ring.

THE MEETING of the Kawakami yakuza clan was called to order.

The back room of Nishiyama Restaurant was filled with cigarette smoke as waitresses brought sake and bottled beers to the men seated at the low tables. Dinner was finished, and the business portion of the evening was about to begin.

Jirō Kawakami viewed the proceedings with his usual dispassionate eye. He was a calm, reticent man, not the typical image one would hold of a yakuza clan leader.

He had inherited the position when the former leader—his older brother Ichirō—had been killed in retaliation for a deal gone wrong. That was twelve years ago.

In the years since then, things hadn't changed much in the Kansai region, as far as yakuza interfamily warfare was concerned. Both the Kawakami clan and the neighboring clan, the Shiromuras, were still at odds, though the reason for it was baseless and therefore the most exasperating reason of them all.

Jirō's nephew, Shintarō Kawakami—Ichirō's only child— had gone to Tokyo University. It had been while Shintarō was at university that his father had been killed. The rumor was that the Shiromuras were behind it, though they weren't the only suspects. Another local clan had been gunning for Ichirō as well. Ichirō Kawakami had been ruthless and was feared and hated by many.

Ryōta Shiromura, the future head of the Shiromura clan, had attended Tokyo University at the same time as Shintarō. Though Shintarō, to all outward appearances, hadn't done anything to provoke young Shiromura, somehow a rivalry had sprung up. From what Jirō could tell, Shintarō had abandoned the rivalry once he graduated, but Ryōta kept up the grudge.

It was stupid things like this that kept Jirō, now fifty-seven years old, from a peaceful sleep at night.

Ryōta kept encroaching on Kawakami territory all over the region: in Kyoto, Osaka, and Nara, pushing wherever he could. Secret meetings held between Jirō and old man Ryōga Shiromura to defuse the situation hadn't helped. The old man was winding down his leadership, and Ryōta was the unquestioned next in line. Jirō would have Ryōta as a headache for years to come.

That is, unless.... He looked toward a sharp-eyed man at his right. Takeshi Kawakami, Jirō's younger brother, was a firebrand in the tradition of their brother Ichirō. Takeshi was a yakuza born and bred; he loved the lifestyle and the traditions. By all rights, it should be Takeshi who should take over once he, Jirō, was finished. As far as he was concerned, Takeshi could take over right now.

But Ichirō had been adamant. His last words to Jirō had been "Make sure it's Shintarō. My son must lead when he is ready."

Jirō closed his eyes.

Shintarō Kawakami was an anomaly among yakuza. Though born to the yakuza life, he had no real attachment to it. After graduating with a business degree, Shintarō had been set up as the right-hand man to Hiroshi Satō, a dry older man who was the clan's saikō-komon, or main business advisor. Shintarō was exceptionally skilled at negotiating and closing real estate deals. Jirō sometimes suspected that his nephew maintained such excellence on the business end so he could avoid having to be involved with the seamier side of the clan's business: drugs, prostitution, and the protection racket.

His nephew was no saint; he indulged in some of the perks that came with being yakuza. Expensive nights out on the town, the occasional high-class bar hostess for an evening's fun. But like water off a duck's back, none of it seemed to cling to him. He was in the family business only because it was the family business, nothing more. If pressed, Shintarō would probably admit to him—in private, of course—that he would just as soon do something else for a living.

Jirō's gaze lit upon his nephew, seated nearby on the left side of the table.

A tall man at six feet, Shintarō Kawakami possessed a face that was both decidedly masculine and beautiful. He looked like a movie or TV star, like a samurai warlord in one of those historical dramas. Jirō could envision his nephew with long flowing hair and in battle dress, leading his samurai into battle with katana aloft.

He shook his head a little, laughing silently at this fanciful image.

FROM THE moment he had disembarked at Osaka's main train station, Michael had been running to and fro in the gleaming modern city.

Tamaguchi-san had given him all the yakuza haunts he knew of in Osaka. Some, as to be expected, were in the glitzy new parts of town, and he ran through those restaurants and clubs fairly quickly.

Going rapidly down the list, he began to hit those in the old Japanese neighborhoods, the places Allied bombers had missed in World War II and which remained relatively intact from the Meiji era. He walked through the crowds down the narrow streets— more like alleys—in the steamy-hot August evening.

A prickly feeling alerted him when he approached the next-to-last on the list, an old family-style Japanese restaurant on a dark side street. He was about a mile out from Osaka's city center at this point.

The restaurant was located on the corner of an intersection of two small streets, with the entrance on one side of the corner. The cloth banners in the entryway said "Nishiyama Restaurant"— West Mountain Restaurant.

A man in a dark suit emerged from beneath the banners. As he glanced curiously at Michael, Michael ducked his head and quickly walked down the street.

He turned right at the next small street and then made another right turn at the first alleyway he came to. As he thought, the alley was narrow, long, and dark, and it led all the way back to the first street. If he was lucky....

Yes. The restaurant's back door opened onto the alley. And farther down, near the street, were the windows to the private rooms of the restaurant and a fire exit door.

As Michael approached the windows, he heard talking and laughter. A large quantity of cigarette smoke wafted out from the room.

The kitchen workers had left some boxes filled with day-old produce and other refuse in the alley. Michael dragged a few boxes over to the windows, which were just above his height.

Testing them to see if they could hold his weight—they did—he stepped up and carefully raised his head to look in.

It was a smaller room than he'd expected. Men in business suits and a few in kimonos with traditional haori coats sat on the floor at several long low tables. It looked like dinner was over and their meeting was about to begin.

He held his breath as he surveyed the room, looking for one face....

There.

Near the end of one table, close to where the older men in haori were seated, was Shinjirō.

Michael gazed at the fine features and noble profile, oddly juxtaposed with the slightly too-long hair—almost to his shoulders—and completely modern clothes. He wore a black leather jacket, which looked out of place next to the traditionally dressed and business-suited men surrounding him.

As he watched, Shinjirō abruptly got up from his seat on the floor and made his way to the doorway.

THE HANDSOME man stepped out into the alley.

He took a deep breath of the Osaka night air, pulling a pack of cigarettes out of his leather jacket pocket.

As he placed a cigarette in his mouth, a lighter flicked on in the dark alley.

He glanced at the small flame, startled, and then at the man holding the lighter.

"Konban wa, Shinjirō-sama."

CHAPTER FOUR

SHINJIRŌ STARED. "Excuse me?" he said in English.

Michael said nothing, only proffered the light again. Shinjirō must've concluded he was no threat, as he bent his head slightly to light his cigarette with Michael's lighter.

He drew in, blew some smoke, and took the cigarette out of his mouth. "Who are you?"

Michael replied, "I think you know who I am."

Shinjirō shook his head politely. "I am afraid you are mistaken. My English is not very good, sorry—"

"Then we can speak in Japanese," Michael said pleasantly, switching to Japanese. "I've been told my Japanese is pretty decent. My name is Michael Holden."

Shinjirō blinked, then laughed softly.

He took another drag from his cigarette. "And what would be your business with me, Holden-san?"

"Your name is Shinjirō. And we know each other."

"My name is Shintarō Kawakami. I am sure we've never met before tonight."

"Then why did you look at me the way you did at Kyoto Station?"

The man started, then regained his composure. "Kyoto Station?"

"Last night. You turned around and saw me."

"Sumimasen. I don't know what you're referring to—"

"You and I knew each other a long time ago. I know that you know what I'm talking about."

"Holden-san, forgive me. You have mistaken me for somebody else. I have a meeting inside that I must return to. Shitsurei shimasu." Shintarō turned to leave.

Michael grabbed his arm. "Wait—"

The man moved swiftly and gracefully, turning Michael's body until he unexpectedly found his face to the wall with one arm held behind him at an awkward angle.

Michael turned to look at him.

"Please don't force me to take further measures. You need to leave here, now."

"What are you afraid of... Kawakami-san? I came from America to see you. I only ask that you hear me out." He flinched and gritted his teeth as the man exerted pressure on his arm. "I'll leave... and return to America... but only after you've heard what I have to say."

He waited for Shintarō's response, barely breathing.

Two men burst out of the restaurant's back door. "Waka-danna, daijōbu desu ka?"

"Yes. I'm fine. Please take this gentleman to the safe house for me." He released Michael to them. "I'll be there following the meeting."

"Hai."

THE ROOM was furnished only with a futon on the floor and a low table. The window was high and barred, reminding him of another cell-like room from long ago.

The two yakuza underlings had taken his jacket and wallet, all the contents of his pockets. His hands were bound behind his back, and his ankles were also bound, and he lay on the futon.

At least I'm not naked this time.

He closed his eyes.

He might have been less certain before now. The glimpse of the man at Kyoto Station had been brief. But now he had no doubts at all.

This was Shinjirō Kaminishi.

He was every inch the daimyō, the man Michael had known in 1851—the man he had had sex with and loved. Physically he was the same man. His voice was the same, the way he moved his body was the same....

It was Shinjirō.

Michael was already half-hard just from being in the daimyō's presence again. He'd been that way since he'd been taken from the alley and pushed into a black Mercedes. He didn't even care if the two yakuza had noticed.

The feel of Shinjirō's hands on him—even if he was manhandling him in a nonsexual way—excited him beyond measure.

He didn't care what happened to him anymore.

Just so long as he could be with Shinjirō.

SHINTARŌ KAWAKAMI finally arrived several hours later.

He entered the room, dismissing the underlings who lingered at the doorway, and shut the door.

The two men were alone.

Shintarō crouched down to untie Michael's bonds. "I apologize for this treatment," he said. "I was unable to conclude our conversation at the time."

He stood up and waited patiently while Michael flexed his hands and felt his ankles. Michael glanced up at Shintarō. "You do remember, don't you?" he said softly.

The man looked down at him expressionlessly. "No."

"I don't believe you."

"Holden-san," Shintarō said, as Michael slowly and painfully got up. "I will listen to what it is you have to say. But after that, you must leave."

He was standing about five feet from Michael. From that distance, Michael took in the black leather jacket, the dark slacks, the air of power and privilege. His hair was neatly and expensively coiffed, and he had the same beautiful pale skin he remembered.

"Please say your piece."

"I am a college student from California. One night in June, when I was studying for finals, I fell asleep at my desk. When I woke up, I found myself in Japan here in the Kansai area, west of Kyoto. The year was 1851."

Shintarō's expression was calm. "Continue."

"I was seized by samurai and taken to the castle of their daimyō, a warlord named Shinjirō Kaminishi. I was held captive for a number of weeks. I then returned unexpectedly to my life in present-day California." He walked slowly toward Shintarō, who merely watched him approach. "I returned twice more to the past. On my last time there, I made my way to Edo along the old Tōkaidō road and met with Shinjirō-sama for the last time. There, I assisted him in ending his own life." Michael stopped, only a foot away now, right in Shintarō's space. He gazed at Shintarō, whose unwavering gaze matched his own. "You are the exact incarnation of Shinjirō Kaminishi. I would never mistake Shinjirō for anyone else. I was his prisoner, and then... his lover. I've come to Japan to be with you."

He moved even closer, their faces now a mere hand's width apart.

"I will never leave you again."

Shintarō stared at him for a moment, then unexpectedly smiled.

"My goodness," he said mildly. "A most amazing story. Are you perhaps planning to write novels once you've graduated from your studies?"

Michael stopped him from saying anything further by closing the last few inches between them. He kissed Shintarō, holding his face between his hands.

The daimyō's lips were the same; the face between his hands was the same beloved face. Beneath the aftershave, he smelled Shinjirō's body musk, and he felt the same feelings surge up as when he'd last been with Shinjirō-sama in bed in the Edo mansion—

Thwack!

The backhand sent him stumbling, then sprawling onto the floor. He tasted blood from the corner of his mouth and looked up at Shintarō.

The man was still calm. "I could have you killed for that," he said. "Who do you think you are? You are a complete stranger to me. Be grateful I'm willing to let you go after that without having my men beat you to a pulp—or worse."

He turned away from Michael and walked to the door.

"I can change your mind."

Shintarō glanced over his shoulder.

"I can prove that what I'm saying is true."

The man Michael knew as Shinjirō Kaminishi froze for a moment. Then he left the room, closing the door behind him.

CHAPTER FIVE

MICHAEL OPENED the locker at Kyoto Station and pulled out his backpack.

The train to Tokyo was leaving in three minutes. He had just enough time to pull out his ticket to show the clerk and run to catch the train.

His mind was a whirlwind of thoughts and emotions.

Shintarō had been gone from the room for about a half hour when the door had abruptly opened.

Shintarō threw his jacket at him. "This is what you are going to do," he began without preamble. "There is a train to Kyoto that is leaving in twenty minutes. You will be on that train. From there, you will take the next available train to Tokyo Narita. Within the next twelve hours, you will leave Japan."

"No."

"Yes. And this is why. If you do not do as I say, I will file a complaint with the Osaka police department stating that I saw you kill a man."

Michael stared. "You can't do that."

Shintarō laughed. "Holden-san. My clan may not be large or extremely powerful, but I hold a high position within it. There are many who owe favors to me. Please trust me when I say this is something I can make happen."

"But you can't say that I killed somebody when—" He stopped, appalled. "My God. You wouldn't."

Shintarō gave him a dead-level stare. "Are you willing to take that chance?"

He came toward Michael, who for the first time felt a small thrill of fear.

"You say you know me from a time long ago. You say that I was a daimyō, a samurai warlord. I say this is nonsense—but can you say what kind of man I am today? Do you know me? I am Shintarō Kawakami, the son of a yakuza oyabun, who will one day succeed him in leading a thousand men. If you do not leave this country in the next twelve hours, you will spend the rest of your life in prison here." The glint in his eye faded, and he spoke normally again. "There is a car outside waiting to drive you to the station. Go."

MICHAEL CLOSED his eyes.

The late-evening train to Tokyo was not crowded; he had almost an entire section to himself.

There had been no time to think, which he was sure was part of Shintarō's strategy. He had wanted Michael to panic, to be able to think of nothing but leaving Japan as quickly as possible.

But flashes of the last twenty-four hours kept running through his head. The startled look in Shintarō's eye when he first saw Michael at Kyoto Station; his calm in Michael's presence, as though he knew Michael somehow; the glint in his eye when he'd threatened him.

That last was telling. He probably thought he had successfully intimidated Michael. He definitely *had* intimidated him—no question. But that actually revealed the truth on a whole other level to Michael.

For a few moments, the façade of the contemporary, educated yakuza businessman had fallen away, and what was revealed was the soul of a warlord. A samurai warlord. For a few moments, Michael had unmistakably seen the soul of Shinjirō Kaminishi showing itself.

A man who led, who commanded without question or doubt. Shinjirō.

He opened his eyes, staring out the train window at the Kansai night landscape rushing by.

At first he figured he would go ahead and leave the country. Shintarō probably had ways to check to make sure that he got on the plane. But obviously he could then just turn around and come back. Shintarō might be able to find out that he'd returned, but before he could do anything to Michael, Michael could work to convince Shintarō of the truth.

And if all else failed, he had *that*.

His trump card.

The dark night flashed by outside. He had ridden in the back of a pumpkin seller's wagon along this same route one hundred and sixty years ago. Only this time he was rushing away from Shinjirō, not toward him.

The thought sobered him. This was the opposite of what he wanted, of why he had come to Japan.

There has to be some way out of this.

He absently felt for his passport in his jacket's inside pocket. He took it out, and it fell open to the first few pages, showing the most recent stamp for his entry into Japan.

He stared at the official stamp. He had arrived at Tokyo's Narita Airport, and on his first night in Japan, in his hotel room in Ikebukuro, he had contemplated (after a few cups of sake, granted) tearing out the rest of the pages in the passport. He knew he wouldn't be needing those extra passport pages. He was in Japan for good, because he would find Shinjirō and then everything would be all right.

Michael turned the blank pages, one after the next. How many entry and exit stamps would these pages eventually hold? Would it take repeated tries to get Shintarō to listen to him? The thought depressed him.

He was about to stop before the final page when something made him finger it. It felt thick, like something was behind it. His heart started pounding as he turned the page over.

There was a folded piece of vellum paper neatly taped to the back side.

He stared at it, mouth going dry.

He gently lifted it off the page, the tape coming away easily, and opened it with shaking fingers.

The text on the page was in handwritten Japanese script with a lot of kanji characters, and Michael fumbled in his pack for his kanji dictionary. When he'd finished the translation, he stared at the page for some time.

It began without salutation:

I do not know when you will read this. I only wanted to leave you with some sense that you were not entirely mistaken.

CHAPTER SIX

HE RUSHED off the train at Nagoya and ran with his backpack up the stairs, across the bridge, and down the stairs to the other platform, the one for trains headed westbound.

He was returning to Kyoto.

Once he'd settled in his seat on the train, he took out the note and smoothed it between his hands to read the characters again.

> *I do not know when you will read this. I only wanted to leave you with some sense that you were not entirely mistaken.*
>
> *When I was a young child, my mother said I talked all the time about living in a castle, and fighting with a sword, and holding the destiny of Japan in my hands. She took it to be the fantasy of a young boy. I myself have no memories now of this.*
>
> *I have, however, had many dreams through the years, where faces of persons I do not know have come before me with such vividness that it is logical to conclude that they were people I knew in past lives.*
>
> *In recent months, your face came to me in such dreams. I have no way of knowing what our past association may have been. I do recall a sense of profound incompletion associated with seeing you.*
>
> *In sum, I cannot say with certainty that what you told me is incorrect. Your feelings for me, however, are misguided. Whether I am in fact the reincarnated soul of this daimyō has no bearing on who I am today. My path in life is set and seems unlikely to change. You*

are a young man and should afford yourself of the
many opportunities available to you in life. Please
forget about me.

    Shintarō Kawakami

Michael took a deep breath, then let it out.
Shinjirō.
He had to trust that he would know what to do once he saw
Shintarō again.

HE SLEPT little that night.
    Having checked in to an expensive hotel near Kyoto Station—not
having the energy to bother looking for anything cheaper or less fancy
that late at night—he lay in bed, drifting off for a few minutes here and
there but remaining restless through the night.
    Morning came, and Michael, exhausted, ordered a room service
breakfast. He finished eating and was paging idly through the
newspaper when a photograph and caption suddenly caught his
attention.
    It was Shintarō.
    The caption read that the distinguished Shintarō Kawakami
would be cutting the opening ceremony ribbon at Kyoto's newest elite
restaurant, the Miyako, that evening at 8:00 p.m.
    He carefully ripped out Shintarō's photograph and tucked it into
his wallet.

THE MIYAKO was only a few blocks from Kyoto Station, so he
waited until 7:45 to leave his hotel.
    He had shopped for clothes and shoes that afternoon, figuring that
dressing well was key to managing to get into the event somehow.
    When the time came, however, Michael found it to be no
problem. Apparently a well-dressed gaijin ducking back inside through

a side door after taking a fresh air break in the alley outside wasn't considered an unusual event by the security guards.

He walked quickly down the hallway toward the party.

MICHAEL ENTERED the restaurant, where a crowd was mingling and music was playing.

The lights were low, which helped, as he didn't want to stand out too much. As it was, there were other non-Japanese there, so fortunately he wasn't the only one.

After getting a drink at the hosted bar, he scanned the room for Shintarō. Most of the men were in dark business suits, and he wondered which of them were yakuza. He wondered if Shintarō had bodyguards around him all the time.

He wondered if that would be difficult to live with.

The opening ceremony looked like it was going to be held in the front of the room, judging by the cloth-covered table, champagne in ice buckets, and podium with microphone.

Michael saw a man enter the front of the room. Shintarō.

He was in a dark suit with white shirt, hair perfectly styled, smiling for the photographers. Michael watched as he made his way toward the podium, where an older gentleman waited to introduce him.

As the man started his introductory speech, Shintarō stood silently by the podium. He was vulnerable, Michael thought suddenly.

Michael looked around the crowd. Where were Shintarō's men? He supposed it was unrealistic to expect his men to stand at his side while he was being introduced, but something about this didn't feel right. Like... something was about to happen—

Far across the room, he saw a man reaching into his jacket.

The glint of metal.

A gun.

Michael was closer to Shintarō than to the man, so he did the best thing he could think of in a split second.

He ran forward and tackled Shintarō to the ground.

Shots rang out in the dimly lit room. People screamed and ran for cover.

Michael was lying on top of Shintarō. "Get off me," Shintarō said. He pushed Michael aside and got to his feet, then ran after the gunman, who'd exited the room through the same door Shintarō had entered a few minutes before.

Michael got up and ran after Shintarō.

THE SUMMER night air in downtown Kyoto was hot and balmy.

Michael caught sight of Shintarō, now with his men, running headlong down the alley, and took off after them.

The alley exited onto a narrow side street lined with izakaya restaurants and bars. At some point Shintarō became separated from his men. Michael kept his eye on Shintarō, who put on a burst of speed and turned a corner up ahead. Michael groaned inwardly. *He's ten years older than me. He shouldn't be able to outrun me....* He did his best to keep up, dashing into traffic after the man to the tune of startled drivers and honking cars.

Down another dark alley... and then... a dead end.

Finally he caught up to Shintarō, who stood staring at the wall that marked the end of the alley. They were in a small rectangular area ringed with large trash cans. Moonlight slanted down and gave a bit of illumination. Dark shadows dominated the dead end.

Michael got a weird feeling all of a sudden. "Shinjirō-sama—"

Then he felt a heavy *thud* to the back of his head.

MICHAEL OPENED his eyes. He was lying on the floor in a room with bars on the windows. Again.

He felt the back of his neck, rubbing it.

"Are you all right?"

Michael turned his head. Shintarō was sitting against the wall, knees to his chest, looking very relaxed, considering the circumstances.

The room had a single lamp on a small low table and tatami mats on the floor. There were two windows, both of which were barred.

It was still night outside. "I think it is around 2:00 or 3:00 a.m., judging by the position of the moon," Shintarō remarked.

"Where are we?"

"I don't know. I woke up in here, the same as yourself."

Michael sat up and moved his head from side to side to get the kinks out.

"My uncle Jirō always says I have a reckless streak. I must conclude he is correct, after this. I don't believe I'll ever live down running straight into an ambush."

Michael started, then stared at Shintarō. "Wait, you're speaking English."

He knew something had sounded odd.

Shintarō laughed. It was a warm sound. "I had an American girlfriend—many years ago," he said. "Though it's hard to keep up with it. It requires practice." He was missing his suit jacket but still wore the white shirt and dark slacks. Michael noticed his own jacket was missing.

"They have our wallets, phones, everything that we were carrying." Shintarō still seemed oddly relaxed.

"I see. You don't seem too worried."

"Well, I think they missed their opportunity," Shintarō said, "and now they're having second thoughts. You see, in this situation, Holden-san, if they were confident of their position, you and I would be dead by now. The fact that it is hours later and no one has come for us means they realized they made a mistake. I expect they are discussing the situation with their superiors, trying to find the best way out of this."

"Who do you think they are?"

"I can guess," Shintarō said, grimacing. "The neighboring clan, the Shiromuras, are not well disposed toward me. Though they have never gone quite this far before. I have no idea what they were thinking, to actually try to kill me. And this after we made a deal with them only last year."

Michael stood up and walked around the room, stretching his legs. He looked out the windows and saw nothing but rice fields, their watery surfaces glistening in the moonlight. There was a doorway into a small dark room that contained a toilet and sink. He saw the door.

"It's locked, of course," Shintarō said, watching him.

He continued to watch as Michael approached him and sat at his side with his back against the wall. Michael's left shoulder was mere inches from Shintarō's right shoulder. "Sumimasen," Michael said. "I have an apology to make to you." He turned to look at Shintarō, who gazed back calmly. "I still believe that you are Shinjirō Kaminishi," Michael said. "But you are also who you are in this lifetime. For me to barge into your life and act as though you are simply the man I knew in late-Edo Japan was rude of me. I am truly sorry, Kawakami-san," he finished, bowing his head.

Shintarō inclined his head politely. "There is nothing to be sorry for," he said. "If you believe all that you've said to me, then your treatment of me is understandable."

"I expect you're just humoring me in this. But I appreciate it anyway."

"None of us knows what came before our birth," Shintarō said. "I would be patronizing indeed if I were just humoring you. What brought you back to Kyoto?"

"I read your note."

Shintarō raised an eyebrow. "Oh. I didn't think you would read it for a very long time."

"Do you believe what I'm saying, since you've experienced some evidence of it yourself?" Michael switched to Japanese, hoping that Shintarō might be more forthcoming with the ease of speaking in his native language.

"I don't know," Shintarō replied honestly. "As I said in the note, I don't have any solid memories of this past life. I can say that yes, I have seen you in my dreams."

"Were we together in the castle?"

"That I cannot say," Shintarō said. "The details are unclear. I did recognize you, however, at Kyoto Station."

Michael waited, but Shintarō seemed disinclined to add anything further. "I came to Japan a few months ago. I knew that you were here and that I would find you. And now, I don't know... what to say to you." He stared into Shintarō's beautiful eyes. "You are... *you*, and yet somebody else. I have no right to be a part of your life, and yet this is why I came all the way here."

"Assuming you were meant to, would you choose to be involved with me? I am gokudō, after all," Shintarō said, using the word yakuza used to refer to themselves.

Gokudō. Gangster.

He opened his mouth to respond but then closed it, lost in thought. When he'd gotten involved with Shinjirō before, though he was a prisoner, it had been of his own free will. Shinjirō was a samurai warlord, as exotic and far removed from Michael's life as things could get, and yet... it was the man he connected with, the man underneath the role.

This man—Shintarō Kawakami—was a yakuza gangster, but there was a man underneath that role too.

And more than that, he was also Shinjirō Kaminishi.

"Yes," he finally replied.

Shintarō held his gaze for a moment, then looked away. "You are an unusual man," he said.

"So are you."

"How do you mean?"

"Most men would react badly to another man's interest," Michael said. "Unless... you are...?"

Shinjirō—Kawakami-san—laughed. "Perhaps our unusual situation at the moment is giving rise to such frankness," he said, his eyes crinkling with mirth at the corners. "This is a topic that many in my family would give their right arms to discuss with me." His eyes grew serious. "I will not, however, discuss it with you at this time."

"Sumimasen. I understand."

Shintarō rose abruptly from the floor and walked to the window. Michael stood up as well but remained where he was. Shintarō stared out at the night. The building they were held in was completely silent;

whoever their captors were, they were either on the other side of the building or had left completely. Being in the room with Shintarō under these circumstances gave the moment a kind of timeless quality.

Maybe our relationship isn't centered in time, but something else.

Michael couldn't even begin to say what that thought meant. He leaned back against the wall and continued to watch Shintarō.

The man sighed and turned back from the window. "We may as well get some sleep," he said, coming back to where Michael stood. "Nothing is going to happen until morning."

Michael looked down as Shintarō settled himself on the floor, propping his back against the wall again. He then seated himself in similar fashion, leaning back against the wall, closing his eyes.

HE WOKE with a start, still sitting against the wall, his face resting on his knees, which were pulled against his chest.

The small lamp was still on, giving off a soft illumination from the corner of the room. Michael turned to see Shintarō standing with his ear to the door, listening.

He waited until Shintarō came away from the door to ask, "Hear anything?"

Shintarō shook his head slightly. "I thought I heard something, but...." He went to the window again and looked out.

Michael got up and joined him at the window. "Still dark out. No sign of dawn yet."

"Yes."

He gazed at Shintarō's profile, knowing the man was aware he was being watched. Shintarō continued looking out the window until he closed his eyes and laughed softly.

Michael caught his breath.

Shintarō's eyes when he turned to face Michael were unexpectedly soft. "You called my bluff about going to the police."

"What?" Michael stared; then he remembered. "I knew you wouldn't do it."

"How so?" Shintarō took a step toward him, into the moonlight shining in through the window. "How can you say you know anything about me? I could be anything—a murderer, a rapist, a pathological liar." He came closer as Michael felt his heart start to pound. "Was I cruel? Did I force you? It was a different world back then. Daimyō could do anything they wanted to in their domains. Their word was law."

"No. You were—" Michael stopped himself. "Shinjirō Kaminishi was... representative of his time. He ruled strictly but fairly, according to what life was like then. He was an exemplary leader. In personal relations, he showed consideration and even kindness."

Shintarō went still for a moment; then he laughed softly again. "He sounds like a character out of a novel. You must be disappointed, finding his soul reincarnated as a yakuza."

"I'm not disappointed at all." Michael stared calmly at Shintarō, who stood very close to him now. "I will accept whatever you are."

There was a pause, and then Shintarō took Michael's hand and placed it on his groin. Michael started, feeling the hardness there. He glanced at Shintarō's face as Shintarō moved his hand against his growing erection.

Michael was getting hard as well. Shintarō's cock swelled, and he held Michael's hand away for a moment as he worked to open his fly with his other hand.

When his cock was free, he pushed down on Michael's shoulder. Michael went to his knees without a word, took out Shintarō's cock, and began to suck.

CHAPTER SEVEN

MICHAEL NURSED Shintarō to a full erection using his lips and tongue, then took him into his mouth.

He heard the man groan somewhere above his head and relaxed his throat to take in even more of him.

Shintarō's hand twisted in his hair, holding Michael's face close. Michael's world was reduced to the cock in his mouth, and he put everything he had into it, reveling in the connection with Shintarō that was being allowed for these few precious minutes.

Shintarō tasted faintly of sweat and urine and his own musk, a familiar warmth that surrounded Michael and flooded him with memories and emotions. His own cock ached as he sucked Shintarō's erection, tears forming in his eyes. *Shinjirō.*

Memories of other Kansai nights, hot and steamy and filled with the feel of slick skin and muscles and burning-hot arousal, echoed in every cell in his body. He remembered every feeling and sensation the daimyō ever aroused in him, and he tried to convey this remembered passion in every movement of his tongue, every bit of suction his mouth could manage.

Shinjirō. Shinjirō. I love you.

WHEN IT was finished and he had swallowed everything and cleaned off Shintarō's cock with his tongue, Shintarō sank down to the floor.

He pulled Michael toward him, gently guiding him to lie with his head on his lap. Michael placed his head on Shintarō's thigh, reaching to hook one arm around his knee.

He didn't need to ask to know he hadn't been Shintarō's first man.

His own arousal was still painfully there, but he focused on breathing deeply in and out, slowing his heartbeat. He was content just to be lying with Shintarō, feeling the warmth of his body on his cheek.

He soon fell asleep.

When he next opened his eyes, it was morning. He was lying curled up on the floor and sunlight was streaming into the room.

Several things happened at once. He saw Shintarō coming out of the bathroom, and at the same time, he heard voices and footsteps approaching the room.

He and Shintarō made eye contact. He stood up slowly as Shintarō walked toward the door and stood there, waiting for whoever it was to open it.

The door opened, and Michael tensed until he saw Shintarō smile and move to greet the older man standing there.

"Jirō Ojisan."

He watched as Shintarō embraced the man affectionately.

MICHAEL TRIED not to cough as Shintarō's cigarette smoke filled the Mercedes's interior.

The Mercedes moved through the suburban Kyoto streets, finally ending up at a familiar site: the house where Michael had seen Shintarō while hiding in the bushes.

The gate opened, and the car pulled up in front of a large but otherwise unpretentious house.

When Michael got out of the car, following Shintarō and his uncle, a small beautifully dressed older woman opened the front door and came out to greet them. Shintarō's mother, he guessed.

He stood by as Shintarō repeated the same thing he had told his uncle at the warehouse—it had been a warehouse where they'd been held—telling his mother that this gaikokujin was the one who'd saved his life when the shots rang out.

Michael accepted Shintarō's mother's thanks, bowing to her as she welcomed him inside.

MICHAEL WAS relieved to learn that no one had been injured at the Miyako the evening before; the shots had missed all the patrons.

Shintarō's mother, Mariko Kawakami, led him to a Western-style dining room table, and they all sat down to eat. Michael found he was starving.

The house was furnished in an expensive but nonostentatious way. The furniture and wall decorations were modern Japanese in style; he noticed a formal low table and tatami mats over in the large living room. Nothing about the house stood out as being a gangster family's home.

Mariko-san had prepared a traditional Japanese breakfast of fish, rice, and miso soup with pickled radishes and green tea. He and Shintarō ate their fill, replenishing their energy after the long and mostly sleepless night.

After breakfast, Mariko asked Michael if he would like to rest in the guest bedroom and take a hot bath if he wanted. To his surprise, Shintarō told her no. "I would like Holden-san to be present while we discuss matters," he said. When both Mariko and Jirō looked startled, Shintarō merely said, "I have my reasons. He knows we are gokudō. We can speak freely in front of him."

He looked at Michael, who could only manage a short nod.

For better or for worse, Shintarō had just included him in the family.

They adjourned to the living room, taking places on the tatami mats around the low table.

Formal introductions were made. Michael understood by now that Jirō was the oyabun, or clan leader, and that Shintarō was the designated heir to the clan.

Jirō had important news. Shintarō's boss, Hiroshi Satō, had gone missing.

Satō was the saikō-komon, or legal and business advisor to the clan, in charge of negotiating transactions and formalizing deals. When they'd found he'd gone missing, Jirō called in their IT expert to break into Satō's computer files. It appeared that Satō had been skimming profits off the top, the money disappearing to who knew where. Also, there was some indication that Satō had been meeting in secret with Ryōta Shiromura. Jirō speculated that Satō may have been extorting funds or other concessions from the future Shiromura leader and blaming it on Shintarō—hence the assassination attempt.

Throughout this discussion, Michael sat in seiza, silently sipping his green tea and contemplating what Shintarō's life must be like. Shintarō had shown not the least bit of shock at any of this. Was this everyday life in the gokudō world? Betrayal. Attempted murder.

All in a day's work.

He couldn't fathom it.

Shintarō said he would check the files himself that afternoon, but Mariko told him that the police would be coming by at 2:00 p.m. to interview him about last night's incident. Michael was dryly amused that the police made appointments to interview people when they were high-level yakuza. "I'll check the files after that, then," Shintarō said. "There's something of importance that I need to say before we adjourn."

He looked at each of them in turn. "I have always considered the interests of our family and of the clan to come first, as my father did. It is with that in mind that I propose the following." Shintarō paused, then glanced at Michael before speaking again.

"I propose that I be officially expulsed from the clan."

MICHAEL SAT curled up in the armchair, staring out at the Kyoto night sky.

He was back in his hotel room. When Jirō had come to release them, they'd found their jackets and personal items left on a table in one of the warehouse's rooms. Apparently the goons had really been spooked by what they'd done. Even their cash was intact.

So he'd had no trouble reentering his room at his hotel. He stared down at the cars and pedestrians on the streets below, lost in thought.

JIRŌ HADN'T seemed surprised by what Shintarō said, but Shintarō's mother was.

There was a long conversation after that, but Shintarō's mind was made up. "This is an opportunity for the clan as well as for myself," he stated. "Ryōta will continue to cause trouble as long as I am here. If it turns out that the information is correct, then Satō-san wronged the Shiromura clan in what he did.

"However," Shintarō continued, "Ryōta really fucked up in trying to have me killed, and their side already knows this. They should be looking for a way to mitigate what they've done to avoid a gang war. If I leave the clan and move out of the Kansai region, this accomplishes two things: one, it takes me out of the equation in dealing with Ryōta, and two, it puts the Shiromura clan in our clan's debt. This family would have an advantage over them for years if it played its cards right."

He turned to Jirō. "Ojisan, you know that I have never truly wished to take over this clan. If anyone besides yourself, that position belongs to Takeshi Ojisan."

"What about you?" Jirō asked curiously. "What will you do?"

Shintarō blinked; then he smiled a little.

"I believe I will be moving back to Tokyo."

SO MUCH had happened, and so quickly, that Michael hadn't had time to absorb all of it.

It was decided that there was no point in Michael staying at the house and being subjected to questioning by the police. The police apparently hadn't discovered Michael's identity, and the gaijin who'd saved Shintarō Kawakami's life wasn't a suspect anyway. Michael agreed to return to his hotel room and wait for further word, as Jirō was going to meet with old man Ryōga Shiromura, head of the Shiromura clan, later that evening to talk over the deal.

Shintarō walked him out to the car, where the driver was waiting. "I'll come by tonight after Jirō's meeting," he told Michael. "Please wait for me."

And so Michael found himself in his room. He'd taken a hot bath and changed clothes, and now he was sitting and waiting, more or less, for his future to be decided.

His future with Shinjirō—the man known as Shintarō Kawakami.

Around 10:00 p.m. there was a knock on the door. Michael went to open it.

Shintarō entered the room, and Michael felt his pulse quicken.

He shut the door and followed Shintarō to the window, where he stood and lit a cigarette. "It's been settled," he said. "The Shiromuras have agreed to what I proposed."

"Are you sure this is what you want?"

Shintarō looked at him, then took a drag. "Yes."

"Isn't it a bit sudden, all this?"

"You mean leaving the yakuza? Not really. I've felt this way for a long time. I expect everything feels sudden to you since you've only known me for a few days." His mouth quirked. "You might give a thought as to how this must feel for *me*."

Michael laughed wryly. "Sorry. Yes, I suppose the story I told you is even more of an adjustment for you than being exposed to the yakuza for a few days has been for me."

He sat down in the armchair. "Though I can't say what I've seen hasn't shocked me. Did you confirm what they said about your boss—"

"Yes," Shintarō said. "He was doing just as Jirō Ojisan suspected. Satō-san left on a midnight flight to Hong Kong last night. No one knows where he went after that."

He stared out the window morosely.

"Were you close to him?"

"No," Shintarō said honestly, "but I did think I knew him better than that."

Michael watched Shintarō silently, taking in every inch of his long lean frame and the beautiful face he feared he'd never see again. Though it was miraculous that he was here with him again in modern-day Japan, the moment felt tenuous. The uncertainty made him say, "If you're moving to Tokyo, I would like to come with you."

Shintarō stared at Michael. "What?"

"I will go with you to Tokyo," Michael said, rising from the armchair and coming to Shintarō's side. "Let me be with you."

"No."

"Why not?"

"Just no," Shintarō said. He moved around Michael to stub out his cigarette butt in the ashtray on the small table.

"I won't ask anything more of you. Just let me be by your side, for whatever comes next in your life."

Shintarō shook his head, but Michael sensed him opening slightly to the idea. "No strings attached. I won't pressure you in any way."

Shintarō grabbed him by the arm, pulling him close. "This is absurd," he said roughly. "You are a complete stranger to me. You have no claim on my life, my time. Why are you doing this?"

I could ask the same of you, Michael thought. *Why are you doing this?* Shintarō's grasp on his arm was painfully tight, and he had pulled Michael to him as if he wanted him in his space. *If you're trying to push me away, why are you holding me like you're afraid I'm going to leave?*

Then it hit him. *You're attracted to me as well. You want me. You may not believe anything I've said, but you want me.*

He lifted a hand to Shintarō's face, gently laying it on his cheek.

Shintarō's eyes widened. His grip on Michael's arm loosened.

Michael took Shintarō's hand and led him to the bed. Somewhat to his surprise, Shintarō came along without any resistance.

Michael sat down on the bed as Shintarō stood in front of him, watching as he began to unzip his fly. "I had never been with a man before," he said, reaching inside to take out Shintarō's cock. "I had no idea what to do. But I wanted to please him." He leaned forward and, with his tongue, flicked the tip. He heard Shintarō catch his breath slightly.

"I didn't realize it at the time, but I already loved him," Michael continued. He gently pulled the foreskin down and opened his mouth, blowing warm air onto the tip before placing his tongue there and lightly dragging it across.

Shintarō moaned softly then, and Michael began to suck, caressing his shaft with a firm, warm hand.

As his breathing grew ragged, one of Shintarō's hands landed on Michael's shoulder, gripping almost desperately.

Michael concentrated on pleasuring him, the occasional wet sucking noise the only sound in the room. When he had nearly brought Shintarō to climax, Shintarō suddenly pushed him down on the bed.

He climbed on top of Michael, removing his own clothing below the waist. He pressed his groin down on Michael's, and Michael gasped.

Shintarō straddled him as he removed his jacket and shirt. In the dimly lit hotel room, Michael saw a dark swath on Shintarō's upper right chest and shoulder—a tattoo. He couldn't make out the design.

Shintarō began impatiently removing Michael's clothes, handling him roughly, shoving Michael's hands aside when he tried to assist.

When Michael was as naked as he was, Shintarō reached behind himself for something, then moved Michael up the bed. He grabbed Michael's hands and yanked them over his head, then secured his wrists together with his belt.

Michael stared at Shintarō's chest as he felt his wrists being tied to the headboard.

Once Shintarō had finished, he moved back down to stare into Michael's eyes. His own eyes suddenly softened, and he let one finger trail down Michael's cheek in a drifting caress.

Michael closed his eyes.

The hand traced to his neck and then his chest. Michael felt his left nipple being rubbed. He arched up slightly, moving against Shintarō's balls. Shintarō grunted softly. He lowered his head and tongued the other nipple while continuing to rub the left one.

Shintarō's hands and mouth were so gentle on his body, Michael wondered at the difference. Shintarō had been almost violent with him before he was tied up, but now he was hesitant in his touches.

Shintarō massaged his flanks lightly, then moved down to touch Michael's balls, caressing the underside with his fingertips. Michael, eyes still closed, gasped softly, and Shintarō took this as encouragement. His warm hand palmed his balls. Michael drew his knees up, spreading his legs apart so Shintarō had better access.

The hand was removed, and Shintarō lowered his face. Then he was licking the underside of Michael's cock.

Michael's breathing quickened. He squirmed lewdly, the sensations maddeningly arousing. Shintarō's fingers tentatively touched his cock, and his tongue moved to the tip.

Michael could feel his hesitation, and realized, *Oh. He's never done this before.* Some of Shintarō's behavior was becoming clear to him now. The mouth on his cock moved from lightly sucking the tip down the side of the shaft, and Michael made a low, encouraging noise in his throat.

At one point Shintarō choked a bit. Michael found himself thinking, *You don't have to do this. There are other ways*—and in that moment, Shintarō pulled himself up and seated himself on Michael's upper thighs, straddling him again.

He took hold of both their cocks in his two hands and began working them, hands moving up and down.

Yes. Michael breathed. *Good.*

He opened his eyes and watched Shintarō manipulate their cocks. The man had his eyes closed, expressions playing across his face with each stroke.

Michael moved against his bonds. Being restrained heightened the tension in his whole body, which made his arousal almost unbearable. He pulled on his bonds impatiently, moving his hips under Shintarō.

Their eyes met then, and Shintarō's eyes darkened with pure lust. Michael lay still, watching him. The tattoo was more visible now. From the front, it was a blue-green fish—a carp—with its body spilling over Shintarō's right shoulder and presumably down his back.

Shintarō began again, slower and more deliberately, his eyes on Michael as he moved his hands up and down their shafts, his fingers squeezing on the upstroke. "Please," Michael said softly, undulating his hips.

He began a slow rhythm, working in time with Shintarō's hands pumping their cocks together, until they were both at the brink.

Shinjirō-sama.

He was more vocal than Shintarō when he came, gasping, the pulses of high sensation coming in waves. He heard Shintarō catch his breath sharply and felt his body still for a moment, his thigh muscles clutching Michael's hips, and then he let out a long sigh.

Michael's eyes were closed as he laid there, his body going slack, his mind not thinking of anything.

He became dimly aware of Shintarō's body over his own; he was reaching up to untie Michael. Then he lay down next to Michael, an arm across his chest to keep him close.

Michael circled his arm around Shintarō's back, holding him.

This Shinjirō was... the same, and yet mysteriously, surprisingly *different*.

He was two men in one, and Michael knew that if he ever forgot this, he would regret it. He was as much Shintarō Kawakami as he was Shinjirō Kaminishi.

He resolved to love them both.

This twenty-first-century man was a man in command like Shinjirō had been, but he was more vulnerable. He was certainly intimidating in his own way, but something about him felt less commanding. The yakuza, as fierce as they could be, were still no match for the samurai.

Shintarō's face was against Michael's cheek, his breathing peaceful. *Perhaps being in the modern age made for a less controlling man—*

"Don't let me sleep," Shintarō said suddenly. He spoke next to Michael's ear, and Michael started. "I have to leave in a few minutes."

—or not.

Michael smiled.

"Hai."

HE LET Shintarō drowse for a few minutes, then gently squeezed his shoulder, the one with the fish on it.

"Kawakami-san."

Shintarō stirred, then sleepily lifted himself off Michael's body.

He sat on the edge of the bed and discreetly used the bedsheet to wipe the semen off his abdomen, then got dressed.

Michael sat up in bed, watching him. For some reason he was content to sit like this instead of assisting Shintarō or getting dressed himself so he could see him to the door. Part of it was postorgasmic lassitude, but it was also the calm that came with relief.

The gamble he'd taken in coming to Japan had paid off. He'd found Shinjirō.

Whatever came next, he could face. The adrift feeling he'd had all his life had come to an end.

He'd found his home.

"Kawakami-san," he said, as Shintarō finished dressing.

"We will have tickets for the 6:00 p.m. train to Tokyo tomorrow," Shintarō said. "Please be ready to leave by five-thirty."

"I have a favor to ask of you."

"Yes?"

Michael held his gaze. "Tomorrow afternoon, there is somewhere that I would like you to visit with me."

IT TURNED out that Shintarō kept a two-bedroom apartment in Kyoto's city center, and he needed to go home to get a few things packed and to leave instructions for the movers. For some reason, Michael had imagined Shintarō lived at his family's house, even though he was thirty-two years old. *You've watched too many yakuza movies.* He grinned wryly at himself.

He packed his things and waited to be picked up in front of the hotel. When the black Mercedes arrived, not only Shintarō, but Shintarō's mother and uncle Jirō were inside.

Shintarō put Michael's bag into the trunk. "We'll not have much time, wherever it is we're going," he told Michael.

"That's all right."

"Then let's go."

THE SMOOTHLY paved road became gradually steeper as it led toward the mountains.

At the top of the road, the foothills began, with an overgrowth of tall grass climbing up the slope.

"Please stop the car," Michael said.

He and Shintarō got out, Shintarō asking his family to wait for them, and Michael indicated that they should walk up the hillside. There was a partially obscured pathway that halfway up became a set of old wooden steps.

This was all shops and small rickety houses. The streets were made of dirt. The fires were dancing in the night sky, lighting the way for the townspeople and farmers to revel in their masks.

And Shinjirō was standing there....

A clearing came into view as they reached the top of the steps. Only a few corners and remnants of stone foundations remained of what had once been Kaminishi Castle.

Shinjirō's castle.

He turned to find Shintarō staring at him curiously. He smiled and glanced at a crumbled piece of wall off to the side. "I think that was probably the southeast corner of the castle," he said matter-of-factly. "I was never in that section, so I don't know what rooms were there."

Michael turned to gaze at a large stone area on the ground. "That was probably the main entry area," he continued. He moved from spot to spot, explaining what room had been there, with Shintarō trailing behind him like a confused tourist.

When he'd found the castle here in Kameoka on his last day before he'd intended to leave for Nagasaki, it was as if a spell had been cast over him.

He'd walked through the ruins, feeling the weight of the past on him like a shroud. Then, the fact that he'd actually found Kaminishi Castle wasn't a cause for celebration, but more like a knife through the heart.

It had all been real. And he had been responsible for Shinjirō's death.

The grief he'd felt had led him back to Kyoto, and every bar he could find. Though he'd known in his heart that it was all real and true and had happened, a small part of him had wished it was only his mind playing tricks in a dream state. But he could no longer hold on to this illusion.

He'd been grief-stricken then. But now, his having found the castle again served another role, another purpose. It might be the thread that led Shinjirō back to him....

He stopped suddenly and felt a strong sensation. This had been....

Michael looked at Shintarō, who had also stopped. Shintarō's face held an odd expression, and he was very still for a moment. Then....

"Maikoru."

Michael stared.

"This was... my room."

He stood still, not daring to breathe. "Hai. Shinjirō-sama."

Shintarō stared at the ground, not moving a millimeter. The wind riffled his hair slightly, and Michael imagined long straight hair flowing from a topknot made of upswept tendrils, moving gently in the breeze.

He watched as the man turned slowly to look at an area a small distance away. "There was running water there—and a garden—"

"—with rocks and sand and grass," Michael finished gently.

"It flowed underground," Shintarō said absently. "My father diverted it to flow through the castle."

Michael shivered a little. The breeze had picked up, and it felt like there was more than wind moving the air. The spirits of Kaminishi Castle surrounded them, greeting them—and saying good-bye.

Norio. Kanosuke.

Misako.

All of Shinjirō's ancestors were present. Michael couldn't see them, but he could feel them.

He lifted his head. *I'm sorry. And I thank you for the enormous gift of knowing Shinjirō. If I can, I will make the rest of his life a pleasant one.*

He felt them start to fade out, disappearing back to wherever it was they existed now.

He closed his eyes.

A small wind passed and was gone.

Michael risked a look at Shintarō. He was still standing in the same spot, but now he was gazing into the near distance. Then a small smile appeared on his face.

"They were all here just now, weren't they?" Shintarō said. "Incredible...."

The look on his face was one of wonder. Tears came to Michael's eyes. He opened his mouth to speak but couldn't get any words out.

"You will have to tell me everything," Shintarō said. "I want to know all that happened when we knew each other before."

"Yes. I will."

He wiped the tears away, then approached Shintarō, who turned to look at him. It was as if he were seeing Michael for the first time.

Michael met his gaze calmly.

I'm ready.

Tell me what you want from me. I'll give it to you. I came here for you.

I love you.

Shintarō suddenly pulled him close, crushing Michael to his chest in a fierce embrace. "I make no promises," he said into Michael's ear. "But stay with me now. We'll see what happens from here."

"Hai."

They stayed like that for a few more seconds, and then Shintarō was kissing him.

It was raw and passionate, and Michael rode the waves of feeling that ran through him. The heat of Shintarō's body pressed up against his own, here in the place where it all began, and his tongue plundering his mouth, literally overwhelmed his senses. He swayed in the man's embrace.

"Yes," Michael softly breathed in English.

THE OLDER man watched quietly from the shadows at the top of the stairs.

He had never been one to shock easily, so it didn't bother him to see his nephew kissing another man. He merely wondered how long Shintarō had known him, since they only appeared to have met sometime in the past few days.

Jirō Kawakami watched as the two men separated—reluctantly—and began to walk toward where he was, side by side.

His nephew seemed to walk with a lighter step than before. He looked more relaxed than Jirō had ever seen him.

I'm glad for you, Shintarō.

His gaze moved to the other man curiously.

Who are you? You, who have blown into my nephew's life like a whirlwind.

What an interesting gaijin.... When he went to Tokyo next month and stopped by to visit them, he'd have to get to know this foreigner better.

He stepped out of the shadows. "It's time to go."

THEY SAT in the backseat of the Mercedes as it swung away from the curb and proceeded down the street.

Neither spoke, but each felt the presence of the other by his side.

Michael couldn't help himself. *This might be the last time we....*

He turned his head to stare out the back window and watched the castle ruins start to grow smaller in the distance.

Out of the corner of his eye, he saw Shintarō turn to look as well.

They continued to look until the car turned the corner and the ruins disappeared from view.

OMAKE

Sapporo, Hokkaido, Japan
Five years later

THE TRAIN to Hakodate was two minutes late.

The old obāchan *tsked* and clutched her ticket in her frail hand.

She glanced around Sapporo's main train station, looking among the crowd for two familiar faces, and sighing a little when she didn't see them.

Ah, well. Soon.

The train pulled in, and she made her way to board one of the train cars. Within minutes, the train moved out of the station and headed toward the southern end of the island.

IT HAD been quite a week.

Four days earlier, her husband had died.

Hideo had been in poor health for the past two years, so in a sense she was at peace with his passing. He had been in pain on and off, and toward the end he'd seemed quite out of it, speaking of things from his childhood and holding long conversations out loud with his older brother, who had died a long time ago.

After phoning people, signing the death certificate, and making arrangements for a funeral in one week's time, oddly she had found herself at loose ends.

People came around, neighbors visited and made her tea. She was coping very well with the situation. Nothing out of the ordinary had happened until the night before last, when she found she couldn't sleep when she lay down in bed.

Either she fell asleep and had a dream, or else somehow she was awake and had been transported to another dimension, because suddenly there was Hideo, hovering in midair over the bed!

"Hey," Hideo said. "You awake?"

"What?"

"Kotori-chan."

She sat up in bed at that. No one but her second husband ever called her "little bird."

"Why are you here?"

Hideo, or his ghost, frowned. "What kind of thing is that to say? Don't you want to see me?"

"Of course. But aren't you dead?"

They had been an unusual couple. People had stared at their bluntness and odd sense of humor. But Hideo had always made her laugh.

"Well, yes. But it's great here. I mean, there's nothing to be afraid of. You wouldn't believe who I've seen here!"

She noticed suddenly that Hideo seemed much younger. He looked around thirty-five, which was how old he'd been when they had first met.

His little twinkling eyes... his big smile.

Oh, Hideo.

"You know, I'm supposed to come and get you pretty soon."

"Really?" Strangely she felt no fear. Life had been interesting, but to be honest, she was eighty-two and had had enough of it. "When?"

"Just soon. Oh—" Her husband turned around all of a sudden and seemed to be listening to someone. "Okay." He looked at her again. "Soon, ne?" he finished.

Then he was gone.

Somehow, against all odds, she had actually fallen asleep after that, or perhaps she had always been asleep. Nevertheless, when she woke up, a new realization came to her.

There was one thing left to do before she could go.

FIVE YEARS before, she'd had a moment of dizziness.

She was standing in the kitchen washing dishes when she felt her consciousness slipping out from under her.

She traveled in darkness for a brief moment, and then she was in a light-filled place with indistinct shadows around her. Though she couldn't see their faces, she knew they were people she'd known in a past life.

They were all in a place that she didn't know, yet which seemed somehow familiar.

This is a castle. The year is....

I was the concubine of a daimyō. My name was....

A stranger entered the daimyō's life—and mine.

Our lives were changed forever.

His name was—

She had a fleeting sense of all of them at the castle saying good-bye—and then she was back, standing at the sink with the water running.

She remembered some additional details over the next few days. Her name had been Misako, and the daimyō was named Shinjirō.

The stranger was a young American named Michael Holden.

Somehow he had traveled from this modern era back to Japan in the year 1851, and in doing so he had changed the course of her life and the daimyō's. But her moments in the light, standing in the castle, had taken place in present time. The two men were together again now, in *this* lifetime.

She never forgot the experience. Like many Shinto Buddhists, she believed in reincarnation, but it was one thing to believe in something and another to have a direct experience of it!

Once Hideo became ill, she thought about it many times. She wondered where the two men were today, if they were doing well. She thought about what came before and after one's lifetime here on earth. And as Hideo's condition deteriorated, she pondered the nature of the soul and what the point of life really was.

She didn't consider herself to be a deep person. But that unexplainable event from five years ago opened her mind to all the possibilities.

That was why she didn't think twice when, for no apparent reason, she felt inspired to buy a plane ticket to Sapporo and a train ticket from Sapporo to Hakodate. She spent the last day in her home cleaning and leaving instructions for people in neat envelopes on the dining room table, and the last night sleeping soundly in her bed.

THE WEATHER was clear and bright in Sapporo that day.

After she got off the plane, she spent the afternoon strolling through the downtown area, enjoying the fresh air. It had been many years since she'd been to Hokkaido, and the air of Japan's northernmost island had always invigorated her.

As she looked in shop windows, she began to notice a strange phenomenon: little glowing trails of light were coming off people. As a person turned, the little trail would come off the person's body and then slowly dissipate.

She stopped and looked at the traffic, the buildings, the bustling sidewalks full of people. Everything suddenly appeared to be made of light. The people and cars and buildings retained their shape and structure, but it was all light, a kind of beautiful, vibrant energy.

She blinked… and then everything went back to normal again.

But she couldn't help thinking that she'd seen beyond everyday reality, to the truth of all things.

AFTER ENJOYING tea and cake in a little tearoom, it was time to catch the train.

Sapporo's main train station was in the center of town. It was large and modern in its design, and she sat in the station and looked around her at the restaurants and shops, relaxing.

She felt at peace.

Soon.

It came to her without any fanfare that today was her last day on earth.

Well, good enough, she thought. *I'm more than ready to go.*

Her only regret was that she'd been unable to have children, but regret faded as time went on and other matters in life came before her.

Many old friends had died.

She would see them again. And Hideo.

The old obāchan stepped onto the train to Hakodate.

SHE SAT down on a bench seat that faced another bench seat. She supposed it was meant for families or business people traveling together, but something inside said she was supposed to sit there, so she did.

Not long after she set her purse down and arranged herself comfortably on the seat, she saw them.

Shinjirō was first, walking down the aisle of the train car. He wore a crisp white shirt with dark slacks and a dark leather jacket and carried a compact overnight bag.

Behind him came the young American man, Michael. He was dressed more casually. He carried an overnight bag and a second tote or shopping-type bag.

As the other seats were taken, Shinjirō approached her and politely inclined his head toward the empty bench seat facing her, and she nodded. He took the window seat, handing his bag to Michael to place on top of the rack along with his own bag.

She turned her face to the window, watching the Hokkaido landscape go by as the two men got settled.

They look well.

Michael took reading material out of the tote bag, a Tokyo newspaper and a food magazine, while Shinjirō looked out the train window.

He was still a strikingly handsome man, now nearing forty she guessed, though he wore it exceedingly well. His short, neatly trimmed hair was still black, and his porcelain skin looked youthful.

Astonishingly she felt something... down there.

A warm little rush of fluid and a pulse of desire.

She hadn't had a sexual thought in years.

Well, you did have sex with him. Many times.

The daimyō Shinjirō Kaminishi had been quite a lover. Her memories as Misako had surfaced in bits and pieces over the past five years, and some of what she remembered shocked and delighted her.

Yes. Quite a lover.

She turned her gaze to the other man. Michael would be nearing thirty now. His light brown hair had grown long enough to be pulled back in a ponytail. When his gentle blue eyes met her own, he smiled. His even features brought back memories of a night's walk through a bamboo grove and the sorrow of betrayal.

She recalled his determination to find Shinjirō in Edo and save him.

How are the two of you together again?

She couldn't figure it out. This was the same Michael she had known, and this was Shinjirō, though there was an overlay of another man that she could discern. The two men, Shinjirō Kaminishi and this modern Japanese man he also was, coexisted in some sense.

She closed her eyes and suddenly got it: *he was a yakuza who turned legitimate and was now a businessman.* She wondered if he knew about his past life, especially his experiences with Michael.

She had a feeling he did.

You both know, don't you.

The obāchan gazed at Shinjirō with a penetrating stare until the man returned the look. His eyes met hers and he blinked, startled.

At that moment Michael handed him his newspaper, and she smirked a little. *Do I look familiar to you, even a little bit?* One never thought about what their lovers would look like old when one was young. Had Misako lived to old age, that is. Her life had ended in her twenties, at the hands of two violent customers in the Yoshiwara.

She repressed a shudder, hiding it by searching in her purse for her wallet. The bento girl was coming round with her cart.

One last cup of green tea would taste very good.

SHE INITIATED some small talk with the two men under the guise of being a lonely and somewhat nosy old lady on a train ride with nothing better to do.

Michael's Japanese skills were excellent now; he spoke with only the slightest trace of American accent, and that just on certain words.

His "friend and roommate" Shintarō Kawakami—apparently Shinjirō's modern identity—had worked in real estate in Tokyo for the past five years after moving from the Kansai region. Michael had supported the business by doing some administrative and secretarial work. He had become interested in Japanese cuisine and was thinking about starting a restaurant.

As she listened to Michael talk—Shintarō remaining silent—she nodded politely to show she was listening, but due to her suddenly increased psychic awareness, she heard clearly what the American was saying beneath the words.

"I decided that I might as well study Japanese seriously, since I was living here." *After the first few years, Shintarō began ignoring me.*

"Japanese cuisine fascinates me. I learned to cook on my own."

He... really left me alone a lot.

"We're going to Hakodate to look at some restaurant possibilities."

He's since come around, though, and is a little tired of Tokyo, as I am. We're thinking this might be a fresh start for both of us.

She nodded in response to Michael's talk, thinking all the while, *I guess you've discovered that Japanese men can be undemonstrative. They don't like to admit that they're dependent on the things you do for them.* It couldn't have helped that the young American placed himself in a sort of wife role to Shintarō. That had to have made things worse, but....

She turned to Shintarō, who was calmly looking out the window. *How does he feel about Michael?* she wondered.

At that moment, Shintarō turned back to the conversation, glancing over at Michael, and the obāchan picked up a sudden infusion of feeling coming from him, directed toward the American. *He really loves him.*

I'm so glad.

So glad for both of you.

She was done here. Everything she'd been curious to see, she'd seen. The train was approaching its next station, Noboribetsu, and she stood up, nodding to both men and wishing them well.

The still-suspicious look in Shintarō's eye as he nodded politely to her didn't escape her.

She wanted to laugh but held it in.

THE STATION at Noboribetsu had a view of the ocean, and the twilight sky was deepening into a dark blue.

The stars came out. She was alone on the platform.

All was still.

The obāchan sat down slowly and heavily on one of the benches and stared out at the ocean and at the night sky.

Suddenly she remembered.

Noboribetsu.

She had met Masanori, her first husband, here. It was at the onsen, the hot springs that the town was famous for.

Masanori, her remote, unemotional, distant, and beautiful husband, who had died of cancer when he was thirty-one—and she was only twenty-five.

Tears rolled down the obāchan's cheeks and were cooled by the night air. A slight breeze moved through the station.

Masanori's face came before her in a flow of light.

Masanori....

"I'm ready," she said aloud.

She turned her face to the southbound train, now far in the distance, headed toward Hakodate. As her consciousness began to fade from her body, she wished she could say to the two men on the train....

Live your lives, and don't be afraid.

Because it's a longer journey than you know.

I wish you both well.

Sayonara... for now.

The obāchan's head fell gently onto her chest as the train continued on its way.

Stay tuned for an
exclusive excerpt from

Kaminishi: Four Seasons

Kaminishi: Book Two

By Jan Suzukawa

Michael Holden and Shintarō Kawakami have put Shintarō's yakuza past behind them and started a new life together in Tokyo. For Michael, the relationship is the joyous reunion he dreamed of. The love he traveled through time for is his again, and this time it's for good.

But echoes from that summer long ago are never far away—and for the two men winter is on the horizon.

From the past to the present and as the seasons turn—love always comes around again when the cherry blossoms bloom.

Coming Soon to
http://www.dsppublications.com

SUMMER

THE FIRST thing he saw when he awoke was Shinjirō's beautiful face hovering over him.

Michael gazed into the daimyō's dark eyes, which crinkled at the edges with a smile. A few tendrils of Shinjirō's long black hair fell into his face, sweeping across his cheek as he lay naked beneath the silk cover on the futon.

"Konnichi-wa, Shinjirō-sama." He smiled up at his lover.

The hot late-summer days in the Kaminishi Han west of Kyoto made Michael sleepy, so after his gardening work with Kanosuke in the mornings, he would return to Shinjirō's room and take a nap.

The best thing was that sometimes Shinjirō would join him there.

He reached up and touched Shinjirō's face, the skin warm and soft against his fingers. Shinjirō was ten years older than Michael, but his face was like pale smooth porcelain.

Shinjirō leaned down and kissed him. The warm, wet sensations of his tongue and lips invaded Michael's mouth, the taste of him intoxicating. Michael's body rose to meet his.

A gentle breeze drifted in from the courtyard, bringing a scent of bamboo and grass. Michael's hands roamed over Shinjirō's back, slipping over the silk kimono, relishing the muscles underneath.

Shinjirō gave a wicked smile, and Michael felt the cover being swept aside. He lay naked before Shinjirō. The sliding door to the courtyard was wide open.

He tried to pull the cover back up, but Shinjirō stopped him, laughing.

A woman's voice sounded from the hallway. The door slid open, and the elderly woman entered, bringing in a tray.

Michael blushed and glared at Shinjirō, who barely hid his laughter. The woman didn't look in their direction but merely arranged the teapot and cups and small plates of food on the tray before backing out, still on her knees, to the hallway.

The door slid shut.

He scowled at Shinjirō again before getting up to retrieve the tray, feeling the daimyō's hot gaze on his naked form.

He returned to the futon, and as he set the tray down, a hand gently lifted his chin and he looked into the daimyō's amused face. "You are a beautiful man," Shinjirō said. "There is no need to hide yourself."

His tone was gentle, and Michael was ashamed at his reaction.

Shinjirō chuckled, leaning forward and kissing him.

"Please," Michael said, handing him his cup.

He lifted one of the small round manjū—pounded rice with sweetened red bean paste inside—to the daimyō's lips. Shinjirō, amused at being fed, bit into it.

"Shinjirō-sama, I would like to cook for you sometime," Michael said suddenly.

The daimyō glanced at him, surprised. "You wish to cook for me?" It was one of the few times Michael saw a raised eyebrow from him.

"Yes. Dinner. Would you like that?"

He expected Shinjirō to laugh, but the daimyō's mouth quirked instead. Michael knew what that meant. *I'd like to see that.*

"Then I'll do it." He put the half-eaten sweet manjū into his own mouth, and Shinjirō laughed.

"I'll look forward to it."

Michael was eager to get to the garden the next morning. Kanosuke looked up and commented in his mild voice that he was quite early.

The kabocha pumpkins still weren't ready, but there was cabbage and negi green onions and daikon radishes. Michael had cooked occasionally while at Berkeley, nothing fancy, but he liked to try new combinations of fresh ingredients, particularly vegetables.

He checked the leaves on the plants for insects and shored up tilting plants, moving his hands in the dirt. The morning sun was warm on his back.

Kanosuke knelt next to him. He picked a long cucumber from a climbing vine and dipped it in a bucket of water before wiping it off on his sleeve. Then he snapped it in half.

He handed Michael one of the halves. "Please," he said, then took a small bite of his own half.

Michael bit into the crunchy green vegetable, the juice trickling down his chin. The flesh was almost sweet.

He loved the smells of the garden. The vegetables and the soil, the fresh air—it was like being released from prison. He had been held captive, after all, in a cell in the castle's lowest level before Shinjirō took him into his bed.

"Kanosuke-san, I want to cook for Shinjirō-sama."

The gardener stared at him, and then his face broke into a smile. "I see. Would this be for a special occasion or...?"

"Just dinner, tomorrow evening. But I've never seen the kitchen here." He glanced hopefully at Kanosuke.

Kanosuke grinned. "I think I can help you with that."

KANOSUKE SHOOED the servants out of the kitchen, then gestured for Michael to enter.

The first thing Michael noticed was the long stone structure along the wall, like an old-fashioned wood-fire oven. The oven had three large openings near the floor. Inside he could see charred wood.

On top were three smaller holes. Two were covered by wooden lids, and an iron pot with handles sat on top of the third hole.

Michael understood the setup. Wood was burned inside the oven and pots and pans were placed on top of the holes. The stone surface was meticulously clean. It was a simple and completely efficient arrangement.

There was a wooden table for food preparation against the wall. A box of knives and other kitchen implements sat on the table.

It was perfect. "Tomorrow night," Michael told Kanosuke.

Later that day, as twilight turned to evening, he sat in the garden next to the stream. The stream Shinjirō's father diverted into the courtyard flowed gently over rocks and through a garden. It wasn't just a beautiful feature, but a water source in case of drought or siege.

He drifted his fingers in the cool water, marveling at how functionality and aesthetics always seemed to go together in Japanese life.

A hand joined his in the stream.

Michael turned his face, only to have it captured by a kiss. The daimyō's hand held him in place so his mouth could be plundered. "Mmph," he said, breaking the mood.

Shinjirō laughed. "Come," he said, bringing Michael to his feet.

The room was lit by a single lantern. The flower pattern on the paper shade cast flickering shadows on the walls.

Shinjirō gently pushed him down onto the futon. "You have been in my thoughts all day, Michael," he said. His warm scent and overwhelming presence made Michael still beneath him, as an animal does when caught by something powerful.

He gazed up at the daimyō, enraptured.

He'd never wanted to hold on to anything harder in his life. Shinjirō and living at the castle—everything was perfect. If nothing changed, Michael would live and die a happy man. "Shinjirō-sama," he said.

Michael reached a hand up to Shinjirō's face.

The daimyō captured his mouth in a deep kiss and lowered himself to rest on Michael. The contact made Michael's body come alive. He opened his legs and hooked his ankles behind Shinjirō's legs to increase the pressure where their groins met.

Michael raised his hips and Shinjirō grunted his pleasure. "You are wicked," Shinjirō said, and Michael laughed softly.

He took Michael's hands and held them down on the futon on either side of his head. Their intertwined fingers felt good. Michael squeezed, and Shinjirō squeezed back, a faint smile gracing his perfect face.

The daimyō dipped his head and nipped at his earlobe, making Michael yelp. Shinjirō immediately tongued the reddened area, then behind his ear.

Michael's cock hardened. He squirmed, wanting more.

Shinjirō sat up, straddling him, and opened his yukata. He circled Michael's nipples roughly with his thumbs.

Michael drew in his breath and narrowed his eyes.

This was a game they played. Shinjirō liked to make him beg for it.

He set his mouth.

Shinjirō moved down, lightly touching Michael through his fundoshi. He pulled the undergarment off, then trailed his fingers along the underside of Michael's cock as Michael shivered.

He tried to move his legs but Shinjirō had him pinned. He wanted to touch himself but that was forbidden.

The daimyō's teasing touch drove him mad. He was fully erect now.

When Shinjirō lightly rubbed the pad of his thumb over the slit, Michael squirmed, shutting his eyes, but Shinjirō was relentless.

He finally gave in. "Please."

Shinjirō smiled.

Michael watched as Shinjirō removed his fundoshi and prepared himself with oil, then lifted Michael's legs over his shoulders.

It was a slow entry. As he was filled with Shinjirō's bulk, Michael breathed slowly and deeply, pushing out with his lower muscles to ease the insertion as much as he could.

Shinjirō still wore his kimono. As he began to move in and out, one shoulder was bared as the material slipped down.

Michael lost himself, Shinjirō's thickness the only reality, an extension of the daimyō's will as much as his body, joining with him in a way that felt sacred.

The lingering heat from the day, the shadows cast on the walls in the darkening room, Shinjirō's kimono flowing over them like a shroud—all induced a kind of altered state in him.

As he climaxed, Michael's eyes filled with tears.

Shinjirō came soon after, driving impossibly deep into him.

Michael felt Shinjirō withdraw after a time, and his sore body was gathered into the warlord's arms.

"I wish I could stay like this forever."

Shinjirō's hand stopped stroking his hair for a moment, then continued on as if he'd said nothing.

HE FELT Shinjirō's eyes on him as he set the tray inside the room, then slid the door shut.

The dinner was easier to prepare than he'd expected. Norio, Shinjirō's longtime retainer, had even stood by the kitchen door to keep the other servants out while he was cooking.

In the end he made a simple meal of pan-fried mackerel with miso soup, rice, cabbage, and pickled daikon radish on the side. The pickled radishes and rice had already been prepared by the servants earlier at Kanosuke's request. It wasn't a fancy meal by any means, but Michael imagined Shinjirō would enjoy it.

He set the tray on the low table next to the futon. Again he felt Shinjirō watching him as he arranged the dishes and poured tea.

Michael looked up and met the daimyō's gaze. "I hope this humble meal meets with your satisfaction."

"It already has. You made it for me with your own hands. That makes it special."

They ate in comfortable silence, the lantern light flickering and making Shinjirō's shadow loom large on the wall behind him.

The sliding door to the garden was open and the air was still pleasantly warm as daylight waned.

The mackerel was flaky and tender, and the cabbage, fresh from the garden, its perfect flavorful complement. "The simplest things are the best," Shinjirō said, and Michael ducked his head and nodded at the indirect compliment.

After the meal, they sat in the doorway to the garden. Michael poured sake into small cups and settled himself next to Shinjirō.

Shinjirō sat with his back against the doorframe, gazing at the garden. Michael loved seeing the daimyō like this, released from the cares of rule for a few precious moments. The planes of that beautiful face caught the fading sunlight and his eyes softened slightly, as if seeing something other than what was in front of him.

Shinjirō pulled him close, and Michael nestled against him with his face in the daimyō's chest. He'd gotten over feeling like a girl when Shinjirō did this and just let himself enjoy it.

They rested for a long time as the evening shadows lengthened, Michael refreshing their cups with the sake bottle as needed.

"You are enjoying this moment, yes?"

"Yes."

"That is what is important." Shinjirō put his cup down, and to Michael's surprise took his cup as well and set it on the floor. "Because it won't always be this way."

Michael froze. He stared at Shinjirō. "What do you mean?"

"Life is about change. The unexpected. The things you think will always be...." Shinjirō smiled. It was a gentle and sad smile. "People come and go. They grow old and die. Nothing stays the same."

He touched Michael's face. "You are young, Maikoru. You are happy now and want everything to stay this way forever. But that cannot be."

Michael was indignant at being patronized. He covered Shinjirō's hand with his own. "Shinjirō-sama—"

"Hush," Shinjirō said calmly.

He brought his beautiful face close to Michael's. "Who you love, you were meant to love. Love with all your heart, but do not hold on. When the time comes, you must let go." He smiled at Michael. "Those who love will see each other again."

Shinjirō brought his lips to Michael's forehead.

"Remember this."

JAN SUZUKAWA started out as a science fiction fan and discovered slash fan fiction several eons before the invention of the Internet. Her tastes turned to yaoi when she became a freelance editor of manga and anime-related books for Digital Manga, Inc., Tokyopop, and other publishers. As an m/m romance author she has combined her slash roots with her love of yaoi, and she is delighted that m/m stories are now considered quite acceptable in polite company these days.

When not reading manga or romance stories, she spends her time studying Japanese, freelancing in two professions—law and publishing—and watching entirely too much anime. She lives in California.

Jan's writing blog—Atypical Romance
http://atypicalromance.blogspot.com
Jan's anime and manga industry blog—Neo-Shonen Fujoshi
http://jansuzukawa.blogspot.com.

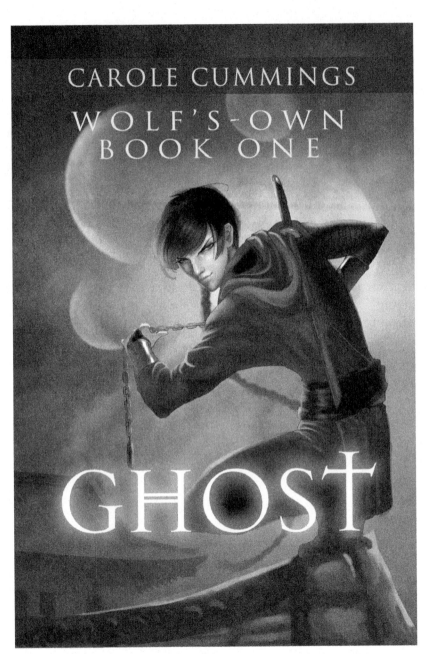

CAROLE CUMMINGS

WOLF'S-OWN
BOOK ONE

GHOST

http://www.dsppublications.com

Ash AND Echoes

Book One of the
BLESSED EPOCH

AUGUST LI

http://www.dsppublications.com

THE
RELICS
OF GODS
YEYU

http://www.dsppublications.com

DREAMLANDS

FELICITAS IVEY

http://www.dsppublications.com

The Bastard's Pearl

CONNIE BAILEY

http://www.dsppublications.com

FORBIDDEN
MONASTERy

RAGE: BOOK 1
SAM C. LEONHARD

http://www.dsppublications.com

PATRICIA CORRELL

LATE SUMMER, EARLY SPRING

http://www.dsppublications.com

"I was smitten, right from the beginning."
-Charles deLint

Greenwode

J Tullos Hennig

http://www.dsppublications.com

THE LONELY WAR

Alan Chin

http://www.dsppublications.com

BRANDON WITT

SUBMERGING INFERNO

MEN of
MYTH

http://www.dsppublications.com

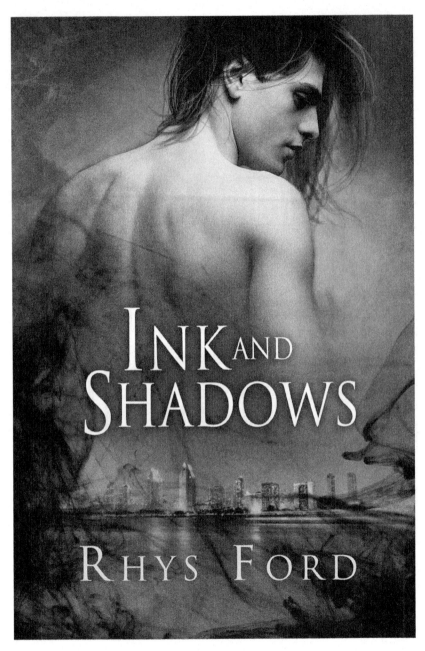

INK AND SHADOWS

RHYS FORD

http://www.dsppublications.com

EVOLUTION

LISSA KASEY

http://www.dsppublications.com

the prince
and the
program

aldous
mercer

http://www.dsppublications.com

http://www.dsppublications.com

For more
great fiction
from

DSP PUBLICATIONS

visit us online.

WWW.DSPPUBLICATIONS.COM